"One of
the
—*BookBrowser*

Praise for Ashley Gardner's Mysteries of Regency England
featuring Captain Gabriel Lacey

The Sudbury School Murders

"This page-turning historical is thoroughly enjoyable."
—*Romantic Times* (4½ stars, Top Pick)

"English country mysteries don't get better than this."
—*The Romance Reader's Connection*

"This fourth Gabriel Lacey mystery is another compelling entry in this outstanding series." —*Fresh Fiction*

The Glass House

"In Captain Gabriel Lacey, Gardner has created an intriguing protagonist . . . a quickly paced read with engaging characters and a multilayered plot sure to satisfy . . . an intricate puzzle that subverts the classic love triangle in a novel way." —*The Mystery Reader*

"A perfect choice for mystery readers who like an intelligent historical as well." —*The Romance Reader's Connection*

"Compelling . . . Newcomers and fans alike will quickly become enamored of Captain Lacey." —*Romantic Times*

continued . . .

A Regimental Murder

"An exciting, read-it-in-one-sitting novel, thoroughly enjoyable with genuine edge-of-your-seat suspense . . . Eminently satisfying." —*Roundtable Reviews*

"Ashley Gardner is a name worth following as this author shows deep talent for vividly recreating the era and people of the Regency period inside a powerful mystery."
                                                    —*BookBrowser*

"Gardner has inhabited this world with recurring secondary characters rich in personalities who continue to evolve. The icing on the cake is the intriguing, masterfully told mystery." —*The Best Reviews*

The Hanover Square Affair

"With her vivid description of the era, Gardner brings her novel to life." —*Romantic Times* (4½ stars, Top Pick)

Mysteries of Regency England by Ashley Gardner

THE HANOVER SQUARE AFFAIR
A REGIMENTAL MURDER
THE GLASS HOUSE
THE SUDBURY SCHOOL MURDERS
A BODY IN BERKELEY SQUARE
A COVENT GARDEN MYSTERY

A
COVENT GARDEN
MYSTERY

ASHLEY GARDNER

BERKLEY PRIME CRIME, NEW YORK

35674 043773895

THE BERKLEY PUBLISHING GROUP
Published by the Penguin Group
Penguin Group (USA) Inc.
375 Hudson Street, New York, New York 10014, USA
Penguin Group (Canada), 90 Eglinton Avenue East, Suite 700, Toronto, Ontario M4P 2Y3, Canada
(a division of Pearson Penguin Canada Inc.)
Penguin Books Ltd., 80 Strand, London WC2R 0RL, England
Penguin Group Ireland, 25 St. Stephen's Green, Dublin 2, Ireland (a division of Penguin Books Ltd.)
Penguin Group (Australia), 250 Camberwell Road, Camberwell, Victoria 3124, Australia
(a division of Pearson Australia Group Pty. Ltd.)
Penguin Books India Pvt. Ltd., 11 Community Centre, Panchsheel Park, New Delhi—110 017, India
Penguin Group (NZ), Cnr. Airborne and Rosedale Roads, Albany, Auckland 1310, New Zealand
(a division of Pearson New Zealand Ltd.)
Penguin Books (South Africa) (Pty.) Ltd., 24 Sturdee Avenue, Rosebank, Johannesburg 2196,
South Africa

Penguin Books Ltd., Registered Offices: 80 Strand, London WC2R 0RL, England

This is a work of fiction. Names, characters, places, and incidents either are the product of the author's imagination or are used fictitiously, and any resemblance to actual persons, living or dead, business establishments, events, or locales is entirely coincidental. The publisher does not have any control over and does not assume any responsibility for author or third-party websites or their content.

A COVENT GARDEN MYSTERY

A Berkley Prime Crime Book / published by arrangement with the author

PRINTING HISTORY
Berkley Prime Crime mass-market edition / July 2006

Copyright © 2006 by Jennifer Ashley.
Cover photo of woman by James Jacques Josep Tissot / Bridgeman.
Cover photo of Covent Garden © Jiri Rezac / Alamy.
Cover design by Marc Cohen.
Interior text design by Kristin del Rosario.

ISBN: 0-425-21086-3

BERKLEY® PRIME CRIME
Berkley Prime Crime Books are published by The Berkley Publishing Group,
a division of Penguin Group (USA) Inc.,
375 Hudson Street, New York, New York 10014.
The name BERKLEY PRIME CRIME and the BERKLEY PRIME CRIME design are trademarks belonging to Penguin Group (USA) Inc.

PRINTED IN THE UNITED STATES OF AMERICA

10 9 8 7 6 5 4 3 2 1

Chapter 1

June 1817

THE young woman buying peaches in Covent Garden had honey brown hair, clear white skin, deep brown eyes, and a faint French accent. The stall owner, a stooped man with a fat red nose and long strands of gray hair spilling from under a greasy cap, was trying to cheat her.

"Ha'penny for two, miss." He planted his fists on the stall and leaned to her. "Best to be had."

He was goading her to take two shriveled specimens. When she pointed to the firm, ripe fruit near the man's hand, he shook his head. "Penny apiece, love."

I'd just seen him sell two fine peaches to a housewife for half that price, but he probably thought he could fleece a foreigner, especially an inexperienced girl.

It was early, and Covent Garden's market was thronged with humanity. The square was bounded on one side by the pile of the theatre, two sides by rows of houses and shops, and the fourth side by St. Paul's Church, Covent Garden.

Houses ran along the outside of the churchyard, people squeezing themselves in any place they could.

Farmers trundled goods to stalls and shops, young women bore baskets of bright, ripe strawberries on their shoulders, milkmaids balanced heavy buckets on yokes across their backs, and all called to housewives to try their wares.

I casually turned toward the peach seller's stall, walking stick in hand. A lady in distress, even over peaches, spoke to my knight-errant instincts.

"Prices have changed, have they?" I asked the peach seller.

He shot me an irritated look. "Happens."

"In a quarter of an hour?" I leaned to him. "Sell her the same as you sold the others."

He glowered at me, a glint in his eye, but he backed down. I had a reputation for possessing a foul temper, although I believe my close acquaintanceship with magistrates and Bow Street Runners decided the matter.

He handed the good peaches to the girl. "Ha'penny," he growled. To me, he said, "I know why your nose is so long, Cap'n. You use it to poke into business 'tisn't yours."

"True." I touched the offending appendage. "Several men have broken it for me."

"I shouldn't wonder." He took the girl's coin, then with another bellicose look at me, turned to his next customer. "Two for ha'penny."

The girl placed the peaches in the basket on her arm and glanced at me shyly. "I thank you, sir."

I had never seen her in Covent Garden before. I had lived in rooms in nearby Grimpen Lane for a few years now, and came to the markets every day. The regulars of the market were familiar to me, and I to them. I did not know her, but I somehow felt as though I should.

She could not have been more than sixteen, with an unworldly air and innocent eyes. Her dress was fashionable, high-waisted, and plain-skirted, the gown of a young, gently born miss. I could not fathom why she walked about Covent Garden by herself at this early hour. She seemed more suited to strolling formal gardens under a parasol while smitten young men vied to walk by her side.

She spoke with a faint accent, though she spoke English well. Perhaps she was an Englishman's young paramour, perhaps the daughter of émigrés who had fled France long ago and elected to stay, even after Louis Bourbon had been restored and the Republic banished.

Whoever she was, she smiled at me, grateful for rescue. Her expression was guileless; too innocent to be a man's paramour, I decided. She must be a dutiful daughter, gathering breakfast for her mother and father.

I tipped my hat. "Captain Gabriel Lacey, at your service. May I escort you somewhere?"

Her smile was crooked, her brown eyes sparkling with good humor. I paused, wondering where I'd seen that look before, not quite the same. Buried memory stirred.

"My father and mother are staying near, sir. I wanted peaches for breakfast, and so ventured to find them."

That they'd let her come out alone in a strange city did not speak well of them. But perhaps they were provincial people, used to places where everyone knew everyone, where no one would dream of harming the daughters of respectable gentlefolk.

She stirred a protective instinct in me. I held out my arm. "What house? I will walk you there."

She blushed and shook her head. "You are kind, sir, but I must not trouble you."

She thought me forward. At least she was that wise, but I could have told her she had nothing to fear from me. She was young, still a girl, and I had passed my fortieth year. She must be about the same age as Black Nancy, my sometime friend and former street girl. But while Black Nancy had the wisdom of a woman far beyond her years, this young lady was little more than a child.

Trust no one, I wanted to tell her. "You can introduce me to your mama and papa," I began, but a shrill voice cut across the market.

"Gabriella!"

My young lady turned, and her smile broadened into one of relief. "That is my mama now, sir. I thank you again for your kind assistance."

I barely heard her. Hurrying toward me, through the milling housewives and maids, footmen, cart men, and cook's assistants, came a ghost from my past.

The last time I'd seen her, she had been thin and frail, a gold-and-white girl looking at me with timid eyes, her dainty mouth hovering between a smile and puckered worry. Time had thickened her figure, but she retained an air of graceful helplessness, one that urged a gentleman to rush to her side and demand to know how he could assist her.

That air had ensnared me as a young man. I had proposed to her within a week of meeting her, wanting to wrap her in my protective arms.

Her face was still pale and flowerlike, though time had not been kind to it. Lines feathered about her eyes and mouth, and her skin had coarsened a bit. The curls that wreathed her forehead, under her bonnet's brim, however, were still golden, perhaps a little darker than they'd been fifteen years ago.

She stopped a few feet behind the girl, her lips parting in shock. Though I must have changed a great deal from the unruly and impetuous young man I'd been, she knew me, and I knew her.

Her name was Carlotta Lacey, and she was my wife.

We stared at one another numbly, while life in Covent

Garden continued around us. A carter nudged his draft horse around me; a strawberry seller, trilling her wares, laughed as she nearly swayed into me. A robust woman with a mobcap bellowed from the stall next to us that her ale was the best to be had.

Carlotta's eyes were blue. When I'd proposed in a country meadow near Cambridge, those eyes had glowed with excitement and delight. She'd let me kiss her, and then, full of confidence in our future, we'd consummated our betrothal there on the somewhat damp ground. I remembered the sweet scent of crushed grass, the tiny star flowers that tickled my nose, the warm taste of her skin.

Whether she remembered any of it as we stood closer than we'd stood to each other in fifteen years, I could not tell. I only knew that she looked at me with unblinking eyes, and that she had deserted me for a French officer a decade and a half ago.

It struck me then, like a boulder thrown with great force, that Carlotta had called the girl Gabriella.

My gaze shot to her, the breath leaving my body. The girl looked back at me, brown eyes innocent and uncomprehending.

Gabriella Lacey. *My daughter.*

Carlotta recovered first. She reached out and closed gloved fingers around the girl's basket. In French she said, "Come away, Gabriella."

"No." The word burst from my tight throat. I stepped in front of Carlotta, blocking her path.

Gabriella looked startled. Carlotta moved her grip to the girl's arm. "Later," she said to me. "Not now. We will come to it later."

She had not changed in one aspect. Anything Carlotta could avoid facing, she would shove away from her with force.

I had recovered long ago from the grief at her leaving

me. I had lived through the anger and the loneliness, then the resignation. I could forgive Carlotta for deserting me. I had been a thoughtless husband, and following the drum had been a hard life, too hard for someone like the innocent and frail Carlotta.

But I had never forgiven her, nor would I ever forgive her, for taking away my daughter. I had not seen Gabriella since she was two years old.

I said, "By the laws of England, she belongs to me."

Mothers had no legal guardianship over their children unless they were granted it, which I had not done. Her taking Gabriella away had been a crime in truth.

The worry in Carlotta's eyes told me she knew very well what she had done and what I could do to retaliate. She looked at me pleadingly. "We must speak of it later. Not here. Not *now*."

"*Maman,* what is the matter?" Gabriella asked in French. "What is happening?"

Carlotta arranged her face in soothing lines as she turned to her daughter. "Nothing, my dear," she answered, her tone too bright. "We will go home."

I pressed my walking stick against the side of Carlotta's skirt. She could not rush away, her favorite method of solving problems, without pushing her way past me and making a scene. Gabriella peered at me anxiously. She no doubt thought me a madman, accosting her mother for whatever diabolical reason in my crazed mind.

I realized then that when I had told her my name, *Captain Gabriel Lacey, at your service,* she had given no beat of recognition. She had no idea who I was.

"You did not tell her," I said to Carlotta.

"Not now," Carlotta repeated. "Please, Gabriel, let us speak of this later. For heaven's sake."

The haze cleared a bit from my mind, and I realized that the denizens of Covent Garden still teemed about us, now watching us with interest. Gabriella looked as though she would shout for help at any moment. The peach seller and the ale seller observed us with blatant curiosity, Londoners always keen for an impromptu drama. A large black carriage with fine gray horses shouldering through the crowd nearly brushed me as it went past.

I moved my walking stick. I could not very well seize my daughter and drag her away with me, much as I wanted to. We could not split her in two, Solomon-like, in the middle of Covent Garden.

"Where do you stay?" I asked.

"King Street," Carlotta answered. "I promise you, we will speak of it. We will settle it."

"We shall indeed. I will send a man round to fetch you."

Carlotta shook her head. "No, there will be an appointment. He will see to it."

"Who will?"

Carlotta grasped Gabriella's arm. "Come," she said. "Your father is waiting."

That statement startled me a moment before I realized she must mean the Frenchman she'd eloped with, the man who'd thought nothing of living with another man's wife for fifteen years.

Gabriella, with one last bewildered glance at me, let her mother lead her away. Carlotta hurried with her to the north and west side of Covent Garden and out to King Street, and the crowd swallowed them.

I stood in a daze, watching until I could no longer see the two women, the younger one a little taller than the older, walking close, heads bent together.

Chapter 2

I did not trust Carlotta not to run away again. She must not have known I lived so close, else she'd never have let Gabriella come here alone to the market. Whatever her plan had been on journeying to London, meeting me here had not been part of it.

I would go to Bow Street and ask Milton Pomeroy, a Runner, to find out in what house in King Street she'd taken rooms and to have one of his foot patrollers watch her. Gabriella was my daughter; by law, she belonged to me. This time, I would not let Carlotta take her away.

I mused on something Carlotta had said: *He* would make the appointment. Who? Her French officer? And what would this appointment be about? I doubted she had brought Gabriella to London to give her up to me.

"Devil take it, Lacey," an annoyed female voice cried. "Have your brains addled?"

A woman leaned out of the black carriage that had

nearly run me down, her fashionable hat tilted back to reveal a quantity of golden curls and a childlike, pointed face. I realized that the carriage belonged to Lucius Grenville. Those were his perfectly matched grays pulling it, his liveried coachman on the roof, his family crest on the door, and his footman on the back. The footman, who had been helping me into and out of Grenville's carriage for the last year, gave me a grin of greeting.

I had been surprised when Grenville began allowing Marianne Simmons to travel about openly in his carriage. He had hidden her away in his house in Clarges Street for a long time, his relationship with her ambiguous, lavishing on her food and drink and clothing, and driving her mad with her confinement.

Then, two months ago, he had finally made her his mistress in truth. London gossip being what it was, all residents of Mayfair now knew that Grenville had given *carte blanche* to a second-rate Drury Lane actress who used to live in tiny rooms near Covent Garden. He'd bowed to the inevitable, openly squired her about, and gave her the use of his carriage.

"Might as well flaunt my folly," he told me dryly the last time I'd supped at his splendid house in Grosvenor Street.

Newspapers had printed scurrilous, mean-spirited stories and cartoons about him and Marianne. *How are the mighty fallen,* they said of a man who had previously only taken high-born courtesans or famous sopranos to his bed. Grenville regarded the cartoons in disgust, consulted his solicitor about libel, and continued escorting Marianne about without flaunting her.

"I was on my way to see you, Lacey," she said. "I didn't realize that was you until we'd near run you down."

The footman on back leapt to the ground, fanned away the beggars who gathered round a costly conveyance like moths round a lantern, and opened the door for me. "I will walk," I said.

"Someone else will run you down if you do," she said. "Get in, Lacey. I want to talk to you."

I obeyed her for two reasons. First, I was still dazed from the encounter with Carlotta, and the real world seemed a bit distant and hazy. Easier simply to obey orders than argue. Second, I knew that Marianne would not come all this way in the carriage if she did not truly need to speak to me. She rarely made any effort without hope of recompense.

The footman assisted me into the carriage, careful of my bad left knee, and I settled myself facing Marianne. He shut the door, and the carriage jerked forward to make its way through the crowd of Covent Garden and the very short journey to Russel Street. I lived in Grimpen Lane, a tiny cul-de-sac that opened off Russel Street, the house with my rooms nestled between the buildings of Covent Garden and the houses of Bow Street.

"You are white as plain paper, Lacey," Marianne said. "What is the matter with you?"

Though I was most distracted, I reflected that Marianne looked well. She wore a blue silk moiré gown cut modestly above her bosom. Dark blue ribbon trimmed the bodice, which was gathered into a high waist. Her skirt was festooned with lace and ribbon, but conservatively so, and the short sleeves ended in lace that cascaded to her plump elbows. She'd wrapped a light lace shawl over her arms to keep off the breeze and wore pretty black leather slippers, the kind in which she could not tramp through London mud.

I saw Grenville's hand in the ensemble. He had exquisite taste and had likely sent her to the best mantua maker in town. He would have told the establishment what he wanted, and they would have gone out of their way to please him, knowing Grenville had plenty of blunt to go with his good taste.

"Who were the women you were speaking to?" she persisted. "Were they blackmailing you?"

The odd question pulled me out of my daze. "Blackmail? What put that idea in your head?"

"Because I know you. You poke your nose into so many things that criminals must want to find something on you to keep you from sending them to Bow Street."

"You have an interesting imagination, Marianne."

"Are you going to tell me what is the matter? Something clearly is."

I wondered why she wanted to pry. Had I had more of my wits about me, I would have put her off, but I found myself confessing, "The two ladies were my wife and daughter."

She started to give me a sardonic smile, as though she didn't believe me, then her mouth became a pink "O." "Good lord."

"I have not seen them for fifteen years."

"Good lord," she repeated. "No wonder you looked poleaxed. I have some brandy. Grenville's best." She rummaged in a side pocket of the carriage and drew out a box I recognized, one that held brandy and glasses. Grenville's servants always stocked his carriage with the best drink in case their master grew thirsty traveling the byways of London.

As she lifted the bottle from the box, the carriage stopped, reaching our destination, and the efficient footman pulled open the door. Marianne shoved the brandy at me and snatched two glasses. "Come along. We'll drink it in your rooms."

The house in Grimpen Lane where I had my rooms was narrow and tall. The first floor held a bake shop, where the landlady, Mrs. Beltan, sold bread and buns and seed cakes to passersby. She did well out of the shop and rented the rooms in the two floors above it. The first floor held my rooms, reached by a dim staircase walled off from the bake shop and opening to the street.

The house had been grand in the time of Charles II, but its elegance had faded. My two rooms, bedchamber and sitting room, had once been a bedchamber and grand salon. Now they housed my eclectic mix of furniture—chest-on-frame and huge tester bed from the era in which the house was built, a writing table and chair from the middle of the last century, a wing chair before the fire from 1780, and a modern bookcase, given to me by Grenville, that was carved and gilded in the Egyptian style.

The rooms above mine, identical but low-ceilinged, had been rented by Marianne before Grenville had taken her away. In the attics above those my valet-in-training, Bartholomew, kept himself as comfortably as possible.

Since March, when I'd returned from a brief stay in Berkshire, two different lodgers had taken the rooms above mine, but neither had stayed more than a month. The rooms were currently empty. I'd thought of taking both floors for myself, so that I'd have an extra room and Bartholomew would not have to sleep in the attics, but Mrs. Beltan and I had not come to an agreement. She was a kindhearted lady, but steely hard about money.

Bartholomew was not in evidence when we arrived upstairs. Likely he'd gone out to shop for supplies for my dinner. He had an amazing ability to find the best foodstuffs at the smallest prices, a trait for which I prized him. Someday, he would be snatched up as valet by an upper-class gentleman who could pay him fine wages, and I intended to enjoy his services as much as I could before that unhappy event.

Marianne plopped herself on the wing chair and held out her glass. I filled it with brandy, then drew up the straight chair from the writing table for myself.

"You knocked me over with a feather, you know," she said. "I had no idea you were married."

"Few people do." I drank a swallow of brandy, savoring its rich, smooth texture.

"Does *he* know?"

"Grenville?" I wondered how long it would be before Marianne could bring herself to say his name in conversation. "Yes, I told him. And the Brandons know, of course. Colonel Brandon helped me procure the special license long ago so I could marry her without having the banns read."

"Thought someone would object, did you?" she asked.

"My father. And hers. Her entire family, in fact. She was quite ready to board the ship that took us far from England." I rolled the crystal goblet in my hands. "In those days, we thought our lives would be fine if we only got away from England and those who wanted to tie us here. Things turned out much differently, to say the least."

"No one's life becomes what they think it will, Lacey. Not even *his*." She cocked her head. "Does her ladyship know?"

"Lady Breckenridge?" I took another sip of brandy. "Yes, I told her."

After the murder in Berkeley Square in April, when I'd found my affection for Donata Breckenridge, a dowager viscountess, growing deep, I'd gone to her and told her the truth. Lady Breckenridge, the least shockable lady of my acquaintance, even including Marianne, had taken the news stoically. I had told her everything, and incredibly, she'd understood. Having gone through a miserable marriage herself had perhaps given her sympathy for my own affairs.

After my confession, I had taken her hand and gone with her to her bedchamber. We'd spent the afternoon together, learning each other's bodies and letting the affection between us grow.

I had not seen much of her since then, her life during the height of the Season being a whirlwind of social gatherings and obligations. Still, gossip coupled our names, somewhat disapprovingly. The daughter of an earl was worlds above a half-pay captain, albeit I was a landed gentleman's son.

But Donata Breckenridge was a widow now. As a debutante she would have been censured for making a misalliance with me, but society now simply shook their heads and called her eccentric.

"This is awkward for you," Marianne said.

The plain statement from anyone but Marianne might imply secret glee at my plight. From Marianne, it meant sympathy.

"Divorce is almost impossible," I said. "I must accuse her of adultery and drag her through several courts, then ask for a private Act of Parliament to dissolve the marriage. A long, expensive, embarrassing process."

"Has she committed adultery?" Marianne asked curiously.

"She left me in France and has lived there since with a French officer. She's borne him several children."

"There you are, then, rush her to trial. I imagine *he* would help you with the expense. He does so like to arrange people's lives for them."

"Grenville would likely help if asked," I conceded. "But Mrs. Lacey was never a strong woman. Making her face hostile juries who will condemn her as an adulteress might break her. I no longer love her, but I cannot wish such an ordeal on her."

"You are far too kindhearted, Lacey."

"Not really. She has my daughter, and I will fight to get her back. But a divorce would hurt Gabriella as well." I paused. "She does not know that I am her father."

Marianne's eyes rounded. "Your wife never told her?"

"It would appear not."

She gave me a look of deep sympathy. "How awful. Are you going to tell her?"

I took a long drink of brandy. "Yes, but not yet." I traced the facets on Grenville's heavy crystal goblet. "My life, as usual, is a tangle."

"As is mine."

I looked up, remembering she had not come here about my troubles. "You wanted to speak to me about something? Grenville, I assume. I thought he had loosened the leash a bit."

Marianne poured herself another helping of brandy. "I want to go to Berkshire."

"Ah." I had discovered, earlier this spring, that Marianne Simmons had a son, a half-wit boy she'd borne years ago and kept in a cottage in the Berkshire countryside. A kindly woman looked after both cottage and son, and Marianne traveled to see them when she could. She'd spent almost everything she'd earned as an actress, plus any money or trinkets gentlemen gave her in appreciation of her pretty eyes and silver tongue, on the keeping of the boy, David.

When Grenville had first met Marianne, he'd handed her twenty guineas. She'd promptly sent the money to Berkshire, and Grenville had gone slightly mad trying to decide what had happened to his gift.

I had learned Marianne's secret by chance when I'd stayed in Berkshire at the Sudbury School in March. She'd made me swear to keep her secret, especially from Grenville. I had no desire to interfere between Grenville and Marianne, and so kept my silence.

"You have not told him," I said.

"No. You know why. I've just declared that Mr. Grenville enjoys arranging people's lives for them. He will take David away from the home he's always known and try to put him somewhere with hordes of people to take care of him. David would be frightened. I cannot let that happen."

She spoke determinedly, but her eyes held worry.

I could not reassure her that Grenville would do no such thing, because not even I always knew what Grenville might do. Lucius Grenville was one of the wealthiest men in England, and the most fashionable. Not a day went by when a story about him did not appear in some newspaper or magazine, and drawings of him hung in every fine tailoring establishment, which gave their shops cachet, whether they earned it or not.

He was intelligent, generous, gossipy, curious, friendly, and frank, although he could turn his cool, sardonic man-about-town personality on those of whom he disapproved and destroy them socially with one quirk of his brow. Gentlemen in clubs all over London feared the cold scrutiny of his black eyes, trembled when he raised a quizzing glass, and went pale when he dismissed them in his chill voice.

It was telling that the two people he claimed to like best, myself and Marianne, were two people who did not stand in awe of his power. Both of us, from very different walks of life, had seen too much and experienced too much to fear Grenville's scorn. He found us baffling, and therefore, fascinating.

But that assessment was unjust. Grenville did have a kind heart and truly wished to help, although he could be heavy-handed about it. He did not know how not to be.

"You need to tell him," I said gently. "Give him a chance."

"I came to ask if you would tell him, while I am in Berkshire. And then send me word whether to bother to come home or not."

"It is no business of mine, Marianne." Since Grenville had taken Marianne to live with him, I had strived to stay out of their lives, but in vain. Both of them liked to confide their frustrations about the other to me and demand my assistance.

"I have considered this well, you know," she said. "If I tell him before I go, he might prevent me. If I am in Berkshire when he finds out, I can simply stay there with David. I do not want his disapprobation to keep me from my son. I have saved enough money and have enough of the trinkets he's given me to live on for a good while. Unless he sets the magistrates on me for stealing them—although I do not think he would. Too embarrassing for him."

While I agreed with her assessment of Grenville's character, I could not let her simply run off and live on money from Grenville's gifts. "Tell him, for God's sake. I can be present when you do, if you like, and try to stop him from disrupting David's life."

She looked stubborn. "You have just told me that you were prevented seeing your daughter for fifteen years. I thought you would have more sympathy."

"Sympathy, yes. But I am not your conspirator against Grenville." I gave her a sharp look "You are fond of Grenville. Can you not show him that you are?"

She gave me a scornful look. "I know better than to let on to a gentleman that I like him. They take advantage, you know."

I raised my hands. "Your ideas on how ladies and gentlemen behave to one another are your own. I cannot agree with them, but I know I cannot change your mind. You may finish the brandy if you like. I must go to Bow Street."

"Consulting with the magistrates again, are you?" She reached for the brandy bottle.

"An errand."

She was too shrewd for me. "If you hire a Runner to watch that your wife does not slip away, you will be as bad as Grenville. He threatened to do the same to me, remember?"

I well recalled the incident. When I had taken the post at the Sudbury School, Marianne had disappeared from Grenville's house, and he'd wanted to take England apart to find her. I had dissuaded him from this action only because I happened to know where Marianne had gone.

"I thought Grenville unwise, but I could not blame him. You tease him and plague him, and I am surprised he does not keep you on a tether."

She made a face at me as I prepared to leave. "Gentlemen always stand together," she threw at me. "Especially those of your class. Rich and poor, if you went to the same school and came from the same sort of family, you band together against the downtrodden."

I shot her an ironic look before I closed the door. "I could never think of you as downtrodden, Marianne. You are the least downtrodden woman I know."

Her answer was to put out her tongue, then I shut the door on her as she raised her goblet again.

I left the house and walked to Bow Street. I made this trip often, strolling out of Grimpen Lane to Russel Street and around the corner to the left to Bow Street. Today I made it under the June sun, which had at last chased away the drear of winter. I preferred warm climates, having grown used to the stifling heat of India and the warm summers of Spain. Grenville had recently invited me to accompany him to Egypt in the fall, traveling so that we would arrive there in December. The desert would still be hot at that time, he said, but not unbearable.

I wondered, as I tipped my hat to a passing housewife, whether Grenville yet had told Marianne he wanted to leave England for several months, and what her reaction would be when he did. He believed Marianne did not care a fig for where he went, but I knew better. I hoped they settled things between them soon, because they were driving me mad.

I approached the Bow Street magistrate's house, a tall, narrow edifice that comprised numbers 3 and 4. The chief magistrate lived upstairs, and the unfortunates dragged in to appear before him in the large room downstairs spent the night in buildings behind the house as well as the cellar of the tavern opposite.

The unfortunates consisted of pickpockets, prostitutes, the drunk and disorderly, thieves, illegal gamers, house-breakers, brawlers, and murderers. Those accused of more serious crimes, like murder or rape, generally saw the magistrate in isolation. Those accused of petty crimes tumbled together in a mass of unwashed and surprisingly good-humored humanity.

"Mornin', Cap'n," slurred a man who was brought in for drunkenness nearly every night. He did not simply drink himself into a stupor—many a man did that and only went home and slept—but Bottle Bill, as he was called, went quite mad when he was drunk, and violence occasionally ensued.

In the light of day, he was a quiet creature, ashamed of himself, smiling gently and apologizing to those he'd hurt the night before. He could not help himself, he said. If he did not have drink, he became wretchedly ill, near to death. A few glasses of gin, and he was right as rain. But then he could not stop drinking the gin, and so he went round again to losing his senses, starting fights, breaking furniture, and ending up at Bow Street.

"Good morning, Bill," I said as I stepped past him.

"How are you this fine day?" Bill went on. He leaned against the wall, his red eyes screwed up against the bright sun I'd brought in through the door. "I like it a bit gloomier, meself."

"I'm well, Bill. What did you do this time?"

"No idea, Cap'n. They say I broke a fellow's arm, but I don't remember. I'm not very big, am I, to be breaking another man's arm?" He put a shaky, thin hand to his brow. "Feel like the elephant at the 'Change is a-dancing on my head."

"You'll likely go home soon," I said. "Is Pomeroy about?"

"Aye, that he is. Hupstairs. With one of those Thames River blokes."

"Thank you." I put a shilling in his hand that was not quite outstretched and made for the stairs.

Chapter 3

MR. Thompson of the Thames River Police was a lanky man whose clothes hung loose from his bony shoulders. He belonged to the body of patrollers who moved up and down the river, protecting the huge ships at the London docks and beyond. The patrollers had been started years ago by those appalled by the number of cargo thefts they endured. Eventually, the Thames River Police, as we now knew it, had come under the same authority as the Bow Street Runners, foot patrollers, and runners from other magistrates' houses.

I liked Thompson, who had a sharp mind and quick intelligence. Normally, I enjoyed a chat with him, but today I wanted to talk to Pomeroy about my wife, not a conversation I wanted to share with Thompson. Pomeroy had known my wife, knew about her desertion, and would understand my present agitation.

"Good morning, Captain," Thompson said as I entered

the room in which Pomeroy generally wrote his reports. The thin man came forward and shook my hand. His countenance, as usual, was smooth and bland, but there was a definite spark in his eyes. Something had happened.

"Was going to come round to see you later today," Pomeroy said. He got up from his writing table and saluted me, just as he'd done when he'd been one of my sergeants in the Peninsular War. Pomeroy was thick-bodied, tall, and athletic, and had a shock of blond hair that he kept slicked down with pomade. His blue eyes were twinkling, eager, and good-humored. He pursued criminals with great fervor and had the reputation for always catching his man (or woman) and getting a conviction. Runners were paid reward money when a conviction went through the courts, and so their incentive to drag criminals to trial was high.

"Why?" I asked sharply. I wondered if he knew Carlotta had returned to England, and I realized suddenly that I would make a mistake asking Pomeroy to keep an eye on her. Carlotta had abandoned me and committed adultery, and for both things she could be tried and convicted to stand in the pillory at the very least.

As much anger as I carried for her actions, I could not let her face the pain and humiliation of the stocks. The condemned could be killed in the pillory if the mob was sufficiently outraged at their crime. The helpless person could be struck by stones, mud, and dung, and even beaten to death if no one stopped it.

"Crime, of course," Pomeroy said cheerfully, breaking my worry. "A missing gel, specifically."

"Oh?" I asked. I had looked for missing girls before, because unfortunately, girls and young women disappeared in London all the time. Procuresses met country coaches and lured girls to bawdy houses where they were forced to work. Sadly, some parents sold their daughters to these same houses for a sum of needed money. Reformers strove to put an end to this trafficking, and they had some success but not enough.

"Yes, Captain," Pomeroy went on. "A street girl. No respectable man's daughter, just a game girl. Her young man is worried about her because she hasn't come home. Went out to Covent Garden one night, then vanished."

"How long ago?" I asked, growing curious.

"A week," Pomeroy said. "I thought at first that she likely found herself a softer bed and a richer man. But the young man is worried she's been hurt by one of her gentleman customers or kept with him against her will. He's been round to all the workhouses and reforming houses, and asked all her friends, but he's not found her."

"Perhaps she has left London completely," I suggested.

"Maybe so, maybe so. But Mr. Thompson, here, he read my report over in Wapping and came to see me. Seems he's heard of one or two game girls a'disappearing from his part of London as well."

Thompson nodded. "Two girls, neither knew each other as far as I can tell. One turned up in the river. She was pregnant, and so might have killed herself. The other was from Wapping—lived with a sailor there when he was in port. He reported her missing after he'd gone to her usual haunts and heard from her pals that she hadn't been seen. Funny thing, she went to Covent Garden one night, to meet a chap, she claimed, and never returned. Her friends thought that perhaps she'd taken up with this fellow and become his ladybird, but now they're worried."

"Neither of these occurrences may mean something wrong," I began. On the other hand, Thompson, a careful man and not likely to chase shadows, had thought enough of it to come round to Bow Street and speak to Pomeroy. "The girls could have gone to work in bawdy houses, although if they had protectors concerned enough to report them missing, I think it unlikely they did." I looked at Thompson. "What is your theory?"

He shook his head, limp hair swaying. "No theories yet, Captain. Or rather, many. The girls might be dead, by their hand or another's, they might be held against their will, they might have found new gents to take care of them, they might have returned to their mothers or fathers, they might have reformed and joined a crusade against prostitution. They might have done any number of things."

"What are you asking of me?"

"Well," Pomeroy said, "the girls what come in here speak highly of you. Quite the gentleman, they think you. I told Thompson that if anyone could pry any secrets from the game girls, it was my captain."

I shot him a weary look. "You are tarnishing my reputation, Sergeant."

Pomeroy grinned, loving to tease, and pleased he could. "You do have a way with them, Captain."

Thompson looked slightly amused, betraying himself with no more than a twitch of lips. "The magistrates are not worried about these missing women, as yet," he said. "Many things could have happened to them, and they are only street girls, after all."

"Unlikely that a large reward will be offered for their return," I supplied.

"Exactly," said Pomeroy. "But if a gent like you were to take a poke around, make sure no man who should be in Bedlam has decided to off game girls, well then, that's a different thing."

I knew how my former sergeant thought—I would investigate, and if a true crime were involved, I would report it to him so that he might find the criminal and reap the reward money. A gentleman did not accept a reward; this was considered beneath him. I was always amused by how

Pomeroy liked to goad me to action, smelling a possible prize. I'd brought him a few already, and he seemed to consider me a source of income.

Thompson was more interested in the crime itself, though he, too, would receive reward money. He did not habitually express emotion, but I had seen, from working with him during the affair of the Glass House, that he had a passionate anger at the men of the world who perpetrated crimes against the helpless. He would worry about missing game girls where his magistrate would not.

I was most distracted by the sudden return of my wife, but I could not turn my back on a matter that Thompson, whom I respected, believed serious.

"I do have resources," I said. I hadn't seen my main resource in about a year, she having taken a post as a maid in Islington. Louisa Brandon, wife of my former commander, would know where I could find her.

"Knew you would understand, Captain," Pomeroy said. "You have a gab and tell us what you discover, eh?"

Thompson looked less optimistic. "The sailor might be willing to speak to you, to tell you about the girl and her usual routine. He's leery of magistrates' houses, though. He could meet you at a tavern, especially if you purchased him ale."

"The Rearing Pony in Maiden Lane," I said. "It's a congenial house."

"Then I will send him round there tomorrow, if it is convenient."

It was. The London Season was nearing its end, and engagements wound down as Mayfair families left for their country estates. Though I was by no means a socialite, I was invited to soirees and musicales held by Lucius Grenville, Lady Aline Carrington, and Lady Breckenridge. Other hostesses, intrigued by the interest of three high-placed members of the *ton,* and by the fact that I sometimes got my name in the newspapers connected with solving a crime, often invited me to their at-homes. As the son of a landed gentleman, I was acceptable, but my father had lost his money, leaving me none, and therefore I was not marriage material for their daughters, which suited me. I had no interest in watching a string of debutantes being paraded before me by hopeful mamas.

When Lucius Grenville, the darling of society, had begun a friendship with me, the *ton* had trained their collective quizzing glasses on me in some bewilderment. Grenville had found me first refreshingly blunt, and then interesting. Our friendship had begun at a New Year's soiree in which the staff hired for the night had turned out to be thieves. I had discovered their purpose, Grenville and I had thwarted them, and our friendship had been born.

At first, he had regarded me as a novelty, but somewhere along the way, he'd begun to like me, and I him. He did not require toadying from me, and I never offered it. His sharp curiosity had been a natural aid during my investigations of several murders in London and outside of it.

I was not certain he'd have interest in street girls who might or might not be missing, but I'd relate the tale anyway. Grenville had been showing restlessness lately, and this problem might just pierce his weariness of London life.

Pomeroy and Thompson could tell me little more. The young man who had approached Pomeroy was called Tom Marcus and did odd deliveries in and around Covent Garden, and I might be able to find him if I looked.

"By the bye, Captain," Pomeroy said when I started to take my leave. "Why did you look me up today?"

I had definitely changed my mind about alerting Pomeroy to Carlotta's presence. I could discover their lodgings in King Street if I looked hard enough and deal with the problem myself. "Passing the time," I said. "The summer days are long."

Thompson sent me a sharp glance, sensing my disingenuousness, but Pomeroy took my words at face value. "The long days suit me after a winter's gloom. The robbers, too, they grow tired of waiting for the dark and attempt crimes in broad daylight. Makes things easier on me." He guffawed.

I smiled politely and took my leave, but Thompson still watched me closely.

THE mystery of my wife's presence in England was easily solved. When I reached home, Marianne, the brandy, and Grenville's coach had gone, but I found a letter waiting for me, written on thick paper, from my uneasy ally, James Denis.

"As you have discovered," he wrote, "Madame Auberge, formerly Mrs. Lacey, has arrived in London. I will make arrangements to proceed with a divorce or annulment as you wish. I suggest a meeting in Curzon Street tomorrow at ten o'clock. My carriage will call for you."

Auberge was the name Carlotta had taken when she moved to France with her French officer. James Denis had given me this information a year ago, and had presented me with her exact whereabouts this spring when I'd been employed at the Sudbury School.

At the time, he'd also offered to fetch Carlotta for me so that I could divorce her or otherwise punish her for her sins. This morning, I had been too startled by her presence and then by the realization that I was beholding my daughter for the first time in fifteen years to think clearly, but I believe I'd known in the back of my mind that James Denis was involved in this. He had obviously decided to take matters into his own hands.

I crumpled the paper. "Why does the bloody man not stay out of my life?"

Bartholomew, entering with my freshly laundered shirts, started. "What bloody man is that, sir?"

I tossed the paper in the grate, though there was no fire on this warm summer day. "Bartholomew, you are quoting *Macbeth*. King Duncan in the first scene, I believe, which is ominous. I mean James Denis."

"Oh, right, sir. I brought the letter upstairs from the messenger what left it in Mrs. Beltan's shop. Bad news?"

"No, more interference. Why will he not keep his fingers from my personal business?"

"Well, he's helped now and again," Bartholomew said in a reasonable tone as he dove into my bedchamber with the shirts. "Nabbed that Frog officer and helped get your colonel out of clink."

True, Denis had provided me with evidence to help clear Colonel Brandon of murder a month ago. He had assisted in all the problems I'd solved in the last year or so—the murder of Josiah Horne in Hanover Square, the murder of Colonel Westin, the affair of the Glass House, and the murder of one of his own lackeys in Berkshire. He enjoyed helping me and making me squirm with the thought that someday I'd be asked to pay him back for his favors.

James Denis was a criminal through and through, a man who reigned at the top of the criminal class. He lived in a fine house in Curzon Street, had power and money and servants to do his bidding, and held many a lord, MP, and respectable gentleman in thrall. He owned them outright—for paying their debts, for gaining their seats in Parliament, for obtaining precious works of art that weren't necessarily available for sale.

He did all these favors for a very high price—the gentleman was obligated to make things happen in the Houses of Lords and Commons that Denis wanted to happen, or to make certain Denis never came before a magistrate. No one could move against him; he held too many in his hand.

He wanted me to work for him. I do not know quite what he wanted me to do, but it could not, in the end, be good. Denis did not help others from kindness—he was a businessman, and he always made a profit. He was simply better at the business than any of the men who paid him.

He had once told me that he thought me a danger to him. I was not certain why, but perhaps because I did not stand in awe of him. I did fear what he could do—to me, to my friends and colleagues—but that fear enraged me still further. If a stand could be made against James Denis, I would be at the head of the crowd.

"He helps only for a price," I said to Bartholomew. "Remember that."

"Right, sir."

He bustled into my bedchamber, where I could see him placing my shirts gingerly into the wardrobe. By the time he emerged, I'd scribbled a note on a half-sheet of saved paper, blew on the ink to dry it, then folded it over once. "Please take this to Mayfair, to Mrs. Brandon. I need her help in a matter."

In the letter, I asked Louisa to have a girl formerly known as Black Nancy to come to speak to me. If anyone knew or could find out what went on with the girls in Covent Garden, it would be Nance. I'd welcome her help.

My pen would not write the fact that Carlotta had returned. That was something I would have to tell Louisa in person. "I will give you shillings for the hackney."

"No need," Bartholomew said, snatching up the paper. "Mr. Grenville obliges."

Grenville paid for all Bartholomew's expenses— Bartholomew and his brother had both been footmen in

Grenville's house until Bartholomew begged to train to become a valet. Grenville had lent him to me, implying that I did *him* a favor. Bartholomew brushed my suits and got my meals, and Grenville paid his upkeep. As Marianne had observed, Grenville did like to take care of everyone.

Bartholomew departed, leaving a draft in his wake. I left the house myself soon after he'd disappeared with his long-legged stride down Grimpen Lane. The summer day had turned hot, and I was sweating by the time I reached Russel Street and walked again to Covent Garden.

The large square that comprised Covent Garden teemed with life on most days, and this fair afternoon was no exception. Market stalls marched down the center of the square and vendors' carts jammed any open spaces they could find. Shoppers swarmed them, and thieves and pickpockets abounded, I knew, awaiting their chance. The game girls usually kept away until after dark, but some of the bolder ones already lingered in shadowed corners, ready to entice a gentleman away for a crown.

The girls liked to tease me, knowing I would neither pay them for a few moments' dubious pleasure, nor turn them over to the Watch or the reformers. I was harmless, and they enjoyed bantering with me. If I had spare coin, I gave it to them in hopes that they'd go home and escape a possible beating from their flats—the customers who sought them— or the men they lived with who took what they earned. Usually, however, they simply pocketed my money, told me I was a kind gent, and moved on to entice their next victim.

Today, I did not see any of the girls I knew as I passed through and turned my steps to King Street; likely they rested during the heat of the day to emerge when the square grew dark.

King Street was a long row, lined on both sides with tall houses. It ended in a warren of small streets that meandered to St. Martin's Lane to the west or Long Acre to the north. The street contained surprisingly respectable houses, not for the gentry or the aristocrats of Mayfair, but for the middle class and those who aspired to be middle class. The easy camaraderie of Grimpen Lane or Bow Street or Covent Garden was here replaced with quiet neighbors and dependable servants who looked after their masters.

I strolled along, wondering which was the boarding-house in which my wife had hidden herself. I had no business chasing her here and trying to find her again, but I could not stop myself. I wanted to see Gabriella. I seethed that Carlotta had never told her about me, but my anger was buried beneath the shock of seeing them both again. My encounter with them in the market that morning had taken on an unreal air, and if not for the letter from James Denis, I might convince myself I'd dreamed it.

Not quite, however. I began to ask the dependable servants which houses took paying guests.

Three of them did, number 37, number 31, and number 19. Nineteen I dismissed because it was above a milliner's shop, and I doubted Carlotta, who had always been a snob about tradesmen, would be found above a shop. Inquiring at number 37, I found that the landlord rented only to elderly military gentlemen, so that left number 31.

The maid who answered my knock replied in the affirmative that Madame Collette Auberge and her daughter and husband were staying here. What name did I want to say?

I did not think Carlotta would see me. I paused on the threshold, wondering whether to send up my card or perhaps give a false name to lure her down. Neither seemed a good solution.

I would have simply tipped my hat, said, "Never mind," and departed, but just then Gabriella herself crossed the hall on her way to the stairs. She saw me standing in the sunshine and stopped.

"You are the gentleman from this morning," she said. She hesitated, no doubt remembering the odd encounter and wondering what to make of it. "Can I help you, sir? My mother is resting."

I drank her in, from her fresh, light brown curls to her pointed chin to her sensible, high-waisted gown now covered with a long apron. My daughter. Lord, she was so beautiful.

"I want to speak with you," I said. "Please."

This morning, I had spoken rudely to her mother, barely restraining my temper, and she must have thought me a madman. I did not believe Carlotta had explained the matter to her afterward, because Gabriella would now look upon me with more alarm. As it was, she displayed the trait that made me know more than anything that she was my daughter. Curiosity.

"Perhaps, sir," she said, "we may converse here in the hall."

She glanced at the maid who had answered the door as though seeking her approval. It was not the thing for a young lady to speak to strange gentlemen, but as I said, she was my daughter. I saw in her that she would bend the rules as far as she could in order to satisfy her curiosity.

I hid a smile and said that would do very well for me. The maid, who looked as though she did not like it but felt it was not her place to say, sent me a warning glance, but opened the door wider to admit me.

I walked into a foyer that was dim and small but scrupulously free of dust and mud from passing boots. The maid closed the door, shutting us into a narrow rectangle with doors opening off one side into whatever rooms lay behind them. At the back of the hall, the staircase rose then twisted back on itself to the next floor.

Gabriella waited politely as I took off my hat and relinquished it to the maid. With a last disapproving glance, the maid trotted off to the back of the hall and down the stairs to the servants' demesne.

Gabriella stood calmly near the foot of the stairs, her hands clasped loosely around the newel post, waiting for me to explain my errand. Her hair, brown with a touch of honey, was pulled into a simple knot on the crown of her head, much as any other young girl would dress it. She wore no jewelry nor perfusions of lace and ribbons that seemed to be fashionable now. In short, she was simple and unadorned, a fresh-faced girl waiting for her life to begin.

I could not speak. I looked at her while she stood poised, very likely wondering whether she'd been wise to let me in the house. Her eyes were brown like mine, and like my own mother's had been. If a man wanted to have a daughter to make him proud, Gabriella Lacey would be that daughter.

Gabriella's look turned puzzled. "Are you all right, sir?"

I suddenly wondered why I had come here. Was it to speak to Carlotta about James Denis, or had I come to feast my eyes on my daughter? I suddenly wanted to tell her the truth, to burst into her world and tell her who I was and what she was to me.

Something held my tongue. I realized I did not want to spoil her innocence. I wanted her to know, but I did not want the knowledge to hurt her.

"Are you well?" I asked her at last.

"Yes," she answered, as though relieved that I had begun speaking on normal topics. "Though I am finding London rather crowded."

My mouth moved in polite response, although I hardly knew what I said. "I am sorry that the peach seller tried to cheat you. It was a poor example of English hospitality."

She smiled. "They did the same in Paris. I believe it is a habit of market sellers to try to take as much coin as they can from the country folk."

"And you have always lived in the country?"

"Always. My father has a little estate near Lyon. He likes farming," she finished with a fond look.

The look broke my heart. I swallowed, my throat tight. "Do you like life in the country?"

"It is pleasant," she said. "But I am excited to be in London, and was happy to see Paris. I have never been farther than Lyon before."

She spoke politely, making the same sort of small talk she might make to an acquaintance of her parents in any social occasion. I barely contained my impatience. I wanted to sit her down and make her tell me all about her life, and what she had learned and who had taught her and what she knew of Latin and Greek and geography. I wanted to know what her favorite color was and what she liked to read and what were her dreams and her hopes. I wanted to know *everything*.

My anger rose. I should already know everything about her. Carlotta had taken from me the joy of watching her grow and learn and become the young woman who now stood before me. I should have been at Gabriella's side for every one of her triumphs and heartaches and everything she discovered in her life. I should have had that.

I had grown used to the fact that Carlotta had left me. The insane rage that had visited me the day I discovered her gone had long since worn down. But seeing Gabriella again brought home the pain of knowing that all the years between then and now could never be recovered.

"You are not called Gabrielle, in the French way," I remarked, my voice soft.

"My mother is English," she said, as though she'd had to explain this countless times. "But you know that, sir. You know her. You spoke to her very familiarly in the square this morning."

I realized, with a jolt, that while I was watching her and trying to discover everything about her, she was trying to discover everything about me.

"I was a captain in the English army. Cavalry, Thirty-Fifth Light Dragoons. I was posted to India at the end of the nineties, and then Paris during the Peace of Amiens. That was fifteen years ago." I stopped.

"Did you know my mother there? I was born in France at the beginning of the Peace."

"No," I answered. "You were born in India."

She looked perplexed. "No, sir, in France. My mother has never been to India."

I fell silent. Carlotta must have constructed a world in which I did not exist, cutting out the six years she had been married to me. In spite of my hurt and anger, I knew why Carlotta had done so—simple lies were easier than the complicated truth, and Carlotta ever sought the easier path.

"She was there," I said. "Your cries used to annoy my colonel. I was not very contrite about that."

I remembered how in the middle of the night, I would walk up and down with Gabriella on my shoulder. Carlotta had hysterics when Gabriella cried too much, certain retribution would come upon her. She had not known what to do with a healthy and robust baby like Gabriella.

I had not known what to do with a baby, either, but I had carried her about the tents and the campfires of the men and told her about all the beautiful things I would buy her when she grew up. I remembered her nonsense words and her laughter, and how she'd stared in wonder at everything on the ship as we'd made the long journey back to Europe.

Louisa Brandon, my colonel's wife, had loved Gabriella. Louisa had no children, and by the time we reached France, she had realized it unlikely she ever would. She had doted on Gabriella, happily playing with her on the voyage while Carlotta was laid low with seasickness. Louisa had been as upset as I was when Carlotta had taken Gabriella away, though she'd had her hands full bringing me back from madness.

"You were there," I almost whispered.

A step on the landing above kept Gabriella from answering. I looked up and beheld a man, not tall but squarely built, descending toward us. He had graying hair, a small head on broad shoulders, and he was bulky, rather than fat. He wore a plain suit of French cut and shoes that would make fashionable Grenville wince. His stance said that he wore his clothes for convenience, not for fashion.

A pale scar creased his face from his ear to his cheekbone, probably earned while serving under Napoleon during the first part of the war. He had a military bearing, and I knew at once that I looked upon the man for whom Carlotta had deserted me.

"Captain Lacey?" he said, stopping behind Gabriella.

I bowed slightly, but made no reply.

"I am Major Auberge. I must ask why you have come."

I answered in French, knowing that language and not wanting any faulty understanding to slow what I wanted to say to him. "There has been an appointment fixed with Mr. Denis for tomorrow."

He nodded. "I received his note. Therefore, we will meet tomorrow. There was no need for you to come today."

"I suppose I wanted to satisfy myself that you were truly here."

He gave another nod, eyes in a somewhat leathery face guarded. "Now you have seen."

"Why did you bring her?" I looked pointedly at Gabriella. "Carlotta could have come alone."

"She could not have made such a journey on her own. I had to accompany her."

"You have other children, do you not?" I asked. "Did you bring the entire family?"

Gabriella broke in. "They stay with my uncle," she said in perfect French. "He has his lands adjacent to ours. We often stay with Uncle."

"Gabriella," Major Auberge said in a father's warning voice.

"Who is he, Papa?" she asked, looking up at him. "Why do you speak to him so? And why does he say I was in India?"

"Gabriella, please return upstairs and attend your mother."

She certainly was my daughter. A rebellious look came over her young face, and she drew a breath as though to argue. Then she seemed to think better of it, made a polite curtsy to me and one to her father, and rushed up the stairs. Her swirling skirts revealed slim ankles and slender calves, the legs of a girl who liked to run, probably more than was ladylike.

She skimmed past her father without looking at him, trained her gaze on me again, then turned the corner of the staircase and ascended to the dim recesses above. Not until we'd heard a door slam in the distance did Major Auberge speak again.

"You will have what you want," he said. "This Mr. Denis says he can make things satisfactory for all parties."

"No doubt he can." James Denis had resources, both people and finances, far beyond what I and a small landholder from Lyon could manage. "Why did you bring her? Gabriella, I mean? Why is she not at home with her uncle and the rest of your brood?"

Red crept into the major's face. "There was a young man. I do not approve of him."

I immediately did not approve of him either. Gabriella was seventeen, too young, in my opinion, for a liaison or engagement. "So you brought her here to keep her out of harm's way? Is that what you told her?"

"We told her we would visit her mother's brother. Which we will." He looked defiant.

"Gabriella will discover the true reason you are here, no matter how you try to hide it from her. She is a Lacey, she will ferret it out."

"She will learn the truth, in time," Auberge said, his brow lowering. "But from me."

"And what truth will you tell her? That I am her rightful father, denied her all this time?"

His expression hardened. "Carlotta was unhappy with you. She told me."

"She was. That is true." After all these years I could admit that I'd expected her to live a life she was in no way suited for. We had both been very young and very foolish, and I ought to have been much more patient with her. "But Gabriella was not miserable. And she belongs to me."

Auberge lost his veneer of politeness. "Do I not know that? Each time I looked at her for fifteen years, I saw another man's child. And now with this telling, I will no doubt lose her, and she is very dear to me."

I scarcely cared. I was jealous and angry and craving to be with Gabriella, and having this Frenchman tell me that he would be heartbroken when she learned the truth was more than I could bear. I planted my walking stick, which encased a stout sword, in front of me. "Then you will have a taste of what you have done to me. Pinching a man's wife and daughter is not the thing, Major."

He only looked at me, anger in his eyes. He knew I was the wronged party, and yet, he blamed me. My fault that I'd lost them in the first place, my fault that now he'd have to face Gabriella with the truth.

I knew I could not stay here and converse with him without rage taking over, without demanding he hand

Gabriella to me then and there. I sent him a hard stare then turned on my heel and marched out the door. He did not try to stop me.

I was so enraged that I was halfway through Covent Garden, the sun shining heavily on my face, before I realized I'd forgotten my hat.

Chapter 4

BARTHOLOMEW had gone by the time I reached home again. He'd left a meal for me on my writing table, but I could not summon any interest in it. Leaving it untouched, I sat down on the wing chair before the cold fireplace and let thoughts whirl through my head.

Not seeing Gabriella all this time had kept the sorrow of losing her at bay, but now that she had reappeared, all the pain and fury resurfaced. I realized after today's visit that Carlotta had effectively expunged me from the girl's life. She'd had no right to do that. By law, a child was related to her father, not her mother, and I alone had the privilege of deciding who had guardianship of her.

I did not know what the laws were in France—perhaps a man could steal another man's daughter and live happily. But those were not the laws of England, and I damn well would get Gabriella back.

I wanted her to know who she was—a Lacey, from a

family of long, blue-blooded lineage. My father had been no saint, and he and my grandfather had beggared the estate with their imprudent living, but the family line had existed for centuries, and I was proud of it. That Carlotta would take away the girl's entire heritage disgusted me. As ever, Carlotta was trying to rearrange the world on her own terms.

Auberge knew the seriousness of it; I'd sensed that in him. He was ashamed of absconding with my daughter, but I do not think he felt any such shame about taking my wife. He'd stated flatly that I'd made her miserable.

I could not refute him. Carlotta had been a delicate creature, not meant to bear the heat of India nor the hardship of life on the move and the dangers of war. She'd been reared to embroider in a quiet manor house or to sip lemonade in a garden with her equally delicate friends.

But Carlotta had married me quickly enough. I hadn't quite believed my luck that day in 1796 when she'd smiled at me and accepted my proposal, then let me kiss her. Carried away with the moment, I had enticed her to bare herself in the tall grass while I made love to her.

I told her I'd met a fellow called Brandon who'd promised he'd help me obtain a career in the army. I would volunteer as an officer and go with Brandon to India without commission or regiment. Many officers started in this way, young gentlemen who had the right birth but lacked funds to purchase a commission. Aloysius Brandon had been very inspiring in those days, young and energetic and with a charisma that made people long to follow him. It was he who'd obtained a special license for me, laughing at my impetuous decision to marry the beautiful Carlotta, although he'd never truly warmed to her.

Carlotta's father had been quietly furious when I announced that I'd married his daughter. I remembered Carlotta trembling and clinging to me, and her father's words,

"Take her, I never want to see her again." We'd boarded ship for India not long after that.

I believe Carlotta began to doubt her wisdom very quickly. I compounded matters by holding Louisa Brandon, whom Brandon had married the day before we'd started for India, as an example for Carlotta to follow. Where Carlotta was shy, Louisa was frank and friendly; where Carlotta was sickly, Louisa was robust and lively. Louisa had a spirit of adventure that helped her through the long, hot ship journey and the unpleasant conditions in India, whereas Carlotta soon wilted. She was almost constantly ill during our five years in India and pushed me away when I tried to be amorous. I had not been very patient with her.

Gabriella was born in 1800, after several disappointed hopes that Carlotta was increasing. The disappointment was on my part, because I believe Carlotta never wanted a baby. I had thought Gabriella's birth would relieve all problems between Carlotta and me, but if anything, having to care for a child only added to Carlotta's distress.

When Gabriella was a year old, we finally escaped the heat of India for a brief but pleasant stay in Sussex, then we moved to Paris during the Peace of Amiens. After we had lived there nearly a year, Carlotta fled me.

I returned to our lodgings one afternoon to find Carlotta out and Louisa waiting for me with a letter in her hand and a distressed look on her face.

I'd searched for them, but Carlotta and her Frenchman had planned well, disappearing into the French countryside. Almost immediately afterward, Napoleon stirred up trouble again, and we fled France and returned to England. I was posted to the Netherlands for that disaster, then France moved into Spain, and the Peninsular War began.

Searching for my wife and daughter had become impractical; after the war it became expensive. I'd had no idea of their whereabouts until James Denis had produced a piece of paper with their direction written on it several months ago.

I remained despondent on the chair for a time, not knowing quite what to do with myself. I'd see Carlotta tomorrow at James Denis's house. A part of me wanted to wait for that encounter to see what would transpire. Another part of me wanted to rush back to King Street and drag Gabriella back home with me.

But the thought of hurting Gabriella stilled me. In all of this, no matter how much anger I felt for Carlotta and Auberge, I did not want Gabriella to suffer. None of the madness that her elders had perpetrated was her fault.

Still despondent, but growing hungry, I rose and went to the meal Bartholomew had left me. A covered plate held beefsteak and potatoes, tepid now. I sat down and ate them, not liking to let food go to waste. The beef was leathery, the potatoes floury, but the Gull was the closest tavern, so we put up with its meals. When I wanted good ale and camaraderie, I took myself to the Rearing Pony, a farther walk, but worth the effort.

Bartholomew dashed back in with his usual energy just as I'd taken the last forkful of potatoes.

"Afternoon, sir." He tossed a cloth-wrapped parcel to the writing table. "Mrs. Brandon sent some cakes and says she'll look into the matter you asked her about directly. And Mr. Grenville would be pleased for you to attend the theatre with him tonight in Drury Lane."

I laid down my fork and wiped my mouth with a linen napkin. "I am hardly in the mood for an outing, Bartholomew."

"He said to come anyway," Bartholomew said cheerfully. "I told him you'd gone off to Bow Street, and he said that if you start investigating anything without him, he'll never forgive you."

I clattered the plates back to the tray. "He needn't worry. I planned to bring him in at the earliest possible moment." Grenville not only had resources, but possessed a clear-eyed intelligence that often cut to the heart of a problem while I grew mired in the emotion of it.

I explained to Bartholomew about the missing game girls and asked him to keep an eye out while he went about his errands for me. He promised to be diligent, and then rushed away to fetch bathwater for me, eager to begin preparing me for my outing with Grenville.

Later, as I walked through the June twilight to Drury Lane, dressed in my best frock coat and filled with the sweetness of Louisa's lemon cakes, I glanced at the shadows, to see whether I could spy out any girls I knew. I saw a few flits of movement, but no one called out to me.

I entered Drury Lane Theatre and gave my card to a footman at the door, who knew to take me to Grenville's box. I had long ago learned not to try to pay for my own ticket when Grenville invited me; it insulted him, and he always squared things with the manager beforehand.

I gave my best hat to a footman who waited inside the box, thankful I'd worn my second best one to King Street if I were going to leave hats about absentmindedly. I had directed Bartholomew to the boardinghouse to obtain it from one of the servants there. He'd seemed slightly surprised I wanted him to fetch it back; when Grenville mislaid something, he simply bought another.

The box was crowded tonight. Grenville stood in the middle of it, a glittering woman in bronze-colored satin on his arm. His cronies from White's stood about, earls and marquises and high-placed men in the cabinet. No wives, however, which made me wonder about the woman, whose back was to me, while I shook hands, greeting those I knew and receiving introductions to those I did not.

By the orange-yellow light of candles in sconces, I saw

that the woman wore a diadem of diamonds in her sleek hair and had a handsome figure hugged by the shimmering gown. When I at last worked my way across the box to Grenville, he turned the lovely creature toward me while I shook his hand.

I opened my lips to ask him to introduce me, then I stopped and stared in astonishment. "Marianne?"

She gave me a sardonic smile. "How flattering you are, Lacey."

Grenville's look was slightly smug, but also wary. They made a fine pair, he with his dark hair and lively brown eyes in a face that was, if not handsome, arresting, and she with her golden hair and forget-me-not blue eyes. Whatever modiste Grenville had her frequent had created a gown to enhance Marianne's greatest assets. The décolletage bared her shoulders and the top of her bosom, but did not make her appear overly voluptuous, and the long skirt, not too much adorned, made her look willowy, but not too thin.

All in all, the gown was a masterwork, the creation of an artist. Her hair, too, instead of hanging in the little-girl curls she liked to sport, had been pulled into a coil of burnished gold and adorned with a net of diamonds. A few gold ringlets fell artfully to the back of her neck. Her only other jewelry were dangling diamond earrings and a tasteful circlet of diamonds around her throat.

The entire ensemble reflected Grenville's elegant taste and restraint. Marianne would no doubt have loaded herself with diamonds so that the actresses below, her former colleagues, could see how far she'd risen.

I realized that this was Marianne's debut. Grenville had been squiring her about in Hyde Park and to races, places where mistresses were accepted, but this was the first time he'd brought her to the theatre as his guest. He had invited all these aristocrats and high-born gentlemen to meet Mar-

ianne and to usher her into his world. That explained the
absence of wives; these men would not bring their respectable ladies into a box with a former chorus actress.

Marianne cocked her head at me. "Aren't I a fine race-
horse?"

Grenville frowned, but I took her hand and bowed over
it, pretending I hadn't heard. Grenville was treating her no
differently than he would any other mistress, but I had a
feeling that Marianne would not be content with being an
ordinary bit of muslin.

The other gentlemen in the box, however, seemed
happy to accept her. The mistress of the most fashionable
gentleman in England had no small influence. She was
quickly drawn into conversation while Grenville looked after her with a cautious eye.

"It is a difficult thing," he said to me in a low voice. "If
I do not flaunt her as though I care nothing for public opinion, I could ruin my reputation. But if anyone learns I will
call out any gentleman who goes near her, like a lovesick
actor in a melodrama, I will *definitely* ruin my reputation."

"The great Grenville cannot fall in love?" I asked.

He gestured me to a chair at the front of the box, and we
seated ourselves. "I must conduct my entire life with cool
detachment." He shot me a hard glance. "And who the devil
said anything about falling in love?"

I did not answer. Grenville had grown fascinated with
Marianne the moment he saw her, a little more than a year
ago. I knew, and Grenville would not admit, that the fasci-
nation had blossomed into something deeper.

His expression softened, and he pinched the bridge of
his nose. "Lacey, how did this happen to me?"

"These things come upon one when one least expects
it," I said philosophically.

He shook his head. "I am wallowing, when I know your
troubles are greater than mine. Marianne told me."

I had assumed she would, which was just as well. I had no wish to explain it again.

He went on, "If there is anything I can do, Lacey, you know you have only to ask."

He looked sincere. Marianne and I had been correct that he was a generous man. "Thank you, but I will wait to see what Denis has to say."

"James Denis?" He raised his brows. "Bartholomew told me you had received a letter. It was about this?"

"Yes." While Marianne held court behind us, I rapidly explained the situation.

Grenville looked thoughtful. "I wonder what his game is."

We both knew that Denis never did something for nothing. "I will find out."

Marianne's throaty laughter rippled to us. She knew how to charm gentlemen when she bothered, and she was busily charming them all. Grenville looked dismayed. "Hell, it's started."

He did not mean the play, which had not begun. A few acrobats cavorted on the stage below, but no one was paying them much mind.

"I promise to second you in any duels that may arise," I said.

He shot me a look. "You do not amuse me. If I drag her to my side, I'll be a laughingstock. But if I do not, some other gentleman might."

"Marianne is no fool. She knows who you are and what you can give her."

"Humph. In other words, she will remain with me as long as I pour gold into her hand and wave trinkets before her eyes." He sighed. "And do you know, Lacey, I am idiotic enough to do just that."

"I do not think it is that simple," I began, but I could say no more, because the acrobats were leaving to desultory applause, and the gentlemen in the box took their seats. Marianne, I was relieved to see, sat down next to Grenville.

The play was tedious. It was a shortened version of *Othello,* rewritten so that Othello forgave Desdemona, killed Iago in a dramatic duel, and danced and sang with Desdemona and the remaining cast. The audience knew the songs and sang along.

At the interval, two more acrobats, more skilled than those of the first group, came out to make jokes, tease the audience, and flip from each other's shoulders. A footman brought me a message, and I stood up and moved to more light to read it.

The note ran, "When you grow tired of sitting in the most gossiped-about box in the theatre, perhaps you could be persuaded to visit the neglected ladies across from you, whom you were at one time pleased to call your friends. D.B."

I smiled, recognizing the handwriting and the acerbic style, and looked across the theatre to the boxes opposite. Even without a glass, I could see the white-feathered head-dress that adorned Lady Breckenridge. Stout Lady Aline Carrington was easier to spot. She spied me looking at them and gave me an unashamed wave.

I bowed back, took my leave of the gentlemen in the box, and made my way to the other side of the theatre.

Lady Aline's box was less crowded than Grenville's, containing only Lady Aline, Lady Breckenridge, and three other women of their acquaintance, two of whom were married to gentlemen in Grenville's box.

"Lacey, dear boy, I knew you would not forget us," Lady Aline boomed. She took my arm in a fierce grip and nearly dragged me to the seat beside her. Lady Aline was a spinster who followed the ideas of Mary Wolstonecraft and had no qualms about her unmarried state. At fifty-two, she declared herself to be well past the age of scandal, and rouged her cheeks, dressed in the first stare of fashion, and went about as she liked. She had more friends than any other woman in London, and was godmother to a good number of children of the *ton*. "Grenville has a new ladybird, and suddenly the gentlemen of London have no use for the rest of us."

I smiled as I sat between her and Lady Breckenridge. Lady Aline was a great friend of Lady Breckenridge's mother, and often took Lady Breckenridge under her wing, as the countess rarely came to Town. Aline was Louisa Brandon's great friend as well, a fact of which she reminded me as soon as I had finished greeting the other ladies.

"I invited Louisa tonight, but she begged off, claiming a headache. Quite right of her. I believe she ought to lay low until next Season, when plenty of other scandals will put her own out of mind. After all, her husband never did kill Henry Turner. We all knew that, of course, but magistrates can be so stupid. You were very clever to prove otherwise."

"You did help me," I answered. Lady Aline's observations and knowledge of her fellow man had assisted me when Brandon had been accused of murdering a dandy in a ballroom in Berkeley Square.

"You flatter me, Lacey. I only answered questions about who did what at the Gillises' ball. You and Donata put the pieces together to find the murderer."

Lady Aline approved of my fondness for Donata Breckenridge. Lady Breckenridge's first husband had been a monster who'd died the summer before. Donata was resilient and bold, but I knew that her marriage to Breckenridge had hurt her deeply. He'd had many lurid affairs, usually under her nose, and was never apologetic about it.

Tonight Donata wore an ensemble almost as elegant as Marianne's. Her headdress dripped feathers down her black hair, which was coiled and curled into ringlets. She'd rouged her cheeks slightly, adding color to pale skin. Her deep blue gown covered her modestly, but like Marianne's, it was cut to enhance her pretty plumpness and hide anything not desirable. I'd had the great fortune to have undressed her myself, and believed that nothing about her was not desirable.

At this moment, she was peering avidly through a lorgnette at Grenville's box. "Is that your Marianne Simmons?" she asked me.

Lady Breckenridge had been the first of the ladies of the *ton* to discover Grenville's current liaison, and to her credit, she'd kept it quiet.

"Yes," I replied. "That is certainly Marianne."

"You know her?" Lady Aline asked in fervent interest.

"She used to live in the rooms above mine. Grenville met her while she was trying to help me find the young ladies who'd been kidnapped in the Hanover Square affair."

Marianne had helped only for the promise of a reward, and Grenville, astounded by her, had given her twenty guineas without thought.

Lady Aline tapped my arm with her closed fan. "You wretched boy. You never told me the most delicious gossip in all of London. I had to learn it from my servants. I shall never forgive you."

I knew from her teasing tone that she had already forgiven me. "It was Grenville's business, not mine."

"And you are a true and loyal friend to keep it so close to your chest. That is what I admire about you, Lacey." Lady Aline flapped her fan, never minding that she'd completely turned around her opinion in five seconds. "She is a stunning creature, is she not?"

I admitted to myself that Marianne had cleaned up nicely. I knew, too, that she was fond of Grenville, and he of her, and I hoped they could tear down the walls of mistrust between them and discover that fondness.

"I prefer the present company," I said politely.

I was slapped with the fan again. "You silver-tongued rogue. And people wonder why I invite you everywhere."

I smiled politely, but my heart was not in the banter tonight. Usually, I should be happy sitting between a lady I considered a good friend and a lady for whom I bore increasing affection, but I was still too dazed from my encounters with Carlotta and Gabriella and preoccupied with the meeting tomorrow.

I had contemplated courting Lady Breckenridge when I was free of my marriage, and in fact, had gained her permission to do so. This summer, I would go with her to her father's estate to meet her family, and I looked forward to the visit. I was at last discovering the peace of being in love without drama.

Yet tonight, I could not be comfortable, and Lady Breckenridge sensed my distance. She behaved as usual, making acid comments about people she observed in the theatre and blatantly watching Grenville's box. She talked of a violinist she'd recently decided to sponsor—one of a string of unknown artists, poets, and musicians she thought had talent and introduced to London society. This one was young, French, and difficult, but his playing had already wormed its way into the hearts of the right people.

I listened and made the correct responses, but she knew she did not hold my interest. She watched me from the corners of her eyes, but asked no questions.

Lady Aline, on the other hand, leaned toward me, all eagerness. "I heard from Louisa that Bow Street has asked you to look into another matter for them. Do tell us about it."

Lady Breckenridge lowered her lorgnette and tilted her

head, letting black curls spill over her shoulders. I glanced behind me, but the three ladies in the chairs in the back of the box had their heads together, tittering over something.

"The reason Pomeroy and Thompson asked for my help is because the matter is unimportant, to the magistrates anyway," I replied. "And it is rather sordid for ladies."

Lady Aline's eyes gleamed. "But we like sordid things, Lacey. It makes us feel morally superior."

Lady Breckenridge slanted me a half-smile, enjoying Aline's joke. "A corpse in a ballroom is also sordid," she said. "And yet we were quite interested in that. Not to mention the goings-on at the Glass House."

She referred to a brothel I had investigated and helped close down at the beginning of the year. Lady Breckenridge had given me information about a few people involved in that problem, and she had been put into danger, through my own fault.

"It involves street girls," I said. "A few have gone missing."

It spoke of the fairness of my friends that neither lady blushed nor grew horrified that I mentioned such a subject.

"You are correct," Lady Breckenridge said. "That is sordid."

"Nonsense," Lady Aline broke in. "It is quite exciting. Life as a spinster is dull, dear boy. Why should these girls be missing? Perhaps they've run off to seek their fortune."

"The men with whom they lived reported their absence with concern."

"Poor things," Lady Aline said. "Perhaps their lovers beat them, and they ran away."

"Or perhaps they found better accommodation," Lady Breckenridge, ever practical, said.

"Either may be the case. I will meet with one of the men tomorrow and ascertain what sort of person he is. That will tell me much about why the girl is gone."

"Louisa said you asked for her help," Lady Aline said. "But she did not specify what sort."

Lady Breckenridge brushed at her dress as though she'd found a stray speck of dust. "I cannot imagine what Mrs. Brandon knows about street girls."

"Oh, she takes them in, my dear," Lady Aline said. "They do not stay, but she's rescued a few urchins in her time, given them employment, and found places for the best of them. A few simply run off with the spoons, but Louisa is not deterred. She has a good heart. Is it one of her strays you are after?"

"A young woman I know who was formerly a street girl, yes," I answered. "Louisa found her a place at an inn in Islington. I wish to ask for her help."

Lady Aline nodded as though it all made sense. I saw Lady Breckenridge's bosom rise sharply, but her expression remained neutral. "You know quite interesting people, Lacey."

I kept my tone light. "I have had an adventurous life."

She said nothing, and I wanted to shift uncomfortably. Lady Breckenridge found it interesting that I was so well acquainted with Marianne Simmons, and now I was admitting counting a game girl as one of my acquaintance. Her good opinion mattered to me, and I sensed it drifting away.

"I wish to ask Black Nancy if she knew any of the missing girls," I put in.

"Of course," Lady Aline said. "Go to one of them. That is good logic."

Lady Breckenridge said nothing. She raised her lorgnette and scanned the crowd, slightly turning her body away from me.

Lady Aline pumped me for more information about the missing girls until she was satisfied she'd heard everything. Then she moved on to other gossip, reporting to me every bit of tittle-tattle about the debutantes, matrons, widows, dandies, and aristocrats in Mayfair. Lady Brecken-ridge made the occasional desultory comment, but stayed rather silent, for her.

Near to midnight, the theatre crowd began drifting away. The ladies with Lady Aline had already departed, as it was Wednesday, and Almack's Assembly Rooms closed their doors at eleven, no exceptions.

The second performance, a comedy, had begun, but no one paid it much mind except those in the pit, who jeered and laughed and tried to look up the actresses' skirts. I pre-pared to take my leave and return to Grenville's box, but Lady Aline stopped me. "I am off home to host a card party for about a dozen friends. You will of course escort us, dear boy. You cannot let a helpless widow and spinster travel across London alone in the middle of the night."

I hid a smile. Lady Aline had her own carriage and ret-inue of loyal servants, and any man fool enough to rob her would no doubt find himself at the business end of her thick walking stick. Likewise Lady Breckenridge was well looked after, and her footmen were stronger and more agile than I.

But Lady Aline wanted me, for what reason I did not know, and so I answered politely, "I will happily escort you to Mayfair, but I will not stay for cards. I have not the head for them tonight, and I have an early appointment tomor-row."

"Pity," Lady Aline said, struggling to her feet. I rose to mine and helped her up. "You are such a splendid conversa-tionalist, Lacey. You do not say only what everyone wishes to hear."

"You mean I am rude."

"I mean that you are refreshing. That is why Grenville favors you; you are nobody's toady, and the poor man must get weary with that. He probably favors the unknown ac-tress for the same reason. Difficult to find novelty in your life when you have everything handed to you. John, my boy, run fetch my carriage."

The youthful footman jumped and ran out, reminding me of a younger version of Bartholomew. Two maids entered a moment later with wraps for the ladies, and we made ready to leave.

I could not simply abandon Grenville, so I sent another footman around to say that Lady Aline had requested my presence. He would understand. When Lady Aline expected a person to do something, they found themselves doing so without argument.

Lady Breckenridge had traveled to the theatre with Lady Aline, so the three of us journeyed home in Aline's carriage, the two ladies facing front, I facing the rear as a gentleman should. The carriage rolled north and west, leaving Drury Lane at Long Acre, then traveling through narrow byways to Leicester Square and beyond to Piccadilly, from which we turned north to Mayfair.

Lady Aline lived in Mount Street, around the corner from Lady Breckenridge's home in South Audley Street. Hers was a typical London townhouse, brick with white pediments over doors and windows and an arched, Palladian front door painted dark green with a door knocker in its center.

The carriage stopped a few feet from this door, footmen swarming from the house to place a stool beneath the carriage door. Another footman unrolled a rug from the stool to the front door so that Lady Aline and her guests never had to tread on the dirty cobblestones of London.

Relieved of wraps, we went upstairs to Lady Aline's opulent sitting room. She bustled out with her servants, bellowing orders like a sergeant major as she chivied them in preparations for her card party. The servants scampered after her, leaving Lady Breckenridge alone with me, which, I realized, was Aline's intention all along.

Lady Breckenridge pulled a gold case from her reticule and extracted a thin, black cigarillo. She held it loosely in her fingers, slightly pointed at me. I took the cigarillo from her, lit it with a candle in the elaborate silver candelabra on a half-moon table, and handed it back to her.

"Thank you," she said neutrally. She drew a long breath of smoke, as though she'd been wanting to do nothing but that all evening. "The theatre is tedious," she remarked. "I long for country walks—or rather walks in the country garden. I am not one to tramp mannishly across wet meadows and scramble through hedgerows and think it entertainment."

"Do you ride?" I asked. My mouth moved, but my attention was on the glisten of candlelight in her hair and the way her lips pursed as they closed around the cigarillo.

"Of course," she answered, as though there should have been no question. "I imagine you have gone off the exercise after living in the saddle for the King's army."

"Not a bit. The one enjoyment I had in Berkshire this spring was riding again whenever I wished."

Her brows lifted. "The groom up and being murdered must have been inconvenient."

"Most inconvenient for him. The one thing I did right in the eyes of Rutledge the headmaster was ride every day. He approved of cavalrymen."

"And yet, in London you remain stubbornly on foot."

"Lack of steed, my dear lady."

"Oh." She inhaled smoke again, drifting away from me as though she'd never thought of this handicap before. "Ride with me tomorrow in Hyde Park. I keep two horses, and one is fat and lazy and in need of exercise. He's a gelding, not a lady's horse, do not worry. I keep him for my son, but he has not ridden very much this Season. My son longs for country air, too."

I had met her son not many weeks ago, a small, dark-haired boy of five, who was now Viscount Breckenridge. A few vicious people drew attention to the fact that six years before, Breckenridge had been in the army on the Peninsula, but the lad had Breckenridge's sturdy build and his somewhat scowling demeanor. Officers did take leave to see family if necessary. I imagined Donata had not been pleased to see her husband return. The thought of Breckenridge insisting on his connubial rights stirred anger in me, although Breckenridge had been dead for a year.

"I hope he dances in hell," I murmured.

She heard me. "Who?"

"Your husband."

She blinked, not having the benefit of my train of thought. "I hope so, too, but I was speaking of riding in Hyde Park."

I shook my head. "I must decline."

"I see."

I saw anger in her eyes. I said quickly, "I have an appointment."

"So you said. Early in the morning."

"I do not know what will develop from it, so I must decline for the rest of the day until I discover more."

She shrugged as though it did not matter. "Has it to do with your game girls?"

"No." I came to her and plucked the cigarillo from her gloved hand. She watched me without expression as I set it on the edge of a table. I cupped her shoulders and turned her to face me. "My wife has returned to London. The appointment is with her, to speak about divorce."

She drew a quick breath. "I remember you said you wanted to find her, to end the marriage."

"If I can. That is why it is complex."

She opened her lips to respond, then she closed them again. I searched her face, looking for what she truly felt, but Lady Breckenridge was a master at hiding her emotions. I'd come to know her well enough, however, to see the tightening around her eyes, the small tug of the corner of her mouth. She was unhappy, but living with Breckenridge had taught her never, ever to show her hurt.

"I should not call on you until I know what is what," I said. "Because I am Grenville's friend, and because divorce is so sordid, it will get into the newspapers. I do not want you to be dragged in as well."

"It is far too late for that, Gabriel. Gossip about you and me is already all over London, and I will get into the newspapers whether you are seen calling on me or if I flee to the wilds of Scotland."

"That is likely true." My fingers tightened on her smooth shoulders. "But I am imagining the cartoons, portraying me carrying on with one woman while busily discarding the other."

"Carrying on?" she asked sharply.

"A poor choice of words, but ones the newspapers will likely use. I hope to do this as quietly as possible, and if anyone can make it happen quietly, it is James Denis. But even he cannot guarantee there will be no damage to you."

"Ah, the intriguing Mr. Denis," she said. "He has promised to help?"

"He has begun helping me whether I consent or no. That is another reason the appointment will be complicated. I do not know exactly what he wants in return for this favor."

She looked at me a moment, her expression guarded. "I observed earlier tonight that you knew interesting people."

"And I observed that I'd had an adventurous life, which is true."

She moved away from me, sliding from my grasp gently but firmly. "My husband led an adventurous life. I soon grew tired of it."

Her voice remained light, but I sensed the tension in her

words. Her husband had given her nothing but misery, and she'd responded by becoming a daring, flirtatious, and acerbic woman with an edged sense of humor. From what Lady Aline told me, she'd made the decision not to become the downtrodden wife forced to look the other way at her husband's affairs, and to do as she pleased. Her bold façade, however, did not mean she had not borne hurt.

"I am not Breckenridge," I said.

"True." She lifted her cigarillo from the table and drew another mouthful of smoke. "But who knows who you really are? I am rather naïve about gentlemen."

I went to her again, and this time, I cupped her face in my hands and leaned down to her. "I never will be Breckenridge. I've told you. If not for you, I would let the entire matter lie, but if I have to prostrate myself before James Denis to get myself free, I will do it. It may be that my marriage is already finished because she abandoned me, but I want to know for certain. I want to start on a blank page with you, no impediments to interfere when the banns are read. I have so little to give you but my heart, and so I want to offer you my honesty."

Her eyes widened during this speech. She held the cigarillo out from her side, and a wisp of smoke wound around the pair of us. "You are quite fervent."

"About this, I am."

We looked at each other, inches apart. She tried to close her expression again, but I saw fear in her eyes, the fear of more pain. Lady Breckenridge was such a strong and intelligent woman that her tiny vulnerability touched the gallantry in me.

I closed the space between us and brushed her lips with mine. When I ended the kiss, her voice grew soft. "Go, then."

I smoothed a stray lock of hair from her forehead. I wanted more than anything to remain here where I could watch her and converse with her and then retire discreetly with her to her home. But my thoughts were in too much turmoil, and I did not want to arrive at James Denis's home unkempt and unshaven from a night of revelry.

"Good night," I said. I lifted her hand to my lips and pressed a light kiss to her glove.

She stepped back, the usual glint of humor in her eyes, and resumed the cigarillo. I bowed, turned, and made for the door.

"Do find out what happened to those poor girls," she said, standing firmly in the middle of the room, watching me go. "And of course, tell me *everything*."

I descended from a hackney coach in Russel Street and looked along the narrow length of Grimpen Lane to see a glow of candlelight from my window, a point of warmth in the darkness.

I had told Bartholomew not to wait up for me but to do as he liked for the evening while I attended the theatre. Usually he met his brother Matthias at a tavern for ale and a good gossip. He rarely used the time I gave him for extra sleep, leaving me with no idea when he stored up the energy he displayed during the long hours of the day.

I did not like Bartholomew to leave candles burning, because they were dear. Now that Marianne no longer trotted downstairs to pinch them, I did have a steadier supply, but even so, frugality had become a habit.

I ascended the stairs and entered my front room.

A young woman sat on my wing chair next to a small table with a lit candle and a half-drunk glass of ale. A fat braid of very black hair draped her shoulders, and her eyes sparkled impishly as she gave me a wide smile.

"Now then, Captain," Black Nancy said. "You look surprised to see me."

Chapter 5

SHE was the same Black Nancy, and she wasn't. The huge smile and cocky manner would never change, and she still had her fall of very black hair. But she was a far cry from the girl I had known last year when she'd been a young woman in shabby but seductive cast-off clothing, desperate for coin to take back to her father so he would not beat her.

She wore a neat cotton gown as plain and modest as any servant might wear, and she was clean. Her air of wary desperation had gone, but as she rose to greet me, I learned that her lewd good humor had not.

"Ain't I glad to see you." She threw her arms around my neck and planted a noisy kiss on my cheek. "Let's look at you now." She stepped back, holding my hands. "As handsome as ever. And such a fine coat. Have a tailor now, do you, just like a nob?"

"Borrowed from Grenville," I answered. "The tailor, not the coat."

"Grenville, now he's a true rich nob, but I like you better."

"You flatter me."

"You're much more interesting, ain't you?" she went on. "I read about you in the newspaper all the time. Captain Lacey, up to his neck in the Berkeley Square murder, Captain Lacey in thick with Bow Street on the Glass House. You do have a nose for trouble."

"And how are you, Nance?" I asked dryly. I broke from her grasp, closed the door, removed my hat and gloves, took up a spill from the shelf near the door, and lit more candles. "I heard you were a slavey at an inn in Islington."

"Aye, that I am." She flicked her braid behind her back, and held a candle steady while I lit it. "I make up beds and plump pillows and carry trays of tea and smile at the guests so they'll leave behind more coin."

"And you like this?"

"Oh, aye. I have a soft bed all me own, food when I want it, a bit of coin, and I don't have to lay on me back for a gent unless I want to." She lowered her right eyelid in a wink. "Don't mean I don't sometimes want to."

"You're incorrigible, Nance."

"Does that mean the same as a bawd? 'Cause I know I am." She glanced at the closed door of the next room. "I'm thinking your bed is nice and soft. Strong, too, I'll warrant."

I wanted to laugh. I'd rather missed her blatant attempts at seduction, and I was pleased to see that she was no longer so needy of kindness. She seemed to have found some contentment.

"I have a lady now," I said as gently as I could.

"I know that. Mrs. Brandon told me. She told me everything about you. She's a good one for a gab, is Mrs. Brandon."

"How unnerving." I blew out the spill and tossed it to the cold grate.

"That we had a chin-wag about you? Naw, it were all flattering. I have a gentleman of me own, you know. He's hostler at the inn. Knows all about horses, just like you. He ain't much handsome, but he's young and very strong and likes to laugh."

This was the first I'd heard of a paramour. "Is he kind to you?" I asked. I had a far more fatherly demeanor toward Nancy than she'd like, but I did worry about her. She was apt to imprudence when it came to men.

"He's kindhearted. He knows he's got a good girl in his Nance." She gave me a sly smile. "Thought I'd ask you, though, on the off chance."

She'd known I'd say no. Nancy had always loved to tease me.

"Did Mrs. Brandon tell you why I wanted to see you?" I asked. "I need your help."

She nodded, suddenly all business, and sat down with a thump. "She said something about missing game girls, but not much else. Want me to have a trot about Covent Garden, do you?"

"I hoped you'd know the girls, or at least know someone who knew them. I want to be certain that they haven't simply moved on and don't want to be found; perhaps they encountered happiness the same way you've found it in Islington."

"That was you yanking me off the street and telling Mrs. Brandon to take care of me. I was that furious at you for doing it. I wanted *you* to take care of me, you see."

"I know you did." I remembered the way she had pursued me with relentlessness, puzzled because I had no intention of taking her to be my ladybird. The fact that I had very little money and was more than twice her age had not deterred her. I suppose that compared to living with her father, the prospect of staying with me in these two rooms must have seemed heavenly.

As though reading my thoughts, she said, "I still think we could have chirped along quite nice in this nest, you and me, but I ain't sorry I went to Islington. Now, who were these girls?"

I seated myself and told Nancy what Thompson and Pomeroy had told me about the two girls telling their friends' their intentions of going to Covent Garden, and then disappearing. As I talked, Nancy lifted her pint of ale and slurped it noisily. She gave me a nod when I finished. "Could be they found someone new. But I'll dig up some of me old pals and have a gab. Can I listen in when you talk to this sailor chap? I'll know how he treated her if I hear what he has to say—whether she scarpered or really is in trouble."

"Tomorrow afternoon at the Rearing Pony. I do not know what hour yet."

"You send your slavery around to Mrs. Brandon's to fetch me. That's where I'm sleeping of nights for now." She looked thoughtful. "Mrs. Brandon seems a bit low. I'm cheering her up."

I blenched, wondering what bawdy jokes Nancy thought would cheer Louisa. "She went through much when her husband was in Newgate."

"She said as much. She's that pleased with you for sorting it all out."

I wondered. That episode had revealed many of Colonel Brandon's sins, and I'd left Louisa uncertain whether she could forgive him. Brandon had walked firmly into the mess himself, but my poking and prying had revealed much that both he and Louisa would have preferred to remain hidden.

Nancy drained the last of her ale and wiped her mouth. "I'll be taking my leave then, if you're not offering me a bed."

I gave her an admonishing look. "I will find you a hackney."

She cackled with laughter. "A hackney? Ain't we fine ladies and gents. I can go on me own. I'll look up me pals on the way. Course, some of them won't speak to me, like as not, since I've landed on me feet."

I shook my head. "Not when girls have been vanishing from the dark of Covent Garden. Look up your pals during the day."

"They're asleep during the day. Deserve to rest, don't they? I've been tramping these streets since I was a tyke, Captain. I know me way about."

"You're not a tyke any longer, nor are you a game girl. Respectable maids do not wander about dark London byways at night. I will fetch you a coach."

She flashed a grin and peeped at me from under her lashes. "Sure you don't want a bed warmer, Captain?"

"You flatter me, Nance, but you are still the same age as my daughter." Thinking of Gabriella made me falter. I had once worried that she'd become like Nancy, selling her body for tuppence in order to buy her bread. That she'd grown into a fine young woman as innocent and well cared for as any English lady made me shaky with relief. Whatever her mother had done to me, she'd not punished Gabriella.

Nancy lost her smile, came close to me, and put her hand on my shoulder. "Aw, Captain, I know you're worried about her."

"It is not that. I have discovered that she is well."

A look of genuine pleasure entered her eyes. "I'm that glad, Captain. Truly I am."

As was I. I held on to that thought as I saw Nancy down the stairs and to a hackney waiting at a stand in Bow Street. The coachman leered at me as I gave him coin, no doubt believing I was sending my bit of muslin home. Nancy did not help matters by flinging her arms around me and kissing my cheek as I lifted her up into the coach.

"You're a fine gentleman, Captain." The coachman cracked his whip and the carriage sprang forward. Nancy stuck her head out of the window. "Always said so, didn't I?"

The horse's hooves threw sparks in the darkness as the coach skidded around the corner. Black Nancy's laughter floated back at me, more merriment than I'd heard on this street in a long time.

I awoke early next morning after a bad night. Bartholomew drew a bath for me and shaved me while I lay in the cooling water and reviewed my dreams. I'd dreamed mostly of small Gabriella running about camp, her golden hair tangled and her little feet filthy with mud. I'd carried her about on my shoulders, proudly displaying her to all and sundry, until my men had started calling me Lieutenant Nursemaid. I never minded.

Speaking with Gabriella yesterday had proved one thing: I still loved her desperately.

My morning correspondence included a note from Thompson, who fixed the appointment with the sailor he wanted me to interview for one o'clock. No doubt the man would expect me to buy him dinner.

James Denis's coach called for me at nine. The carriage, with its parquetry and velvet squabs, was as opulent as anything Grenville owned, except that no coat of arms reposed on the polished black door.

I sat in the splendor alone, in my regimentals, brushed and carefully cleaned by Bartholomew. I could have chosen to wear my best frock coat, but for some reason, I'd wanted to remind Carlotta exactly who I was and what I had been most of my life.

London traffic, always thick, seemed particularly difficult this morning. We traveled slowly through Pall Mall to St. James's, and waited for a long time while a broken coach in St. James's Street was hauled out of the way, the horses cut from their tangled traces.

The tall houses on this street were the abodes of bachelor gentlemen, all likely snoring hard in their bedrooms above. They would not rise until late morning and then saunter to their clubs in early afternoon. The traffic at this moment consisted of servants and workmen and all the people who earned their living catering to the wealthy of St. James's and Mayfair.

Once we started again, we rolled past White's, its bow window empty this early, and turned to Piccadilly. The coach rattled past Burlington House and its columned entrance, near which the young man that Brandon had supposedly killed had taken rooms. We turned up Half Moon Street, then onto Curzon Street, and traversed its length to number 45.

My throat tightened as Denis's cold footman helped me from the carriage. Denis's house was plain on the outside, its façade betraying nothing of Denis's vast wealth. The hall inside was like the carriage, unadorned, but obviously costly. He'd left the house in the airy Adams style, white paneled walls, black accents, marble tile, and straight-legged satinwood furniture.

I followed the footman, a former pugilist by the bulk of him, up the stairs and to Denis's study.

I'd entered this room many times in the last year and a half since I'd had my first appointment with James Denis.

As with the floor below, he had furnished it sparsely, but with elegant furniture—a mahogany desk, bare but for a few sheets of carefully placed paper, a bookcase between the windows, a half-round table holding brandy and cups, two Louis XV chairs in front of the desk for visitors.

Today, he'd brought in a Turkish sofa as extra seating. As usual, another former pugilist, one who'd given us a good piece of information about the affair at Sudbury School, stood near the window.

My wife was seated on the sofa, dressed in her best, holding a cup of tea and a saucer. Major Auberge sat next to her, minus the teacup. He'd chosen civilian dress, a plain frock coat and trousers and shoes, nothing of the army about him at all.

Denis rose from behind his desk. He was nearly as tall as I was, dark-haired and long-faced. Denis was barely in his thirties, but the chill in his blue eyes was that of a much older man. I wondered, not for the first time, what his life had been before this, and what had made him into the ruler of the underworld that he was. He had most of the London magistrates in his pocket with only a few exceptions. Any criminal who tried to cross him found himself quickly and mercilessly dealt with.

He and I had an uneasy truce, forged after he'd had me trussed up and beaten as a warning not to interfere with him. Since then he'd helped me solve murders, but with the understanding that he wanted me beholden to him for his help. He'd decided to tame me not with violence, but with obligation.

For this reason, he'd hunted up my wife in France and had her brought over to face me.

"Lacey," he greeted me with a neutral expression. I bowed just as neutrally.

My daughter was nowhere in evidence. "Where is Gabriella?" I asked Carlotta.

"We left her behind," she answered in a shocked tone. "We certainly would not bring her here, to discuss *this*."

I gave her a hard look. "You left her in a boardinghouse in King Street, alone?"

Carlotta shifted. Auberge said, his accent thick, "She is being looked after. Madame Seaton, the landlady, said she would look."

I shot a glance at Denis. He gave me an almost imperceptible nod. "One of my men is watching the house."

I exhaled, somewhat more relieved. I knew he had a man who watched me and reported my activities, and I knew that his pugilists could keep Gabriella as safe as could be. With girls going missing from Covent Garden, I disliked my daughter being near the place alone. "Why could you not find them better accommodation?" I asked Denis.

"I did offer to put them in a hotel in Mayfair. They declined, preferring to pay their own way."

"It is better, I think," Auberge put in.

Carlotta said nothing. She bent her head to drink tea, then halted with the cup at her lips, as though she could not make herself swallow. She ran her tongue across her lower lip and set the teacup aside.

Denis gestured me to sit. "Shall we begin?" He took his chair behind the desk and shifted the papers in front of him as I settled myself and rested my hands on my walking stick. I noticed Carlotta glance curiously at the stick and then the leg that I limped on. She had been gone long before I received my injury, which was a souvenir of my feud with Aloysius Brandon.

"I have consulted with a solicitor at length on this matter," Denis said. He sounded as dry and matter-of-fact as any lawyer in Lincoln's Inn. "Separation—divorce *a mensa et thoro*—is possible, given that there has in this case been abandonment and adultery, but it is not a dissolving of the marriage. Neither of you could marry legally with only this sort of divorce. And I take it that marrying again is what all parties have in mind?"

"It is," Auberge replied stiffly. I said nothing. What I chose to do afterward was not Carlotta's business.

"Annulment is the easiest route," Denis went on, directing his words at me. "But unless you can prove that either of you has insanity or that you are too closely related or were married to other parties when you contracted your marriage, there are no grounds. Impotence, another cause for annulment, is also out of the question?"

He looked at me without embarrassment, waiting for me to answer, as though I should not be uncomfortable discussing whether I could father a child. I supposed that I could claim Carlotta had left me because I became impotent after she'd produced Gabriella, but the fact of impotence would have to be proved. I scarcely wanted to know how I'd produce the proofs that I could not copulate with a woman.

I shook my head. "Out of the question."

"That leaves a parliamentary divorce," Denis went on. "You, Lacey, will go through the process of the *a mensa et thoro* separation, then sue for adultery—a case of criminal conversation between your wife and Major Auberge—and then you will request a private Act of Parliament for the complete divorce. This will allow both of you to marry elsewhere." He folded his hands. "A long and, needless to say, expensive process."

"How expensive?" Auberge said tentatively.

"Several thousand pounds."

Auberge waited while he translated to French francs, then his ruddy complexion paled. "I think I have not this money."

Denis straightened a paper minutely. "I will be happy to furnish the cost of the procedures."

Auberge looked surprised. "You are a great friend to the captain, then?"

Denis did not answer that. "Are you agreed?"

Auberge glanced at me. It seemed unreal, after so many years, to have Carlotta in the same room with me, and for me to at last be able to take my vengeance. But the vengeance was flat and stale, like bread left too many days, tasteless and unpalatable.

"What must we do?" I asked.

Denis answered, "We go to the Court of Doctors' Commons and begin with the separation. Then we go to Common Law court with the trial for adultery."

I saw Carlotta wince. A naturally shy woman, the thought of standing in open court while a charge of adultery was read out must be repugnant to her. I could not imagine that Auberge would be any happier with it.

"No," I said.

Denis glanced at me. If he felt surprise, nothing showed on his damnably blank face. "She is obviously guilty. She has had children with this man while still being married to you, so there will be no question."

Carlotta's gaze became fixed to the floor.

"There must be another way," I said. "Annulment. I will claim to be insane; half of London thinks it anyway."

Denis did not smile. "You must be proved to be legally insane, and no matter what the newspapers insinuate, it is not enough. You have said you are not, nor were, impotent. Perhaps you could find a way to prove you are too closely related?"

"No." Carlotta looked up, her face white. "I know we are not. My father tried to prove that when he discovered I'd married Gabriel. He failed."

I hadn't known that. So, her father had tried to have our marriage annulled, and Carlotta had never mentioned this interesting fact. My annoyance stirred, but it was all so long ago. I made a "there you have it" gesture.

"Annulment also would mean that any children of your

marriage would be declared illegitimate," Denis pointed out to me.

"That is out of the question," I said quickly.

"Another alternative," Denis continued in his monotone, "is to send Mrs. Lacey and Major Auberge back to France, and declare Mrs. Lacey missing and presumed dead. She will live out her life as Madame Auberge and no one will be the wiser."

"Unless someone, like you, discovers her again," I said.

"If you and Major Auberge cooperate with me, I could erase any trail to her. Mrs. Lacey would, to the world, be dead. You might even inscribe a headstone," he finished, with chill humor, glancing at me.

The idea tempted me. To simply send Carlotta away, to tell the world she'd died in France, would be the simplest route, for her and for me.

Uneasiness pricked me. I pictured myself ten years hence, happily married to Donata Breckenridge—that is, if she did not turn me away over this business—and having some busybody announcing to her that the first Mrs. Lacey was still alive and well. I would be arrested as a bigamist, Donata humiliated.

"I dislike that solution," I said. "Though I realize it is likely easiest. But there is more here at stake than our marriage." I looked at Carlotta. "I want Gabriella. I do not want her to disappear with you, never to be seen again. I want her to stay in England with me."

Carlotta looked up swiftly. "No."

"She is my daughter."

She gave me a desperate look. "She is *my* daughter. I will not let you take her away from me."

My anger rose. "You had no qualms taking her away from *me*. I am her legal guardian, Carlotta, not you. I decide her fate, not you."

"She does not even know you are her father," Carlotta said hotly. "She believes that Henri is."

"I gathered that," I said. "It does not matter what you told her, the fact is that I am her father, and by law, you have no right to her."

"You would take her?" Carlotta began to cry, tears pooling on her cheeks. "You would do such a thing? Take her away from her mother and the father she knows and her brothers and sisters?"

My hand closed on my walking stick. "Of course I do not mean to rip her from the bosom of her family. I am certain she has affection for all of you. But neither do I intend to let you shut her away from me. She is mine, and I claim her. If that means I do have to drag you through every court in England to get her away from you, I will."

"And I will fight you," Auberge said quietly, "if you do."

"You have no rights at all," I told him. "You stole my wife and my child, and left me nothing. I find that your threats do not concern me."

"I was driven away," Carlotta choked out.

"That does not matter," I said. "I would have let you go, because I know that in the end you hated me. But you should have left Gabriella."

"Abandon my child?"

"*My* child," I said savagely. "But you cared nothing for that."

She balled her fists. "Was I to leave her to your horrible life following the drum? With mud and filth and sour food and the danger of being massacred at any time? What sort of life was that for a child?"

"I might have given up the army and taken her home to England. But you never gave me the chance."

"You had no intention of living in England. You hated it. You loved the army. I remember."

I could not argue this point. In England, I had my father's house to return to with my martinet father in it. I would rather submit a child to the dangers of army life than to my father and his insane rages.

"Louisa Brandon would have looked after her— gladly," I said.

Carlotta shot me a look of pure hate. "Mrs. Brandon. Always Mrs. Brandon."

"Please," Auberge broke in. He looked at me in anguish. "Please stop."

I closed my mouth in a firm line. Carlotta collapsed back on the sofa, sobbing, her hands pressed to her face.

Denis had sat through the exchange impassively, watching us without expression. He must have been used to listening to histrionics, especially when called upon to dispense his own form of justice.

"I am afraid Captain Lacey is right," he said in his clinical tone. "He is Miss Lacey's legal guardian, no matter what you, Madame and Monsieur, or even Miss Lacey herself, feel about the matter. I am certain we can come to some sort of arrangement after the marriage has been dissolved."

Carlotta continued to cry. Auberge sat like a miserable lump next to her. My heart burned. They had wronged me, but I could not help but let Carlotta's pathos touch me. She had never been a strong woman, and from the look of things, she'd leaned heavily on Auberge throughout the years. Now Auberge was at a loss, and Carlotta could not master herself.

Denis moved the papers aside again, and nodded to his stolid footman, who'd said not a word or moved during the entire encounter. He was no doubt used to histrionics as well.

"I will have the solicitor begin the *a mensa et thoro* proceeding at the very least. You need do nothing for now,

Mrs. Lacey, but wait in your boardinghouse for my instruc-
tion. I know enough people in the right places to make this
as painless as possible."

I had no doubt. He would call in favors all over London
from men too terrified of him to disobey.

Auberge rose. He gently took Carlotta's elbow and
pulled her to her feet. "We will go now. Come."

Carlotta wiped her hand over her face. Her cheeks were
smeared with tears, her eyes bright red, her nose swollen.
She was not a pretty woman, I realized. What I'd been
smitten with as a lad of twenty was young limbs and a shy
smile and large eyes.

Auberge, however, looked at her with a tenderness that
said he did not care a fig what she looked like. He loved
her, doubtless more than I ever had.

The footman gestured Auberge and Carlotta out of the
room. They went, Carlotta clinging heavily to Auberge's
arm. When I tried to follow, however, the footman blocked
my path to the door, which made me know that Denis had
instructed him beforehand not to let me leave.

"I do not like this," I said, once the door had closed behind them. "And I do not like your offer to foot the bill."

Denis shrugged. "You want this divorce."

"You may think nothing of destroying a woman for
gain, but I must have compassion for her. If not for
Gabriella, I'd turn my back on her actions and let her be
dead." I paused, sighed. "No, truth to tell, I do not know
what I would do. I am sorry, in a way, that you found her."
That was not true either, because I was gladder than I'd
ever been in my life to find Gabriella whole and well.

"There is another way," Denis began softly, his eyes
cool, "that we have not discussed. One that would make
you free with the least amount of fuss."

A chill crept into my bones. He stared back at me, blue
eyes impenetrable.

He could do it. He could order Carlotta murdered and never turn a hair. He had enough pull in London to hire someone to do it quietly, send Auberge home, and keep the magistrates away from him.

I took a step closer to him. The footman bent a watchful eye on me, but I ignored him. "If you harm a hair on her head, I will kill you. I do not care how you'd try to stop me, I will do it."

We shared a look. I saw him assess what I was capable of and make his decision. He did not decide out of fear; he simply decided. "Very well."

Damn the man. He could coolly stand and contemplate murdering a man's wife as a favor to him and think nothing of it. Another reason why I could never bring myself to work for James Denis.

I straightened up and set my walking stick on the floor. "I would be the first man suspected, in any case."

"Very likely," Denis said, his mouth straight. "Very well then, Captain. We will begin with the courts."

I left his house in a foul mood. I waved away the carriage that waited to take me back to Covent Garden and tramped on foot northward. I could not bring myself to go home and brood. I needed to walk, I needed to think, I needed to talk to someone who would understand.

Not surprisingly, my footsteps took me up South Audley Street, past the home of Lady Breckenridge, who was no doubt fast asleep—a lady of fashion did not rise before noon—and through Grosvenor Square to the Brandon house in Brook Street.

Chapter 6

MY knock was answered by Brandon's correct butler. I knew that the man had once been a corporal in the Thirty-Fifth Light, had joined the army to escape a shady past, and had gotten himself into trouble in the army more than once. When he was on the point of desertion, Louisa rescued him, promising him protection if he reformed his ways. He'd taken to being a servant quite well, rising from footman to butler quickly after our return to London.

He peered at me down his once-broken nose, his hauteur genuine, but conflicting with his thick body and criminal-class stare. "Mrs. Brandon is not at home, sir," he said.

"At eleven in the morning?" I asked skeptically. "Is she at Lady Aline's?"

"I beg your pardon, sir. I mean that she is not at home to you."

I stared. Louisa Brandon had never before instructed her servants to send me away. "Is she all right?"

"Perfectly fine, sir."

I closed my mouth with a snap and looked him up and down. "Let me in, Matthews."

His eyes widened. One eye had been hurt badly in a fight long ago and was perpetually half-bloodshot. "And disobey the mistress? Never, sir."

"Tell her that I forced my way past you, which I will do if you do not stand aside."

Matthews thought a moment. Louisa would be furious if he let me in, but at the same time, I was desperate and angry and had a stout walking stick. He had witnessed my famous temper on the Peninsula, and though he probably matched me in strength, he always watched me warily.

He deliberately took one step to the side. "Very well, sir. I will tell her that I held out manfully."

"Good." I strode past him. As he shut the door and reached for my hat and gloves, I asked, "Why does she not want to see me?"

"She does not want to speak to anyone in connection with the colonel's recent incarceration, sir. She is most sensitive about it."

"And where is the colonel?"

"At his club. He, for one, has decided to bluff it out."

I could imagine. Brandon and I belonged to a fledgling club for cavalry officers in a tavern in St. James's. I pictured him sitting in the taproom with his newspapers, casting his chill blue gaze over anyone who tried to bring up the embarrassment of his brief stay in Newgate. Brandon had a fiery and compelling personality, and if he willed people not to talk about it, they would not.

I knew where Louisa would be at eleven in the morning. I trudged upstairs to her yellow sitting room, where she liked to take breakfast and go over her correspondence on mornings that her husband was out.

She sat on a low sofa, wearing her favorite yellow, a

gown of soft muslin. She had not yet dressed her hair, and it hung down her back in a loose golden braid. I'd always thought her lovely, with her crooked nose, wide mouth, and light gray eyes. Those eyes flashed irritation, however, when she beheld me entering, unannounced.

"I believe I will have Matthews flogged," she said.

"I bested him in a fair fight." I sat down on a sofa next to her, tossing my walking stick on the floor. "Do you deny me your door now?"

"Am I not allowed a few moments' solitary peace?" she challenged.

"How long have we been friends, Louisa?"

"Above twenty years, I believe."

I nodded. "Exactly. And have we not shared hardship as well as good times? Have we not helped one another over the worst in our lives?" I leaned forward. "Do not shut me out now, Louisa. I need you."

She attempted a smile. "I found Black Nancy for you. Was that not enough?"

"Carlotta is in London," I said abruptly. "I've just come from a meeting with her."

Louisa's irritation vanished in an instant. Her face lost color, and her gray eyes grew sharp and hard, like many-faceted diamonds. "Where is she?"

"I spoke with her at James Denis's, but she is staying in a boardinghouse in King Street, Covent Garden."

"Did she come back to find you?"

"No. Denis brought her here, to facilitate a divorce."

"Oh." Her voice was as hard as her eyes. "I would like to see her."

"She has changed," I tried to say lightly. "I believe life in the French countryside agrees with her."

Louisa's mouth flattened. "She had no right to leave you. I saw what it did to you. She had no right to do that."

Her vehemence startled me. Louisa had been very angry when Carlotta left me, but I had no idea she still clung to the anger. "I forgave her, Louisa. The leaving of me, I mean. I made her terribly unhappy."

"She was a bloody fool. If she'd opened her eyes, she would have seen what a blessing she had in you, what a worthy man you are. But she was always selfish." She broke off and held up her hand as I began to protest. "Do not worry, Gabriel, I will not beg you to run off with me to Paris again. When I asked you that, I was hurt and confused by Aloysius's betrayal. That must have been extremely awkward for you."

Her cheeks were flaming now, embarrassment at her outburst in my rooms several months ago. She, after learning of her husband's infidelity, had asked me to take her on a wild liaison to France. I would have been more flattered had I not known she wanted only to punish her husband. I had reasoned her out of the rash action.

"You were much agitated," I assured her. "What happened that day is no reason to bar your door to me now."

She softened. "I do hope you did not hurt Matthews."

"I battered him only metaphorically. I needed to see you."

"About Carlotta." She frowned. "I truly wish to bully *her*. What of Gabriella? Where is she?"

"She is well." I paused. "I saw her. Louisa, she is so beautiful."

Tears welled in my eyes again, and I saw matching tears in Louisa's. She moved to me and took my hand, and we sat thusly, each of us thinking of Gabriella.

I loved Louisa, my dearest friend, who'd helped me through every heartache. I knew now that we never would have been happy as husband and wife, or even as lovers, but I thanked God for her friendship.

She kissed the top of my head and sat back, drawing out her handkerchief and wiping her eyes. "We are a pair of boobies," she said, sniffling. "Nancy told me you'd said you knew Gabriella was safe, but I thought you referred to the information Mr. Denis had given you this spring."

"She is well and safe, and a father could not be more proud of a child," I said. I retrieved my own handkerchief, mopped up the damage, and stuffed the cloth back into my pocket. "My task now is to decide what to do about Carlotta."

I outlined everything Denis had told us. "I dislike his hand in this. His solutions to problems are to cut ruthlessly to the quick, no matter who he ruins in the process."

By the firm lines around Louisa's mouth, I realized she shared Denis's opinion. "Why be gentle with her?" she asked. "She certainly was not to you. Divorce her and be done."

"The scandal will taint me as well as her."

Louisa waved this away. "She will return to France and be Collette Auberge. No one in her French village will worry about the divorce of Captain and Mrs. Lacey in faraway London. You are protected by the reputation of Grenville—if he says you are in, you are in. You could stand on Piccadilly in your shirtsleeves and chuck bricks at passersby, and still society would fawn on you because you are Grenville's favorite. Likewise, Lady Breckenridge and her family are quite powerful. No one will dare shun her for favoring you."

"Possibly not," I conceded.

"Take Carlotta to court, Lacey. She deserves it."

I studied her a moment. "You have become vindictive."

"Well, when my innocent husband can be accused of murder, why should a woman guilty of adultery be let free?"

I thought I understood. This spring, a woman Louisa's husband had confessed to having an affair with had dragged him firmly into the murder at Berkeley Square.

Louisa had not forgiven her, and she likely had not yet forgiven Brandon. She was extending this anger to Carlotta, another woman who'd broken a marriage.

"I wish I were vindictive," I said. "It would give me a clearer path. As it is, I do not know which direction to take. I came here for your clearheaded thinking."

She flushed. "About this, I cannot be clearheaded. I do not know what you will think of me, but I am afraid I wish her to suffer a little." She paused, her demeanor softening. "Might I see Gabriella?"

"Of course. I have an appointment this afternoon to interview a sailor from Wapping, but after that, I will be free. Come to Grimpen Lane this evening, and I will take you to her."

"Carlotta will not permit it," she predicted darkly.

"As I reminded Carlotta not an hour ago, I am Gabriella's legal guardian. She will permit what I say she will permit."

Louisa sent me an odd look. She opened her mouth, then shook her head, as though she'd been prepared to say something and thought better of it. "I am sorry I cannot help you on the matter of Carlotta."

"There are no simple answers. That is not your fault." I squeezed her hand, then got to my feet. "Is Black Nancy here? She wants to meet the sailor and quiz him about his lost ladybird."

"She is downstairs." Louisa rose and rang a bell. "I quite enjoy having her here. She is an excellent conversationalist. Very diverting."

"She said the same about you. I do apologize for bursting in and burdening you with my problems. I seem to always be doing so."

"We are friends," she answered. "Naturally, we seek one another when we are troubled. I hope that it may always be so."

She smiled a little, and I was pleased that she'd decided to put her embarrassment over our encounters during the Berkeley Square matter behind us. Perhaps anger at Carlotta and joy at Gabriella's return had united us again.

Louisa sent the footman who responded to the bell to fetch Nancy, then she accompanied me down the stairs, her hand tucked through my arm. We reached the ground floor to see Matthews pulling open the front door as a carriage rolled to a stop before it. A footman sprang to open the coach, and then Colonel Brandon descended and strode into the house.

Colonel Aloysius Brandon had black hair, graying at the temples, keen blue eyes, a trim physique, and a brusque manner. He had been a competent commander, earning respect as well as rank. He had gotten me my first commission by knowing the right men and pulling in favors and possibly using outright bribery. He'd helped me up the ladder in the army, though I'd moved no farther than captain. Beyond that I truly did need influence and wealth, and generals did not always appreciate my forthright manner and frank opinions. My own fault, but I never learned to scrape and bow.

Brandon stopped short as Louisa and I came off the last stair. "What are you doing here?" he directed at me.

I inclined my head. "I am well, thank you."

He transferred his blue glare to his wife. "I thought you said you were not allowing him into the house."

"I pummeled your butler," I said, not really in the mood to spar with Brandon. "But I am leaving."

I took my hat and gloves from the footman, noting that Matthews had made himself scarce. Black Nancy came from the back of the house just then. "Ee, Captain, don't you look fine, all in your blue and silver." She took my arm. "Me pals will be pea green when they see me with you."

Brandon scowled at her. Despite his own indiscretions, he did not approve of Louisa's strays, especially not game girls. He said nothing, only turned his back on us all and ascended the stairs.

LOUISA insisted that her own coach take us back to Covent Garden. Nancy rode in it like a queen, staring regally out the window, pretending to be a lady of fashion. She looked down her snub nose at me and drawled nonsense in a ridiculous parody of an upper-class accent. At least her antics made me laugh, and I felt a little better.

I would think over my choices concerning Carlotta and come to a decision about what best to do. I would consult Grenville—a true neutral party. He could put his fingertips together and narrow his eyes and examine the problem objectively. He also likely had solicitors at his beck and call who might find another solution. I did not necessarily have to use James Denis entirely in this matter.

I bade the coachman put us down in Maiden Lane, in front of the Rearing Pony. We'd arrived a little before time, and I saw no sailing man awaiting us. I recognized the regulars, who nodded at me. The rest of the room was filled with reedy clerks or drovers stopping for a nourishing pint of ale.

They all rather stared when I led Nancy to an inglenook and slid into its more private benches. The landlord's wife, Anne Tolliver, brought us overflowing glasses of ale, cast a curious look at Nancy, flashed a smile at me, and departed.

"She fancies yer," Nancy said. She took a deep, satisfying pull of ale and licked the foam from her lip.

"She fancies every gentleman who gives her a tip."

"Naw. She don't give a smile like that to the others." She grinned at my discomfiture, and took another drink of ale. "What's your lady like?"

"Very posh," I said. "She's a viscountess."

"Oo-er," Nancy said, exaggerating the exclamation. "I know that. Mrs. Brandon told me. A widow, very handsome, very la-di-da, and quite taken with you. But I mean, what is she like? Is she all smiles and laughs and a good heart, or is she cold and snobby?"

"Neither. She speaks her mind, but she is kind, in her way."

Nancy looked doubtful. "Sounds peachy. What will she think of you sitting here slurping ale with a game girl?"

"Oh, I am certain she will have plenty to say about it. But she knows that you are helping me with an investigation. She wants to help as well."

"Well, then, perhaps I'll look her up and we'll talk all about it."

I imagined an encounter between Lady Breckenridge and Black Nancy and shuddered. "Perhaps you will not."

"Maybe not. But I like to tease you." She glanced up. "I think that's your sailor, Captain."

A short, rather square man had come into the tavern and stood looking around uncertainly. I rose and beckoned, and he, seeing me, made his way to the inglenook. He was bow-legged and walked like a man expecting a ship to roll under him at any moment. I realized when he neared us that he was not very old, perhaps in his mid-twenties, although his weather-beaten face made him look older. His blue eyes held an air of worry, and he greeted me with an awkward bow. "Mr. Thompson tol' me I should speak to yer."

I signaled to Anne to bring another ale. I bade the man sit down, then Nancy and I slid onto the bench across from him. He watched us with a blank expression until Anne set a tankard in front of him. He lifted it, set the rim to his lips, and poured at least a third of it down his throat.

"Thank ye," he said, wiping his mouth. " 'Twas a thirsty journey from Wapping Stairs."

"I thank you for making it," I began. "Mr. Thompson said you were very worried about your young lady. Tell me why you should be so."

"Because it ain't like her." He shot me a belligerent look, as though daring me to disbelieve him. "She wouldn't walk out and not tell me, or me landlady. She'd 'uv sent some word to me."

"When did anyone last see her?" I asked.

"Week ago come tomorrow. She was there when I woke up in the morning. Went out again at four. Never seen her since."

"She came to Covent Garden, to meet someone, Thompson tells me," I said.

"Said she had something special. Said she'd make a few guineas from it. Said she'd bring them back to me." He swallowed. "But she ain't come back."

Nancy leaned forward, her bosom resting on the table. "What do you do with the money she usually brings you?"

The sailor glanced at me, blue eyes troubled. He had a blue-black tattoo on the inside of his arm, an intricate pattern that looked oriental. I nodded at him to answer the question.

"Well, goes to housekeeping, don't it? Me wages and hers, we buy the bread and our bed. Our landlady ain't much, but she leaves us be."

"But she's a game girl, you know that," Nancy went on. "Means she goes with blokes what fancy her for an hour."

"Only thing she knows how to do," the sailor said reasonably. "And she always comes home to me."

Nancy nodded, as though she was satisfied. "I don't think he did her in, Captain. And maybe she liked him well enough."

He scowled at her. "Course she did. My Mary, she's always waiting for me when I sail in, and there to send me off again."

I held up my hand. "We believe you, sir. What is her name? Mary—"

"Chester, sir. I'm Sam Chester."

"She is married to you?"

He looked evasive. "In a manner of speaking. That's the name we give the landlady, and I don't know no other. She was with another sailor when I came home three year ago, and she didn't like him. But he wouldn't let her go. So I said, if I win at dice, she's mine. And I won. She been with me since. I only ever knew her as Mary."

"Very well. What does she look like?"

Hope sparkled in his eyes. "You'll look for her?"

"Yes." I drew a breath. "I cannot promise to find her, but I will try. She is not the only girl who's gone missing."

"That's what Mr. Thompson said. Magistrate didn't believe me, but Mr. Thompson said he knew a chap what could find her if anyone could."

I pushed my ale glass aside. "I am pleased he has such faith in me."

"She's a bit of a thing, on the plump side," Sam said. "Has yellow hair, but she dyes it and it don't look very good. I like it brown, like natural, but she says it has to be yellow." He thought a moment. "Brown eyes, big smile." He stopped, his voice faltering. "Such a pretty thing."

I glanced at Nancy, letting the man recover himself. She shook her head. "I don't know her, but I never get to Wapping. But one of the girls at Covent Garden might 'a seen her. I can ask."

"Why should you help?" He looked at me in sudden alarm. "You ain't the Watch, are you? Wanting to haul her off for trying to make a bit o' coin?"

"I am not the Watch, Mr. Chester. I simply don't like to see girls hurt."

Nancy ran her hand up my blue-coated biceps. "He looks after us."

I slanted her an ironic glance, and she grinned back at me. Chester obviously didn't know what to make of this teasing, but he sagged against the bench. "Thank ye, sir. I've been so worried."

I asked for another ale for him, which he drank gratefully. Pressing him on questions, though, did not bring much more information. Mary Chester's habit was to leave the house at five or six in the evening, prowl around Wapping getting what customers she could, then returning home around midnight to share a meal and a bed with Sam. The only thing Mary had done differently the day she disappeared was to leave earlier than usual and to travel to Covent Garden. Sam did not know where she met the man she was to see there, or what he looked like, or who he was. Questioning her friends in Wapping had produced no answers. The girls had not known; Mary had been rather evasive about it.

I asked Sam where I could send him word, and he gave me a direction of a boardinghouse near Wapping Stairs, not far from the magistrate's house where Thompson did his work. He said he would stay in London a little longer than he usually did, though he might be shipping out on a merchantman in two weeks' time. I told him I hoped I would know something by then, at least.

The three of us left the tavern together, and I sent Sam off a good deal more hopeful than when he'd come. Finding a lost girl in London was like finding the proverbial needle in the haystack, but I did have several ideas about where to start looking. Black Nancy would be a help as well.

"Poor gent," she said as we watched him weave his way up Maiden Lane toward Southampton Street, which would take him to the Strand. "I met up with a girl last night who might can help us. The hackney driver didn't want to stop, but I made him. You take your time; I'll run fetch her."

Before I could object, Nancy ran away in the opposite direction from that which Chester had taken. I saw her black head bobbing along through the crowd, then she was gone.

I made my way after her slowly, turning north when I reached Bedford Street. Sam had not told us much, but Black Nancy seemed convinced that Mary would not have run away from him. I agreed that they seemed happy, although we had only heard Sam's version of the tale.

The odd thing was, Mary had agreed to meet some unknown man in Covent Garden and had been giddy with the promise of guineas. Who was the man and why Covent Garden? Had he been responsible for her disappearance, or had she met someone else? Or had she been robbed of the guineas she'd so looked forward to and died fighting for them? Anonymous bodies washed up in the river all the time.

But a random robbery would not explain the other disappearances. The incidents may or may not be connected; Thompson and Pomeroy expected me to find out whether they were.

When I reached Covent Garden, it was at the height of its activity. Later risers had joined the throng among the packed stalls and the mass of humanity who wanted to buy fruit or flowers or hens or milk or gewgaws or whatever else the vendors were selling. The shops ringing the square were likewise full of middle-class young ladies with their mothers and maids, shopping shoulder-to-shoulder with unwashed lower-class women with coarse hands and weathered faces. Young male servants swarmed about trying to purchase their masters' dinners, hucksters sidled to passersby trying to entice coins from them, vendors called, trying desperately to pitch their voices above those of their rivals.

The sun shone hot, and sweat dripped freely from faces

young and old, thin and round, ruddy and pale. A water
seller did a fair business letting passersby stop and refresh
themselves with a dipper of well water from his bucket. A
man selling cool ale in the shade of a brick building also
plied a good trade.

I searched the crowd for Nancy, wishing she'd waited
for me. She was nimble and young and easily evaded me,
and I had no wish to tramp all over Covent Garden searching for her. I smiled a gentle refusal at a hopeful orange
seller, then made my way across the south side of the
square, heading for Russel Street.

I spied Nancy standing in the shadow of the back of a
stall halfway along the square. She waved when I saw her,
and I stepped toward her, dodging a scurrying maid carrying two squawking ducks by their feet.

Another girl stood with Nancy, dressed in brilliant
green velvet. Her skin was the color of cream-laden coffee,
and her hair, shiny black, cascaded from a broad-brimmed
hat in a riot of fantastic curls. As I neared, both of them
grinned at me, the black-skinned girl with a gap in her
teeth that was very fetching. She had chocolate-colored
eyes that skimmed up and down my regimentals, a narrow
face, high cheekbones, and arched brows. Her smile
widened when I bowed to her, and she dropped into the
perfect parody of a fashionable lady's curtsy.

"This is Felicity," Nancy sang. "A fine lady and a fair
friend. This is him, Felicity."

Felicity looked me up and down again with a bold gaze
that made me want to blush. "I've seen him about," she
said. "You are right, Nancy, he is a fine one."

My face heated still further. I was used to the game girls
and their teasing banter, but Felicity's gaze seemed to burn.
She was a little older than Nancy, perhaps twenty, and her
greater experience showed in her eyes. She knew about
men's desires and how to stir them.

Black-skinned girls were common in London. Some came here from Jamaica as slaves with their owners, or they worked their way over as free women, or they were the daughters of former Jamaican slaves. They became servants if they were lucky, and if they were unlucky, they plied Felicity's trade. Black mistresses were quite sought after, and a clever girl could become a rich man's paramour.

Grenville had had such a mistress—Cleopatra, she was called—whose origins had been obscure. I'd never met her, she and Grenville having parted ways before he'd befriended me, but apparently, she'd taken London by storm. She'd been the mistress of Grenville, then of the Prince Regent, and then married to a country squire with whom she'd fallen in love. Grenville apparently had assisted in pulling off that wedding, and he claimed she now lived in wedded bliss surrounded by fat children.

Felicity, on the other hand, would likely remain on the streets unless she happened to catch a wealthy man's eye. That is, if she were not unfortunate enough to be transported to the West Indies. It happened from time to time that a person wanting to make quick money kidnapped black women and boys to sell to plantation holders in Jamaica and Antigua. This was not legal, especially when the women and boys in question were free, but it still went on. My reforming friend, Sir Gideon Derwent, wanted to stop this deplorable practice, and it had slowed, but they still had much to fight.

"At your service, madam," I said to Felicity.

"Don't I wish," she answered, but with a brash smile to show that she teased.

"Felicity never saw the yellow-haired wench," Nancy broke in. "But she might a' seen the other one. Name of Black Bess."

Felicity nodded. She folded her hands across the sash

that hugged her bosom, a fair imitation of a debutante at her first ball. "Black Bess is rather a friend of mine. I haven't seen her in a while, and her lad's been around looking for her. I thought maybe she'd taken up with a protector, but Nancy says maybe not."

Felicity spoke in a more cultured voice than Nancy, as though someone had taught her middle-class English, or she'd carefully learned it. There was nothing to say, however, that she was not a middle-class girl herself. White fathers bore children with their black servants or slaves, sometimes raising the sons and daughters alongside their legitimate children. Felicity's father could have been from any background, from small farmer to royalty.

"No," I said. "Pomeroy thinks she might have been kidnapped."

"Pomeroy the Runner?" Felicity asked, suddenly alert. "Last time I saw Black Bess, Captain, she was in the company of Pomeroy of Bow Street. And they weren't simply having a chat, if you know what I mean."

Chapter 7

"WELL," Nancy said, eyes bright. "Ain't that interestin'?"

It was indeed. Pomeroy had neglected to mention this fact. "How long ago was that?"

"Week and a half, I'd say," Felicity answered. "Bess liked to turn Mr. Pomeroy up sweet, so he wouldn't take her in. Let him kiss her if he liked, no coins changing hands. Last time I saw her, she was *there*." She pointed to a small gap between stalls in the middle of the square. "It was late, and dark, and she was with him, laughing in her way. Couple of days later, Bess's man comes through Covent Garden, looking worried. But I hadn't seen her since."

I would definitely have to speak again to my former sergeant. "Are you certain it was Pomeroy with her? If it was dark?"

"No mistaking the Runner, Captain. Tall man, big, bright yellow hair, laughs like 'haw haw haw.' "

Her mimicry of Pomeroy's bellowing laugh was so comical that I nearly laughed with her. "Where does Black Bess live? With her lover?"

"She and her Tom have rooms in a passage between Drury Lane and Great Wild Street. Not much, but clean and their landlady doesn't cheat them."

"Is he still there?" I asked.

"Likely. I'll take you if you wish."

"I do wish," I said. I wondered why the devil Pomeroy hadn't mentioned that he'd known Bess, although he might not have wanted to admit such knowledge in front of Thompson.

"Tom won't be there now," Felicity said. "He labors for a builder, moving bricks and such. Tonight, you come here, and me and Nance will take you down."

Nancy grinned her compliance. I was not certain Louisa would be pleased at Nancy lingering in Covent Garden until dark, but I did need her help.

"I'll see you home, then," I said to Felicity, "and meet you later."

Felicity's grin widened. "I can take care of myself, Captain. Have for ten years."

"If young women are disappearing from Covent Garden, I do not want to risk you disappearing yourself, especially now that you've offered to help me."

"Told you he were a gentleman," Nancy said with a wink.

They laughed at me, but my concern was genuine. No one cared much for prostitutes who plied for trade in the streets. High-born courtesans and women like Marianne with wealthy protectors fared better, but even so, when gentlemen no longer had interest in them, they had nowhere to go, unless they'd been prudent with the money their protectors had given them. Even the much-celebrated Lady Hamilton, mistress of Admiral Lord Nelson, had lived in near poverty after Nelson died, waiting for the pension Nelson had asked be given her, which never came.

I pondered where to take them while we waited. Mrs. Beltan would never forgive me for bringing game girls to my rooms while her shop was open. Likewise, having them sit in her shop, with its respectable clientele, would also be out of the question.

"Well," I began, but Nancy was staring in a puzzled way at some commotion behind me, and I turned to see what she looked at.

A young woman hurried through the crowd, pushing people this way and that, blindly running, earning curses from men and women alike. One matron caught her arm, shouting at her to watch her manners and behave decently, but the girl twisted away and continued her journey.

Without a word, I left Felicity and Nance and pushed my own way through, my path parallel to the girl's until, with my longer stride and more forceful nature, I managed to move in front of her and halt directly in her path.

Gabriella was sobbing. Her red face ran with tears, and her eyes were screwed shut. She reached to push past me, but I remained stolidly in front of her, and she had to open her eyes and look up at me.

"No, not you," she cried. "I do not want to see *you*."

"Gabriella." I caught her elbow as she tried to sway away from me. "You cannot run pell-mell through Covent Garden market. Come with me, I will find you coffee."

"No! I do not want to go with you."

Her vehemence drew attention. Fortunately, I was well known in the market, and no one made to dash off for the Watch.

"Stop," I said sternly. "Do not make a scene. Come with me and tell me what is the matter."

She seemed to realize she could not fight me, not in the crowd. She jerked from my grasp, but allowed me to lead her to Russel Street, and from there, while she wiped her eyes with the heel of her hand, to the bakery below my rooms on Grimpen Lane.

Mrs. Beltan raised her brows high when I pulled Gabriella inside, her face swollen with weeping, her hair straggling from its knot. I handed Gabriella my handkerchief, sat her down on a bench in the empty shop, and asked Mrs. Beltan for coffee.

She brought it, still staring curiously at the young woman. But Gabriella could not be mistaken for anything but a respectable miss, and Mrs. Beltan said nothing.

"What has happened?" I asked gently, once Mrs. Beltan and her assistant had returned to her kitchen.

Gabriella glared at me. I pushed the mug of coffee toward her, but she ignored it. "My mother told me you were my father."

I drew a long breath. "Oh."

"She did not mean to tell me. She and my father . . ." She faltered.

I sat still, wondering how to proceed. I wanted her to know the truth, but truth was a delicate thing. One wrong word and I could shatter anything I wanted to build with her. "I met with your mother and Major Auberge this morning," I said. "Were they discussing that?"

"Yes." She bit off the word. "They did not know that I could hear them. But I wanted to hear them. I asked them what they meant about the divorce and you wanting me back. And so they told me." She balled her hands and stared at me in fury. "It is a lie. It must be."

"I married your mother twenty-one years ago," I said slowly. "You were born four years later, in India. Carlotta is still married to me."

"That cannot be." She stared at me in a stunned manner,

as though she'd hoped I'd laugh and agree that her parents and I had decided to play a cruel trick on her.

"I regret that she never told you," I said. "I regret many things, believe me, Gabriella."

"Stop calling me that."

"You were named for me."

Fresh tears ran down her face. "Stop. Please."

I closed my mouth, mostly because I had no idea what to say. I wanted her back, I wanted her to know about me, but it hurt me to watch her hurting. My anger grew at Carlotta, and also Auberge, for keeping the truth from her too long.

She cried silently for a time, and then sat still, as though too exhausted to rise and leave the shop. The coffee cooled, untouched between us.

Two customers came in after a time, plump matrons in mobcaps with a maid listlessly trailing them. Mrs. Beltan bustled out to serve them. I leaned to Gabriella. "Come upstairs and talk to me."

She nodded, likely not because she wanted to stay with me, but because the two ladies and Mrs. Beltan were throwing curious glances at her. She pushed her loosened hair behind her ears, and rose and followed me out, her breathing uneven.

I opened the door next to the bakery and took Gabriella up the stairs to my rooms. I wished I could take her to better accommodation, but she did not seem to notice the faded paint and the shabby surroundings.

Bartholomew was sprawled on the straight-backed chair in my sitting room, polishing a boot and reading a newspaper spread on my writing table at the same time. He glanced up when I came in, closed the paper, and jumped to his feet. "Afternoon, sir." He caught sight of Gabriella and stopped in surprise.

"Bartholomew, go and fetch us some dinner. Not from

the Gull, bring us some good bread and perhaps fruit and a decent cut of beef. And wine, not ale."

"Right you are, sir." Bartholomew set the boots by my bedchamber door and departed. Gabriella remained in the middle of the room, staring about her as though she did not know what to do. I suspected she did not yet want to return home to her parents, but at the same time, did not wish to remain with me.

"Some food in you will help." I gestured to the wing chair. "Please, sit down."

Gabriella might have been furious and confused, but she was still a gently bred young miss, trained to obey her elders. She sat gingerly on the chair, her hands resting in her lap, her head bowed.

I wet a handkerchief in the basin in my bedroom and brought it to her. "Wipe your face."

Sniffling, she took the cloth and dabbed her eyes. Then she unfolded it, pressed it to her face, and inhaled a long breath.

"I am truly sorry you had to find out like this," I said. "You were born after your mother and I had been married four years. We'd tried to have a child several times, but nothing happened, and then at last, we had you. I was pleased and proud of you; you were such a lovely thing. A year later, the Thirty-Fifth Light Dragoons—my regiment—left India for England. We were to train in Sussex, in case we were needed in the war with France, which was heating up on the seas. Then came the Peace of Amiens, and we went to France with the Brandons, ostensibly as part of the party negotiating the peace between France and England." I smiled. "Really, I think Louisa and your mother had a hankering to see Paris and insisted we go. Colonel Brandon and I obliged. There, your mother met Auberge, and eloped with him. I had not seen you nor her from that day until yesterday morning, when I came upon you in Covent Garden. We never properly divorced, and your mother and Auberge never properly married."

She never moved during this lecture, breathing deeply behind the handkerchief, shaking once in a while as her body wound down from emotion. Quiet fell in the room, punctuated only by the slam of a door below and the shrill voices of the matrons as they left the shop, one snapping at the maid to stop lagging.

At last, Gabriella lowered the handkerchief. She delicately wiped the hollows under her eyes, her eyelashes still wet. "So he is not really my father."

I realized that she was grieving. She was losing the man she had always believed had sired her, the man who had raised her and looked after her, had kissed her good night and paid her dressmaker's bills, and had no doubt given her the fine gold chain that she wore around her neck.

Auberge had done all the things I should have done. "No," I said. "Do you love him?"

She gave me a fierce look. "Of course. He is my papa."

"I never want to take that away from you, I promise you, Gabriella."

"Then what do you want? You sent for us, Mama said so."

"Not exactly. Mr. Denis did, although I did not tell him to. He knew I wanted to find you, and so he brought you here."

"Why?" She balled the handkerchief in her hands, her anger erasing her compliance. "If you are my father, why have I not seen you all these years? Why did you let me grow up believing I was French, believing that my papa was my papa, that they were married to one another? Why did you never write me a letter?" She met my gaze with a furious one of her own. "Why did you never come for me if you love me so much?"

"I never had the chance," I said as patiently as I could.

"I did not have the income to make a thorough search for you, and for much of the time, England was at war with France. I spent years on the Peninsula, coated in mud and dust, fighting. When it was over, I was still too poor to try to find you, and I had thought it hopeless."

"You ought to have tried."

"I know." I looked at her limply. "I know, Gabriella. It hurt me so much when Carlotta took you away from me. I never recovered from it. You do not know how much it hurt to lose you."

"That was a long time ago. I am not a child any longer."

"You are the same." I studied her mussed golden brown hair, her soft dark eyes, the nose and cheekbones that were pure Lacey. "You used to hug my boot, and I'd walk with you on it, and make you laugh. You kissed me good night when your mother put you to bed. You used to sit on my lap and pull at the braid on my uniform." I touched the silver cords that crisscrossed my deep blue jacket. "When you were ill or restless, I carried you about all night so you would not cry."

Her hands tightened. "I do not remember."

"I know. But I remember."

She drew a breath. "It is not the same thing. You know nothing about me."

"I want to know about you." I leaned forward, put my hand on her clenched ones. "I want to learn all about you, I want you to learn all about me. You are my daughter."

"I do not want to be your daughter."

Her answer cut me to the heart, but I did not give up hope. She was upset now, but when she grew used to the idea, I firmly believed she would accept the situation.

Deep down, I knew I was being a bloody fool, but I so wanted her that I would make myself believe anything.

"But I want to be your father," I said. "I want you to stay here with me for a time, so that we can learn about each other. I want to show you London, take you to Egyptian house and the theatre and the menagerie at Exeter 'Change. I have a friend who has traveled the world, and his house is filled with amazing curiosities. He would be happy to show them off to you. He likes an audience."

I tried to smile, but Gabriella gave me an appalled stare. "*Stay* with you?"

"Not here, of course." I glanced at the arched ceiling, from which flakes of plaster were wont to fall if the door was slammed too hard. "I will look for larger rooms in a better house. You would need a chamber of your own in any case."

"I will not stay with you," she said quickly. "I am re-turning to France with my mother and father."

I shifted. "I'd like you to remain here. Not for long, a few months only. The summer perhaps. I have another friend, a viscountess, who has invited me to her country es-tate this summer. I imagine it is quite fine; apparently peo-ple come for miles and pay a shilling to see the gardens."

I hoped she would smile eagerly, but she only sat silently, digesting the information. I had seen the same look on the faces of soldiers on the Peninsula when they learned they had to lose one of their limbs.

"I do not want to stay."

I exhaled slowly, trying to keep my patience. What had I expected, that she'd brighten with joy and eagerly drag me out to look for rooms of our own? She was angry and con-fused, and she had decided to direct the anger at me.

"Gabriella, losing you nearly killed me. It left an empti-ness inside me that has never gone away. Please, let me know you."

A flicker of surprise crossed her features. In her anger, she probably had not realized that the situation caused pain in me as well.

She spoke haltingly, as if choosing her words with care.

"I have always been readily obedient as a daughter. I have always done what my mama and papa have asked me." She hesitated, her eyes darting sideways, and I almost wanted to smile. If she was anything like me, she'd have learned how to evade obeying when it suited her. "Will they ask me to do this, too?"

I had to shake my head. "Carlotta does not want you even to speak to me. I am sure Auberge does not either."

"But you will ask it."

I could force Carlotta to let me have her if I wished, but I hardly thought Gabriella wanted to hear that I could use the weight of the law to have my way. "I do ask it."

"I must say no."

I fell silent. I did not want to tell her that I could simply not let her make the choice. She would be in London for a time while I sorted out what to do about divorcing Carlotta, in any case. I could use the time to persuade her to stay with me. As much as I chafed, I sensed that forcing her now would do me no good.

Bartholomew opened the door and came in briskly, not looking at us. I wondered whether he'd waited outside the door for our voices to die down before interrupting. He banged a tray to the writing table. "Best bread I could find, sir, courtesy of Mrs. Beltan, and sweet butter to go with it. Roast from the Pony and some potatoes Mrs. Tolliver said were best of the barrel today."

So saying, he clattered the plates onto the table and forks and a sharp knife beside each one, all borrowed from the Rearing Pony. At the smell of the roasted meat and fresh-baked bread, Gabriella lifted her head and gazed at the repast with the hunger of a young girl.

"Eat until you feel better," I said. "And then I'll take you back to King Street."

Gabriella reached for the hunk of bread Bartholomew

had dropped on her plate and lifted the knife to smear it with butter. "No need. I will go myself."

"Best not, miss," Bartholomew broke in. "Covent Garden's not the place for a lone young lady. Pickpockets at best. Robbers and procuresses at worst. Very unscrupulous ladies and gentlemen they are."

Gabriella nodded as though heeding his wisdom and began chewing the bread. Bartholomew poured a glass of wine for me, and lemonade he'd brought from Mrs. Tolliver for Gabriella.

I, too, was hungry after our emotional exchange and fell to eating. The two of us dropped the subject while we consumed the beef and bread and potatoes, and Bartholomew bustled about cleaning the place, humming a buzzing tune in his throat. "By the bye, sir," he said presently. "Mr. Grenville sent word around with my brother asking would you please call on him. If it is not too inconvenient, he says, and if you can bother to remember."

Bartholomew's neutral tone betrayed none of Grenville's sarcasm, but I knew it had been there.

"Mr. Grenville is not gifted with patience," I observed.

"No, sir. But he's interested in this new problem." Bartholomew grinned at Gabriella. "The captain solves crimes. Him and Mr. Grenville. Better than Bow Street Runners."

Gabriella eyed him curiously, her eyes still red with weeping. "What is a Bow Street Runner?"

"Only the best in crime investigators in England," Bartholomew answered. "But Mr. Grenville and Captain Lacey, they've uncovered criminals when the Runners and the magistrates were baffled. They've solved murders and kidnappings and fraudulent activities. I was shot once."

He spoke proudly. Whether he was trying to bolster my

standing in front of Gabriella or boast of his own accomplishments, I could not tell.

"Were you?" Gabriella asked with flattering interest.

"There." Bartholomew pointed to his thick leg. "And there," pointing to his left biceps. "Laid me low a long time. But we got the murderer. Crazy devil, he was."

She flicked her gaze back to me, as though reassessing me. "Why do you catch criminals?"

"To help people," I said, sawing at my beefsteak. "Most were crimes that the magistrates ignored or did not know about."

"Bow Street's calling him in now, to help them," Bartholomew said.

"Oh?"

"Some young—ah—ladies have gone missing from Covent Garden," he went on. "That's why it ain't a good place to go walking alone."

"I see." She looked at me again. "How will you find them?"

I shrugged, relieved we'd found a neutral topic, one not charged with emotion. "I am speaking to others who knew them. Once I know where they usually went, I will follow what they did until I find more people who saw them. Then I will simply look everywhere."

She sipped her lemonade and carefully set the glass back on the table. "Why should you? I mean, why should you dash about London, when you have an injury, to find these young ladies? They are not respectable ladies, are they?"

She'd been intelligent enough to discern that. "They do not deserve to be hurt or lost," I said. "I dislike seeing anyone abused."

"He is a friend to the downtrodden," Bartholomew put in.

"All right, Bartholomew. You may cease now."

Bartholomew grinned. "He is that humble; he don't like to be praised."

"Enough," I said. Bartholomew subsided, but his grin did not diminish. Gabriella, on the other hand, continued to study me as she finished her food, as though I'd suddenly become a human being, much to her surprise. She ate with good manners, using the knife in the French way to push things onto her fork.

She finished quietly and seemed to wait for my direction. She was not happy, but she was resigned and, likely, tired of emotion.

Leaving the remains of our repast, I took Gabriella back downstairs, out along Grimpen Lane, and through Covent Garden toward King Street. Evening was approaching, although with summer, daylight could linger well past ten o'clock. Stalls were closing, and maids and cooks hurried to buy the last vegetables for supper. Flower sellers lingered, their posies wilting, determined to make as many pennies as they could before returning home. The square was littered with lettuce leaves, squashed cherries and strawberries, fowl droppings, and newspapers torn from wrapping flowers, fish, and greens. The square of St. Paul's Church, Covent Garden, sat at the west end of the market.

I headed with Gabriella to the right of the church, to the base of King Street. Bartholomew had accompanied us, declaring he needed to purchase some last-minute things for tomorrow. Since he was a genius at finding foodstuffs, candles, thread, and bootblacking at bargain prices, I let him browse.

I escorted Gabriella halfway down King Street, then stood aside and let her traverse the rest of the way to the boardinghouse alone. I saw her square her shoulders, preparing to confront Carlotta and Auberge on her return.

Just before Gabriella reached the boardinghouse, the door flew open, and Carlotta herself dashed from it. She flung her arms around Gabriella, then took a step back and began to scold. Gabriella's stance remained tall and straight; she would not wilt. She pointed back at me. Carlotta followed her outstretched finger, saw me, and gave me a look of rage that I could feel where I stood three houses away.

Carlotta swung on her heel and dragged Gabriella back into the house. I tipped my hat at the closed door, and turned away.

I caught up with Bartholomew on his way back to Grimpen Lane, his basket filled to the brim. "She yours, sir?" he asked as he fell into step with me on Russel Street. "Your daughter, I mean."

"Yes." I glanced at him. "I do not remember telling you that."

"Didn't have to, did you?" He gave me a broad smile. "She's the spittin' image of you, sir."

The answer pleased me, and I suppose I smiled foolishly, because his grin widened in response.

I forced my thoughts back to my promised investigation. I would speak again to Gabriella, gradually bringing her around to agreeing to stay with me while Carlotta and Auberge returned to France. I did not want to force my rights as her father; things would be easier all around if she stayed by choice.

I needed to find Felicity and Nancy after I'd unceremoniously left them behind in the market. I assumed the two had either retired to Felicity's lodgings or to a pub to catch up on old times.

Also, I'd told Louisa to visit me this evening so that I could take her to see Gabriella. I wondered now whether Carlotta would even let us in, and more so, whether Gabriella was ready to see Louisa. I thought not; I would try to persuade Louisa to postpone the visit.

I was reminded not twenty minutes after Bartholomew

and I returned to my rooms that I needed to tend to other people as well. Bartholomew's brother Matthias rapped peremptorily on my door and announced that his master, Lucius Grenville, had tired of waiting and come to pay me a call.

Chapter 8

"I have learned, Lacey," Grenville said as Bartholomew let him in, "that to stay in thick in an investigation with you, I must insinuate myself. So, I am insinuating myself." He thrust his hat and stick at Matthias, then planted himself on the straight-backed chair and stretched out his feet.

As usual, Grenville dressed in the first stare of fashion; or rather, what he wore today would become the first stare of fashion tomorrow. He advocated monochrome colors, as had the famous George Brummell, black frock coat and tightly fitting trousers, ivory waistcoat, and glaring white neckcloth. In deference to the afternoon, and the fact that he intended to hunt criminals, he wore a stock rather than a collar, and his neckcloth was tied loosely. He wore low-heeled boots under the trousers and serviceable gloves, not the fine kid he'd wear to a ball or theatre.

"You did not happen to see Black Nancy on the way, did you?" I asked.

At my abrupt question, his famous dark brows rose. "Black Nancy? The creature that Denis hired to lure you into a trap on one occasion? The young lady for whom I rowed about on the cold Thames, ruining my gloves, while you rescued her?"

"The same," I said.

"The answer is no, I did not. I had thought her in Islington in any case."

"She has graciously returned to the heart of London to help me look for these missing girls."

Grenville put aside his dandy hauteur with a suddenness that was nearly comical. His dark eyes gleamed with interest. "Excellent idea. She will, of course, know many people in this part of the city. Have you met with her yet? Has she found anything?"

So speaking, he reached for the bottle of wine I'd left half-empty and motioned Bartholomew to bring him a clean glass. Bartholomew did, taking the wine from Grenville's hand and filling that glass and mine. Grenville's observant gaze darted about the table, taking in the remains of the meal and the two plates.

"Nancy has already been of help," I answered. "She introduced me to a young woman called Felicity who knew one of the girls, Black Bess as she is called. I do not know yet whether they named her that because of her black hair, like Nancy, or whether she has black skin, like Felicity. Sergeant Pomeroy, it seems, was not amiss to kissing this Bess in dark passages, a fact he neglected to mention."

"Oh ho," Grenville said. "That is how many of these girls avoid facing the magistrates, you know—they bribe the Watch."

"Pomeroy is an elite Runner, not the Watch. I do not

mean that I wish to see these girls in the dock, but I dislike Pomeroy exploiting the situation."

"Many men do exploit the situation. That is why you do not see more game girls in Newgate."

"Yes, but Pomeroy I can put my hands on and shout at."

"I am certain he will be pleased about that," Grenville said dryly.

I drank some of the wine, reflecting that Bartholomew had managed to procure a decent bottle of hock. "Nancy and Felicity told me of Black Bess's young man, who lives off Drury Lane. They promised to take me to him, but I dashed off and left them, and was about to go hunt for them again, when you turned up."

Grenville eyed me over the rim of his glass. "That is most unlike you, to run off in the middle of an investigation."

"Not really, sir," Bartholomew broke in. "The captain was helping his daughter."

Grenville had started to drink. He coughed, then swallowed hastily and set the glass down. "Indeed?" he asked, eyes bright with curiosity.

I shot Bartholomew an irritated glance, then apprised Grenville of what had happened.

Grenville gave me a look of compassion, which he then strove to hide, because he knew I did not like pity. "A difficult situation," he said.

I agreed. "If not for Donata, I'd say the simplest solution is to send Carlotta and her Frenchman back to France, and do nothing. They have been living in their supposed wedded bliss these fifteen years; they may as well continue. I can turn my back and say she is dead, and no one would be the wiser. But in that case, I would never feel right about marrying again. It would be bigamy, and I would know it."

"I once read of a convicted bigamist who was branded

in the thumb," Grenville said after a thoughtful sip of wine. "But the iron was cool and the punisher was bribed to hold the iron to his skin only a second or two. This tells me that the law is unconcerned about bigamy."

Matthias said, "Bet his wives branded him good, though, when they found out about each other." He and his brother shared a chuckle.

"Sometimes bigamy is the only answer," Grenville said. "With the difficulty of ending marriage in this country, a couple who want to part and go their separate ways can only live happily by breaking the law."

"But all parties are agreed in that case," I pointed out. "They agree to say nothing."

"Have you asked Lady Breckenridge her opinion? She is not the most conventional of women, you know."

"She might draw the line at bigamy, or perpetual adultery."

"Possibly," he conceded. "Well, I will quiz my solicitor, thoroughly and at length. There must be a way to resolve this, without resorting to a trial for crim con." He shook his head. "This is precisely why I have never put my own head in the noose. What happens if you awaken one morning and realize you've both changed your mind? And in my case, every debutante's mama wants her daughter to be called Mrs. Grenville. The young lady would not be marrying me for my excellent character, and we'd know it."

"Marry Marianne," I suggested, "and let the ambitious mothers mourn. Dukes and statesmen marry actresses, why not you as well?"

Grenville's look turned ironic. "Dear Marianne has insisted I give her more allowance. I would upbraid her for extravagance, except she does seem to practice good economy." His brows drew together. "Much as it pains me to admit, it might be time to let her go. Give her a large lump sum, since she enjoys money so much, and have done."

"And I will ask you not to," I said.

He gave me a sharp stare. "Why? Would you like to watch her drain me dry? I had not thought you so cruel."

Very aware of Matthias and Bartholomew avidly listening, I only shook my head. "She could not drain you dry for many years, even if you doubled what you give her. I promise you will understand everything about her, as soon as I can arrange it."

His eyes darkened, and his fingers tightened ever so slightly on his glass. "I will be agog to learn," he said, his voice deceptively soft.

I set down my glass. "For now, let us hunt for Nancy and her friend. I am anxious to interview this Tom, paramour of the missing Black Bess."

Grenville gave a chill nod, and we let the touchy subjects of Marianne and my divorce drop.

While we readied ourselves to leave, I told him of my interview with the sailor and what he'd said about Mary Chester. After we spoke to Black Bess's gent, I said, I'd hunt up Pomeroy and quiz him thoroughly about Bess.

We stepped from the house into evening air that had cooled somewhat. It was eight o'clock, the sun just slipping behind tall London buildings. I liked this part of the evening, when the heat of the day abated, and the sky was azure, just barely streaked with gold.

As we neared Russel Street, where Grenville had left his carriage, I saw, to my astonishment, my wife dash around the corner onto Grimpen Lane. She wore no hat and no shawl, her hair was mussed from the slight summer breeze, and the hem of her skirt was muddy. She ran straight for me, shouting before she even reached me.

"Where is she?"

"Where is who?" For a moment, I thought she'd seen me with Nancy, then I saw the stark anger and fear in her eyes. "Do you mean Gabriella?"

"Of course I mean Gabriella. I know she came to find you, and everyone in Covent Garden was eager to tell me where you kept rooms."

"I took her home," I said, puzzled. "You saw me bring her back to King Street. I watched her go into the house with you."

I was aware of Grenville and the two towering footmen behind me, looking on, but Carlotta seemed to neither notice them nor care. "Yes, *then*," she snapped. "She has gone again, without a word. I know she must have come to you, so where is she?"

"She is not here, Carlotta. Are you certain she did not simply want to buy something in Covent Garden?"

She shook her head fervently. "I came through the market on the way. I never saw her."

Alarm touched me. "If she is not with you, and she did not come here, then where has she gone?"

"Perhaps she went to the bake shop," Grenville broke in. "Perhaps she wanted to come upstairs but heard me there and decided to wait. She might be there right now, she and Mrs. Beltan having bread and a gab."

He spoke lightly, but I heard the thread of concern in his voice. With girls going missing from Covent Garden, we could not simply shrug things off. I decided he had a good idea and led the way back to the bake shop.

Mrs. Beltan was there, but not her assistant, and not Gabriella. To my inquiry as to whether Gabriella had returned, Mrs. Beltan said, "No one's been in, Captain, in the last hour. I've been back scraping ash from the ovens, but if someone comes in, they generally sing out."

"She might not have wanted to sing out," I speculated. I scanned the bake shop, but my daughter was not hiding in the shadows. The shop was small, merely six feet by about ten feet with a counter and shelves from which Mrs. Beltan sold loaves of bread and seed cakes.

A door led from the shop into her parlor, but it was shut and, when I tried it, locked. "No one's been in there all day," Mrs. Beltan said. "Not even me. I've been run off my feet with custom."

I turned to Carlotta. "Go back to King Street. I will ask about here and in the market. We will find her."

She gave me a belligerent stare, as she had done of old. "How do I know you have not hidden her upstairs?"

"Of course I have not," I began heatedly, but Bartholomew broke in. "She might a' gone there, sir. She might have slipped upstairs to the empty rooms above or even the attics while we were jawing in your rooms."

I stifled my impatience long enough to agree that it was a possibility. Gabriella might have wanted to speak to me without Grenville or the two servants, and decided to wait. Perhaps she'd fallen asleep and not heard us begin to leave.

Mrs. Beltan came with us. The rooms above mine were locked, since they weren't being let at the moment, and she wanted no vagrants sleeping there. But a young girl with determination might have been able to find her way in.

Mrs. Beltan unlocked the door on the landing above mine with her keys. Stuffy, close air enveloped us when we entered; obviously no one had been in the rooms since Mrs. Beltan had sent her assistant to sweep a few days ago. We found the broom the assistant had left behind, but nothing else.

The attics were likewise empty. One was dark and close, the other, warm with sunshine from a skylight. Bartholomew slept in the warm one and kept his bed neatly made. His clothes were folded on shelves, his nightshirt and extra coat hanging from pegs.

Gabriella was nowhere in the house.

By the time we had emerged into the street again, Carlotta was fearful. "She was coming to see you," she said.

"Did she say that?"

"She said nothing. I never saw her go. But I *know*."

"We'll look, sir," Bartholomew offered. "Could be she went round the wrong corner. Streets here can be a warren, you know."

"What does she look like?" Matthias began. Bartholomew beckoned him on. "I'll tell you," he said as the two of them loped away to Russel Street.

"My coach is at your service, madam," Grenville said, in his smooth, polite voice. "I will escort you back to King Street. Best for you to stay there, and let my lads do the searching. It is very likely she has already returned there on her own."

Carlotta had not changed in one aspect; she responded well when someone told her what to do. Her flush of anger receded slightly, and she thanked Grenville with manners that reminded me of the debutante she'd once been. Grenville touched her arm and led her to his opulent coach, which waited for him at the corner.

His coachman sprang to his feet from where he'd lounged against a wall, drinking from a flask. Grenville nodded at him to open the door, and he handed Carlotta in with as much aplomb as if he'd been escorting her to the theatre. He climbed in beside her and looked back out at me. "I'll see her home safely, Lacey." He did not ask me to join them.

The carriage rolled off toward Bow Street, probably to take the roundabout route to King Street. I walked in the opposite direction, back to the mass of humanity that filled Covent Garden on this warm summer evening.

I scanned the crowd, looking in vain for Gabriella's golden brown hair in the sea of hats, caps, mobcaps, and bonnets. She'd worn a small, flat, ivory-colored hat with ribbons when I'd met her yesterday morning, and I tried to spy something like that.

I passed the peach seller who had tried to cheat her. He remembered the encounter and bent a surly eye upon me when I asked if he'd seen the girl I'd been talking to the day before and snarled that he had no interest in seeing her again. I nearly grabbed him and shook him, but the vendors on either side of him, one for needles and the other for greens, interrupted, confirming that Gabriella hadn't come nigh since yesterday morning.

I asked at every seller down the line, to no avail. I asked the strolling vendors, the strawberry girls and orange sellers, flower girls and knife grinders. None had noticed or remembered Gabriella.

Bartholomew and Matthias were no doubt right, I thought. She probably had simply taken a wrong turn and could not have gone far. I might turn on to Henrietta Street and find her asking her way from the boy who swept paths across the street for tuppence, or chatting with a maid.

With this picture in place, I hurried to Henrietta Street, my walking stick tapping the cobbles, my leg protesting my frenzied pace. I saw only carts and drovers, horses and mules, wagons and carriages. Maids and footmen and women and men and boys and other urchins swarmed about, but no Gabriella.

I began to ask passersby if they'd seen her. Those who bothered to respond to me answered in the negative. A plump, fiftyish woman said to me, "She's your girl, is she? I'm that sorry to hear you can't find her. Best go to Bow Street, you know. If I see her, I'll take her there myself. Don't you worry now."

I thanked her and went on my way.

I walked to Bedford Street and turned north, pausing halfway along at the churchyard of St. Paul's, Covent Garden. This was a quiet passage with the church looming at the end, elegant in its simplicity. The church itself was open, dim and cool, but I did not find Gabriella wandering here as a reprieve from the hectic pace of Covent Garden.

I continued north to King Street and turned east again. Grenville's carriage was just pulling away from Carlotta's boardinghouse, and I waited until it drew alongside me.

The coachman stopped, and Grenville opened the door. Major Auberge was in the carriage with him. The major peered down at me worriedly, his round face pale.

"She is not there?" I asked.

Grenville shook his head, his dark eyes troubled. "The major wanted to join the search. I said I'd take him through the streets, though I am certain Bartholomew and Matthias can cover them more quickly. Come with us."

I refused. "I am heading for Bow Street to ask Pomeroy to send out his patrollers. They know the area better than anyone. Go through Maiden Lane and make your way down to the Strand." I pushed my hand through my hair. "It might be that she was simply curious to see more of London. There are so many unusual shops in the Strand, perhaps she became mesmerized by them."

"She does like exploring," Auberge said. His eyes met mine, he, too, wanting to believe that she would easily be found. "She wished to see all the sights when we were in Paris."

She was a Lacey, all right. "She might have wanted to have a look at the river. There are many confusing lanes south of the Strand. Look there if you do not find her shopping." I hoped she'd not gone to the winding lanes on the river, some of which had an unsavory reputation.

Grenville nodded. I shut the door for him and stepped back as the coachman slapped the beautiful grays with the reins. As the coach rattled away through traffic, I strode back to Covent Garden, skirting it to James Street, its outlet leading north, and around the bulk of the theatre to Bow Street.

Pomeroy was not in, but he was expected soon. I did not care for this information, and I managed to bully the direction of Pomeroy's digs from one of his patrollers. I realized that in the two years Pomeroy had been back in London, I had not known where he lived. He'd simply been at Bow Street.

I told the patrollers of my problem. The one I'd bullied said he could do little until Pomeroy's return, but promised to send out a few lads right away.

As I emerged from Bow Street, ready to find the house off Long Acre that Pomeroy called home, I saw Black Nancy and Felicity coming from the direction of the theatre.

"Captain," Nancy called cheerfully. "You ran off so fast and never said good-bye."

I caught up to them, and regardless of what it looked like to passersby, I seized Nancy by the shoulders. "Where have you been walking? Did you see the girl I took away to my rooms?"

Nancy stared at me in amazement. Felicity looked on, her black silk brows rising on her handsome face. "No," Nancy said. "You looking for her?"

"Yes, she's gotten lost."

Felicity's brow cleared. "That one? She's a young miss, Captain. She won't do well around here."

"Precisely why I am trying to find her. It could be she's simply taken a wrong turn, gone the wrong direction trying to fetch up in King Street and the boardinghouse at number 31."

I tried to speak calmly, as though she was simply an ordinary girl who might have wandered away and would be back soon. But the tremor in my voice betrayed me. Nancy looked worried, and Felicity put a calming hand on my arm.

"We'll look out for her, Captain," Felicity said. "You come with us now."

"I do not want to go anywhere with you, I want to find my daughter."

Nancy and Felicity exchanged a glance. "Coo," Nancy said. "I didn't know that was her."

"I know when a man needs a gin," Felicity said firmly. "Now, you come with us."

So saying, she steered me across the busy street and into a tavern. I had not come to this one before, preferring the Rearing Pony or the Gull, and heads turned as I entered in the company of game girls. But after one curious glance, the clientele, most of them well into their cups, looked the other way without rancor.

They sat me down at an empty end of a long table, and Felicity sidled to the landlord and asked for three glasses of gin.

Nancy gave me a sympathetic glance. "You're worried that she got snatched by the same man who's taking the game girls."

"I don't know." I drew a breath, resting my hands flat on the table. "She is obviously a girl from a respectable family, and we do not know whether the game girls were snatched, as you say. They might have decided to work in a house, or they might have found a protector."

"Well, they ain't in any houses round here," Nancy said. "Felicity and me had a look into all the bawdy houses, and neither Black Bess nor this Mary Chester has been there."

"You can be certain?" I asked. My entire being was focused on finding Gabriella, and at this moment, I hadn't much interest in girls who wandered away from their regular lovers. I knew I ought to be concerned, because the two events might be connected, but I did not want them to be. I could coolly search for game girls, feeling a stranger's sympathy for their plight, but I did not want my daughter and her disappearance to be lumped with them.

"Fair certain," she answered. "They treat Felicity with some respect, and I don't think they'd lie to her."

Unless a house was keeping the girls for some unknown purpose.

Felicity sat down and shoved a glass of clear, noisome liquid under my nose. "You drink that, Captain. It'll stop your shaking."

I hadn't realized I was shaking. But I saw that I had pressed my hands tightly against the table to still their trembling, and I was having difficulty catching my breath. I obediently raised the glass and gulped the gin.

The liquid burned fire through my gullet, and I wanted to cough. Foul stuff, but it warmed my blood and calmed my agitation a trifle. Felicity sipped her gin as though it were a delicate glass of champagne. Nancy took one drink, made a face, and set it down. "I like ale, meself."

I took a long breath, my mouth tingling from the gin. "I need to organize a search. We are all running about half-cocked at present, and might miss her coming or going. I did reconnaissance in the army; I can certainly do it in London."

"What do we do?" Nancy asked, eager.

"Find Grenville for me. I sent him to the Strand. Tell him I will need a map. One of Horwood's will do, the man must have marked every house and every privy in London. I'll round up Grenville's footman and get Pomeroy to lend me his foot patrollers. I will look in every house in every street in this damn city if I have to."

"She might have already found her way home," Nancy pointed out.

"True. Then our effort will be for nothing." I paused. "I hope so."

I could see that Felicity was not as sanguine as Nancy.

She was a little older, perhaps a little wiser. Nancy had been lucky; Louisa had saved her from a short life and early death as a prostitute. Felicity had already spent years on the streets and knew what a very harsh place they could be.

She laid her hand on my arm. Her skin was not really that much darker than Nancy's, but the essence of the color was different; olive and bronzed tones shone through whereas the tone of Nancy's skin was pink. My own tanned hand was more yellow.

"We'll find Mr. Grenville for you," Felicity said. "I know his fancy carriage." She ran her fingers up my arm, her touch suggestive, though she said nothing. The unspoken offer was there, however. There was no desire in her eyes, only pity, as she offered comfort in her own way.

"Thank you," I said, answering both her words and her silent gesture. "Send anyone you see to Grimpen Lane, and I will await you there."

If Nancy noticed the exchange, she said nothing. Felicity smiled at me, a look of understanding, and withdrew her hand.

I sent them off and continued to Long Acre, hoping that every corner I turned would reveal Gabriella. None did.

Chapter 9

TO my annoyance, I found Pomeroy not at home. His landlady, a comely woman of about thirty, her three small daughters busily cleaning the downstairs hall, told me he was looking into a death in Marylebone, trying to decide whether it was suicide or murder. She seemed proud to have a Runner staying in her house.

I left my card, writing a note on the back to Pomeroy to look me up at Grimpen Lane immediately on his return.

My leg aching with all my walking, I hired a hackney to return me home. The hackney moved through the crowd about as fast as I could walk, and I spent my time gazing across people and horses and down passages between tall slabs of houses to see if I could spy my daughter.

I pictured in my head that Gabriella would be at the bake shop when I returned, with Carlotta there, scolding her. Everything would be all right, and we'd laugh at the fright she'd given us.

I held on to this vision, certain that by thinking of it hard enough, I could make it true.

When I arrived at the bake shop, it was shut and dark, Mrs. Beltan gone home. Upstairs, empty rooms awaited me, with no Gabriella. To keep myself from thinking, I retrieved paper and sharpened a pen, and began making a list of likely places I could check and people I could call upon to help me.

My list grew lengthy, and I looked in surprise at all of the people with whom I'd forged ties since arriving in London: Sir Gideon Derwent, Leland Derwent and his friend Gareth Travers, Lady Aline Carrington, Sir Montague Harris, magistrate at the Whitechapel house, Thompson of the Thames River patrollers, Lady Breckenridge, Louisa Brandon and the many people she knew, Grenville of course, and James Denis.

I looked at the last name and felt my mouth dry, the gin having left a foul taste behind. If Gabriella were truly missing, I would be a fool not to go to Denis. If any man could turn the city inside out, it was he, a man with resources I could not begin to match. And, I thought with dawning hope, if he'd had a man watching me as usual, that man might have noted Gabriella and where she had gone.

I could not fathom what price Denis would ask of me. Would he want money, or would he expect me to pay him back in kind? He wanted me to be under his obligation, so that I would not be a threat, and he had more than once hinted that he wanted to employ me outright. If Gabriella had truly disappeared, would enslaving myself to Denis not be worth her return?

I thought it might be.

Grenville arrived not long after I'd finished my list. Bartholomew and Matthias came upstairs with him, as did Major Auberge. By the grim looks on faces all around, none of them had found Gabriella.

Nancy and Felicity arrived soon after, with two of Pomeroy's patrollers in tow. "First time I ever told Bow Street to come with me," Nancy cackled as they all entered my sitting room.

Fortunately, my rooms, while sparsely furnished, were large, the architects of the house over a century ago having a liking for grand salons. My makeshift army fitted inside with ease, though we would have been hard-pressed had more joined us.

Grenville unrolled a map sheet of Covent Garden and surrounding areas on my writing table. He had not bothered to send home for one; he'd simply walked into a shop on the Strand and purchased it. That particular shop had just closed for the evening, but the proprietor had opened it again for Grenville.

I leaned on the table, looking at the streets I had walked not an hour ago, laid out in neat lines and squares. London looked so clean from this bird's-eye view, but the map could show nothing of the tall buildings, each with its own characteristic, streets that could narrow into crooked medieval lanes in three steps, the smell of unwashed people and dogs, the startling snorts of horses or pigs tucked into unseen yards, the noises of cart and carriage wheels, clopping horses, shouting men, laughter and anger, joy and heartache.

With a pencil, I squared off a part of the map, from Lincoln's Inn Fields in the east to St. Martin's Lane in the west, High Holborn in the north to the river in the south. It was a large area, but easy enough for a healthy young woman to walk.

"I am dividing this area into squares," I said. "In pairs, we will each take a part of the grid, where we will walk every street and check every alley and ask everyone we see if Gabriella has been there. I plan to recruit more patrollers and Pomeroy and send word to Thompson. If you find her, you will latch on to her and bring her back here immediately, and stay with her. We will check here every hour to see if any of the others have made progress. Do you understand?"

"Aye, Captain," Matthias said, touching his forelock.

I would have laughed any other time, but the matter was too pressing. "Bartholomew and Matthias, I want each of you to take Nancy and Felicity with you. They know people and they know the streets. Listen to them if they think of a place to look. Grenville, you take a foot patroller, for the same reason."

"Jackson, my coachman, is willing to help," Grenville put in. "He can speak to other coachmen who might report something."

"Excellent. Have him pair up with this fellow," I said, pointing to the other patroller. I folded the expensive map and tore the sheet into pieces around my gridlines, handing one to each pair. "Leave no stone unturned. I want to find Gabriella before some unscrupulous person does. Bartholomew and Felicity, since you will be taking the southwestern part of the grid, check the boardinghouse in King Street every once in a while to see whether she has returned."

"Understood, sir," Bartholomew said.

I stood up, my stance unconsciously becoming like the one I'd taken when readying my men for an upcoming battle. "Go to it, then."

They dispersed and departed, very much like my soldiers when I dismissed them. They squared shoulders and stood straight as though determined to obey orders to the best of their abilities.

Major Auberge did not follow them. "You did not give me a map," he said.

"Because you should go back to the boardinghouse and wait. Gabriella might return there, and I am certain Carlotta will be at her wit's end."

In truth, I was as angry as I could be at Carlotta and d[id] not care much about her anxiousness. She should ha[ve] watched Gabriella and not let her out alone. But I used h[er] worry as an excuse to send Auberge away, because [I] wanted nothing to do with him. Also, if Carlotta had ups[et] Gabriella enough for her to dash off once, there was not[h]ing to say that she would not do so a second time.

Auberge gave me a stubborn look. "She is my daught[er]. And I suspect, like you, that harm has befallen her. I cann[ot] sit like an old woman and wait for her to be found. Y[ou] have no second person. I will go with you."

I opened my mouth to tell him to go away, but [I] stopped. His eyes mirrored my own anguish. He ha[d] known Gabriella all her life, had raised her from bab[y]hood, had held her hand when she walked. I was furio[us] with jealousy because of it, but I had to concede that h[is] fear was as sharp as my own.

"Very well. But do not talk to the people we meet. T[he] Londoners around here are suspicious of foreigners, esp[e]cially Frenchmen. I do not want to waste time extricati[ng] you from a brawl."

He nodded once, his face set. "I understand."

"Let us be off, then." Snatching up my corner of t[he] map, I ushered him out the door.

A hard lump had formed in the pit of my stomach by t[he] time we reached Russel Street, which, if I let it, would i[n]crease to full-blown panic. But damn it all, Gabriella w[as] not a fool. She should come to her senses and return hom[e.] She must know that London was not safe for her, and she[']d heard Bartholomew talk about the missing girls. If s[he] found herself lost, she'd seek out a trustworthy person a[nd] ask the way to King Street.

Even this logical thought could not comfort me. S[he] was lost, and London was dangerous, and we had to fi[nd] her.

I had chosen the northwest corner of the map, where Broad Street cut through the warren of St. Giles to High Holborn. I had chosen it because it was close to Pomeroy's lodgings, and I wanted to lay my hands on him. Also, the area was a bit dangerous, and I hadn't wanted to send my friends into the rookeries where they would be ripe for plucking. I had little to pluck, and Auberge, like me, was a soldier. We could hold our own.

I hired a hackney to where Broad Street met High Street, and we began the search there.

Leaving the hackney, we walked through crooked alleys on soiled cobbles, passing closed shops and houses that had stood in the narrow lanes for several hundred years. Walls had been shored up and repaired as necessary, and the different colors of bricks and plaster gave them a piebald look. In one lane, the upper stories of the houses leaned to each other over the street, making the dim passage darker still.

Nowhere did we find a sign of a girl in a sensible cotton frock, lost and trying to find her way home.

We walked slowly but purposefully, looking in every passage, in every darkened doorway. In one lane, a young woman with a soiled apron held a boy of about five in her arms. He was naked but for a shirt that exposed his backside and spindly legs. She held her hand out for coin, and Major Auberge stopped a moment and dropped some to her palm. She thanked him in a weak voice.

Major Auberge and I had spoken little since leaving Grimpen Lane, except to decide where exactly to began. Now, we walked in silence, saving our energy for our search.

We angled south from Broad Street on another King Street, my idea being that perhaps Gabriella had confused this King Street with the one that led off Covent Garden. Auberge followed my lead without argument. As I had instructed, he said nothing to the people I questioned, only listened to my conversation, observing without offering comment.

As we angled toward Little Earl Street and Seven Dials, he said to me quietly, "She likes so much to explore. When she was a little girl, she would go to the stream below our farm and follow its course as far as she could. She said she wanted to learn where it came from. I explained that it came from mountains far away, but she was certain that around the next bend she would find a fountain that spilled the entire stream into the valley. One day she had walked for five miles, and a farmhand had to carry her home. She was asleep in his arms, as you say, soundly."

I imagined my golden-haired daughter trudging sturdily along the bank of the stream, determined to find its source. "She showed the propensity even at two years old," I said. "She always wanted to come with me when I talked to my men, to see what Papa did as a soldier. One day, she crawled under the canvas of the tent to follow me to where I was meeting with one of the generals. I explained to the general when she popped up that she was eager to learn to be an officer. Fortunately, she amused him, and he simply ordered his batman to carry her home. Carlotta, on the other hand, was not amused. She was quite hysterical about the incident, certain the general would throw me out of the army in disgrace."

"Yes, Carlotta becomes very worried."

I closed my mouth on my reply, not wanting to grow too comfortable with the fact that I shared a wife and child with this man. Perhaps that was why divorce was so difficult to obtain, so we'd be spared these kinds of strange conversations.

We continued the search, slowly moving in a circle through the streets, heading south. When we turned into

Long Acre, I stopped at the house in a lane opening from it where Pomeroy had rooms.

This time, I caught Pomeroy readying himself to go to Bow Street.

"Well then, Captain," he said cheerfully. "My landlady said you had come to call. Couldn't think why, unless it was to do with the game girls."

Auberge looked slightly confused, not understanding the expression "game girls." My worry about Gabriella had superseded my annoyance about Pomeroy's involvement with Black Bess, and I told him quickly what happened.

Pomeroy looked at Auberge in sympathy, but resignation. "Not a good thing to hear, a respectable girl gone missing. Any number of procuresses wander up and down the streets, looking for such an innocent. It's a sad fact, but virgins fetch a nice price in the bawdy houses."

Auberge's face went white as Pomeroy's flat words made the awful possibility that much more real.

"I want to borrow your patrollers," I said. "Put every man you've got to searching the streets."

He gave me a dubious look. "Can't spare that many, that's a fact, Captain. There are more crimes all over London than one missing girl."

I stepped close to him, the fruitless search having raised my fears. "The girl's name is Gabriella Lacey."

His eyes widened. Pomeroy remembered Gabriella and Carlotta. "'Struth, sir. Your little Gabriella?"

"Yes," I said tightly. "She is not so little now. She's about the same age as your Black Bess, I would guess."

I thought I detected a flicker of uneasiness in his blue eyes, but with Pomeroy, it was difficult to tell. "You think the disappearances are connected?"

"I do not know what to think. And I want to have a discussion with you about this Black Bess, including the fact that you did not tell me you knew her, nor that she was paying you in kind to look the other way."

He bristled visibly this time. "Now, as to that, sir, I'd say it was my business."

"I'd say it might have something to do with her disappearance, and if you want me to find her, you will be frank with me. But first, go to Bow Street and send out your patrollers. I have people working already, but the more the better."

"Have to check with the magistrate first," he began.

"Send them, Sergeant. I do not want to call in James Denis, but I will if necessary. I'd rather use Bow Street, but I might not have a choice."

"Are you threatening me, sir?"

"I am happy to threaten anyone who does not assist us in finding Gabriella. You said yourself she hadn't much chance. Instead of bleating about a dismal future, do something to ensure it is not dismal."

He stared at me a long moment. On the Peninsula, Pomeroy had argued with me if he thought my orders daft, and a few times, he was right. The times I was right, however, I stared him down until he wilted and did what I pleased. He seemed to remember those days, because his bravado deflated. He saluted. "As you say, Captain. I'll get on it." He let his hand drop and gave me a serious look, the usual bonhomie gone from his eyes. "I won't let you down, sir."

He trotted off toward Long Acre and turned in the direction of Bow Street.

"Will he do it?" Auberge asked me.

"He will," I answered, my mouth set. "Shall we resume?"

After another hour of walking, we had uncovered nothing. If Gabriella had come this way, no one had seen her. We took another hackney back to Grimpen Lane, Auberge generously counting out the shillings for the fare. I met Grenville and the foot patroller in my lodgings. Both shook their heads unhappily. They had found nothing.

The others that straggled in as the four of us left again had nothing to report. Black Nancy touched my arm. "I'm that sorry, Captain. None of the girls I passed the time with had seen her, or the other missing girls either. But we'll keep trying. I swear to you."

They were giving up. I heard it in their voices when they promised to continue. They were beginning to fear the worst.

Outside, in darkening Russel Street, I sent a street sweep running off to the boardinghouse with news we had not found her. Auberge and I returned to the streets north of Long Acre and tediously trudged down every lane again.

"I am a stranger in London," Auberge said. "Tell me what can have happened." He stopped me near the wall of a shabby house. "Tell me in plain words."

I hesitated, then explained, hating the words as I said them. "She might have fetched up in the river. Either fallen in or thrown in after she was robbed. As Pomeroy said, a procuress could have taken her to a bawdy house. A gentleman could have taken her in his coach, and be far away by now." I stopped, and he nodded, trying to make himself face these possibilities. "I was involved in a case a little over a year ago," I said, "in which a gentleman had asked for young respectable girls to be brought to him. He had an expensive house in Hanover Square."

Auberge looked grim. "Should we go to Hanover Square?"

"The man involved was killed. I could not be terribly sorry about his death." I did not explain what had become of the particular girl I had sought, and I did not like thinking on her fate.

"We must keep looking, then," Auberge said.

"Yes," I agreed.

We fell into step, and resumed the search.

At eleven o'clock, we returned to Grimpen Lane to news. Bartholomew, Matthias, Nancy, and Felicity were waiting, the latter eating strawberries she'd bought cheap from a strawberry girl wanting to rid herself of her last wares for the day.

"We found something, Captain," Bartholomew said, his blue eyes subdued. "Not your daughter. By the new bridge, near to Somerset House. A young woman, dead."

"Not Gabriella?" I said, my voice strained. "You are certain?"

"I saw her clear, sir. Wasn't the same girl. She had golden hair, but not natural."

"I think," Felicity said, "from what you and Nancy said, it could be Mary Chester."

I sent Matthias bolting off to fetch Pomeroy. Bartholomew told me that they'd left Grenville's coachman and his patroller to guard the spot, and when Grenville himself came in, we took lanterns he had filched from his coach and made our way down to the Strand. The new bridge rose near Somerset House, arched and lighted with flickering lanterns.

Bartholomew led us through the darkness to a passage near stairs that led down to the water. Pomeroy had joined us, his tow-colored hair bright in the moonlight. The stink of the river was strong here, covering us in the odor of fish, mud, and human waste.

The ground was hard-packed dirt; the cobbles did not extend here. Grenville's coachman, Jackson, a tall, muscular man with hard eyes, waited sturdily near a pile of debris, holding a lantern that was a bright pinpoint of light in the

gloom. The patroller stood by him, somewhat more nervously.

Bartholomew bent down and moved a wet and grime-
covered board. Beneath was the torso of a young woman,
her hips and legs still covered by rubbish.

Grenville lifted his lantern high, shining the light onto
her. She was dead without doubt. Her face was blue-white,
and a knotted sash was wound about her neck. Her hair,
now dirt-streaked, had been golden blond, but Bartholomew had been right about it not being natural. The roots
of the hair that swept back from her forehead and temples
was mostly dark brown, her own color starting to grow
again.

I crouched next to her, looking at another life too soon
snuffed out. "We need Thompson," I said. "I want him to
see her."

"And a coroner," Pomeroy put in.

I switched my glance to the foot patrollers. They
glanced swiftly at Pomeroy, and at his nod, they loped off,
no doubt to find the requisite gentlemen.

I remained on one knee next to her, bracing myself on
my walking stick. Gingerly, I hooked one finger around the
knotted sash and eased it an inch downward. Her neck was
covered with bruises.

Nancy hissed a breath through her teeth. "That how she
died? Strangled with her own sash?"

I looked at the girl's face, which was straight and
serene. "If she was strangled, she certainly didn't struggle
for breath." I studied the bruises, which were in the exact
pattern of human fingers. My own fingers fitted over them
easily. "A man did this. One with large hands."

"Then why the sash?" Grenville asked.

I eased the cloth back over her neck. "Perhaps the
bruises had nothing to do with her death. Perhaps she was

in a struggle with a man and got away, and wore the sash around her neck to cover the bruises until they healed."

"In that case, how did she die?" Grenville wondered.

"Coroner will tell us," Pomeroy said confidently. "They're amazing at that sort of thing." He sighed and scratched his head. "Will have to be an inquest, her dead back here, injuries like that."

I got stiffly to my feet. Felicity was standing at my elbow, looking down at the corpse with an odd expression on her face. "Are you all right?" I asked her.

She looked up at me quickly, as though surprised at the question. "Wasn't expecting to find her dead, is all."

A shiver ran through me. I prayed with all my strength that Gabriella wasn't lying under another pile of rotting boards, cold and blue and dead. God, let her be all right. Let her be waiting in a tavern for someone to find her, with a kindly landlord's wife feeding her homey soup and coffee.

"Looks like I should be asking whether you're all right, Captain," Felicity said softly. She touched my hand, again with the unspoken offer of bodily comfort if I should need it. The gesture did not disgust me; she meant it from kindness, offering to soothe my hurts like Mrs. Beltan might offer me a cup of tea. I gave her a faint smile and shook my head.

"Jackson," Grenville addressed his coachman. "Take the lads and the two young ladies and find yourselves a steadying pot of ale. You've earned it."

"So have you," I told him.

He shook his head. "I'll wait for the coroner and Thompson with you. I'm curious what he has to say." He withdrew his watch and looked at it in the light of his lantern. "Eleven thirty. Ah, well, I was not looking forward to Lady Featherstone's ball in the slightest. I will be the talk of Mayfair for not appearing." He sounded rather pleased with the prospect.

Auberge, who had been watching from the back of the alley, said, "I will resume the hunt for my daughter."

"I'd rather you didn't," I told him. "Not alone. Or we'll be hunting for you as well."

He smiled faintly. "Perhaps you would not be so troubled to have me go missing, eh?"

He met my gaze, his hazel eyes flickering in the light of Grenville's lantern. "Not so," I said. "I want your help. I know that you are the only other man who will be as adamant as me about finding her."

He hesitated a moment, then he nodded. "As you say, I have no knowledge of these streets. I will wait."

Grenville sensed that the exchange had been personal. As though ignoring us, he tucked his watch away and straightened his frock coat, which he'd been wearing since early evening. It was unusual for Grenville not to change his clothes at least twice in the course of an evening, sometimes three times. He seemed livelier, however, at the prospect of investigating a murder. He made to lean against the wall behind him, then looked at the smears of mud on it and thought better of it.

I turned to Pomeroy, who was gazing down at the girl. "While we are waiting," I said to him, "tell me why the last time Felicity saw Black Bess, you were with her in a dark passage such as this one, kissing her."

Chapter 10

GRENVILLE jerked his head round, interested. Pomeroy flushed. "I believe I told you that was my business, Captain."

"You did, but the girl is missing. A second missing girl has just turned up dead. I'd like to know everything you know about Bess so that we might find her before she has a similar fate. Am I right? Was she paying you in kind?"

"I wouldn't say that, sir."

"What would you say, Sergeant?"

He bathed me in a light blue glare. "I would say we wasn't in the army anymore and you can leave off bullying me. But I know that will do no good." He ran his hand through his already slick hair, pushing it behind his ears. "The thing with Bess, Captain, is she weren't paying me to look the other way. We're sweet on each other."

"She has a lover," I said. "He lives with her near Great Wild Street. I planned to interview him."

"I know that. Tom Marcus. But she didn't like him. He didn't treat her well enough, she said, and he clung to her something fierce. Like having a child, she said."

"Did she want to leave him?"

"Don't think so, not yet. She wanted to have something fixed for sure before she left him. He has some brass from working in a brickyard, and he's good at stretching the money both of 'em made."

"I can wish you had told me this before," I said sternly. "She might have threatened to leave him, and he might have grown angry with her, do you not think? Enough to harm her or at least to make her run away?"

Pomeroy's brows lowered. "She wouldn't have run away without coming to me. She knew where to find me. He didn't hurt her, because when he came and reported her missing, I shook him up a bit, to find out whether he'd hit her, and I'm satisfied he hadn't. Besides, if he'd done her in, he like as not wouldn't come to Bow Street, would he?"

"Unless he wanted to direct your attention elsewhere," Grenville suggested. "Perhaps he killed Bess as well as Mary, then reported Bess missing to make it look as though he was concerned about her. He killed Mary as a blind for the death of Bess, perhaps trying to make it seem as though a madman had decided to kill game girls."

"You are reasoning ahead of yourself," I said. "We haven't found Bess, and there is no reason to believe the two incidents are connected. Besides, Thompson told us that Mary had come to Covent Garden to meet a man."

Pomeroy held up his hands. "Well, it weren't me."

I looked at him. "If you say Bess was sweet on you, why did she not decide to come and live with you instead?"

"Would look fine, wouldn't it, Captain, a game girl living with a Bow Street Runner? She wanted to give up her trade first, find a proper job and become a proper girl."

I traced the head of my walking stick. "Felicity told me

that Bess allowed you privileges without paying in order to keep you from arresting her."

I thought that would anger him. I thought he'd puff himself up, offended, and tell me to go to hell and dance with the devil. Instead, to my surprise, his grin flashed, teeth white in the darkness. "Thing is about Felicity, Captain, you can't always trust what she says. She's a clever one. Has to be, don't she? But she'll tell a tale, wind a chap around her finger, so to speak. I'm not calling her a liar, but you have to question her version of the truth."

I mulled this over, realizing that I had been ready to believe Felicity, probably because I felt a bit sorry for her. She exuded confidence in herself and her ability to please men, but because she was a game girl and she had black skin, the world thought nothing of exploiting her. She must have come up with plenty of defenses against that.

"What is the truth, then?" I asked.

"What I said. Me and Bess, we like each other. She was working to leave her man and take up with me. I last saw her when your Felicity spied us. I was a-kissing her good-bye."

"Good-bye? Where was she going?"

"Good night, I ought to have said. She was off home, and I went to Bow Street. Last I ever saw her." For the first time, he looked troubled. "So I would thank you, Captain, if you could help find her. I never want to see her like this." He looked back down at the corpse of the girl.

I understood. I did not want to find Gabriella like this either, and by the look on his face, neither did Auberge.

We waited in the warm night for Thompson and the coroner. Grenville had brandy in a flask, which he shared around. After midnight, one patroller returned with a plump man wearing an expression of curiosity, followed not much later by the second patroller and Thompson.

The coroner of the parish seemed in no way distraught

that he'd been dragged from his comfortable home to examine a young woman's corpse in a back lane near the river. He spread a cloth on the ground and knelt on it, asking the patrollers to move the rest of the boards out of the way.

Thompson stood looking down at the young woman, his tattered-gloved fingers at his mouth. "Yes, that is Mary Chester. I'll have to have her Sam tell us for certain, but I believe it's her."

The coroner gently untied the sash and removed it from her neck. "Her initials are on the dress," the coroner said, pulling back a fold of bodice. "M.C., embroidered on the seam, nice as you please."

"Was she strangled?" I asked, leaning down.

"Not a bit of it." He turned her head, examining the bruises. "This was done before she died. Maybe a day or two. She's been dead I'd say a few days, but she can't have lain here all that time. Someone would have found her, at least the dogs and the rats."

"How pleasant." Grenville took a handkerchief from his pocket and dabbed his lips.

"So she was killed elsewhere and brought here," I mused. "If that was so, why wait so long to move her here?"

"Perhaps the gent had hidden the body in one place," Pomeroy broke in, "then had to move it or risk it being discovered."

Grenville patted his lips again. "Then why not tip her into the river? He'd carried her this far; the stairs to the river are only a street away."

"Perhaps he was seen, or thought he was seen," I suggested. "He leaves her at the first place he can find and flees." I turned back to the coroner. "Do you know how she died?"

"Well," the man answered, taking his time. He turned

her head again, lifting the hair from the back of her neck. "So far, I've seen no sign of injury, but I'll have to examine her more thoroughly in better light. She might have suffocated, or been poisoned, or perhaps died naturally. I cannot say until I take her elsewhere."

"My carriage is at your disposal," Grenville said.

The coroner climbed to his feet. His hand went to his back, and his face creased in pain. "Get a bit stiff on the hard ground." He grinned. "There's not many gentlemen that would offer his fine carriage to a corpse, Mr. Grenville, but there's no need. I brought my own conveyance. I just need a strong gentleman to lift her."

The patrollers, with Pomeroy watching, did the job. They moved the rotted boards, hoisted the girl between them, and carried her out of the passage. Her gown trailed to the ground, and neither of the three thought to lift the skirt out of the mud.

Thompson looked about the lane a little after the coroner had gone, his face somber. "I believe he is right that she was killed elsewhere and left here. That poor sailor of hers will take it hard. I don't think he murdered her."

"Would he have tried to throttle her?" Grenville asked.

"Possibly, if she angered him. But the fact that she didn't die of that points in his favor, because he stopped before he killed her."

"Or she managed to get away from him," I said.

"True. But then he would simply have tried again. I doubt he would have come to me, worried, if he'd wanted her dead."

The same argument could be applied to Black Bess's lad. Had he known she was seeing Pomeroy behind his back? And if so, why would he have gone straight to Bow Street? I had the feeling that neither of these girls' lovers knew anything about their disappearances or deaths.

Thompson sighed as we emerged from the passage.

"Have to look up Chester and tell him the bad news. I'm not relishing that. Would you like to come with me, Captain? Not to break the news, but to see if he knows anything further?"

"No." I told Thompson about Gabriella and that I needed to hunt for her.

His expression darkened. "If I find the bastard who is doing this . . ." He shook his head, his thin frame moving. "I'll tell the magistrate of the Bow Street house and the others to put as many men as they can spare onto it. I'll even lend one of my own." He held out his hand for me to shake. "We'll find her, Captain."

His resolution only worried me further. Everyone except Auberge had offered the explanation that Gabriella had merely wandered off. Thompson, like me, believed something more sinister had happened. Hearing my fear confirmed only increased the coldness in the pit of my stomach.

AUBERGE wanted to return to King Street and speak to Carlotta. He and I and Grenville and Pomeroy walked back to the Strand, Grenville fetching Jackson from the tavern to which he'd taken the others. Grenville ordered him to drive Auberge back to King Street, while he volunteered to remain and help the others renew the search for Gabriella. Thompson departed for the coroner's house to learn the outcome of his examination.

I decided to leave them and ride with Auberge, hoping against hope that Gabriella had returned to the house while we'd been distracted with the body of Mary.

Gabriella was not there. When we entered the house, Carlotta flew down the stairs, wild for news. When Auberge merely shook his head, she flung herself into his arms, crying madly. I do not believe she even noticed me there.

I left the house, uncertain where to turn. I told Jackson to go back to Grenville and the others and continue the search. I tramped back to Covent Garden alone after he'd nodded and driven away, drawn to the place, as though I could find the answers there in the middle of the night in the pitch dark.

The stalls were shut and quiet, the market closed. That did not mean the place was deserted. Game girls wandered the shadows, their high-pitched laughter promising a merry time, and thieves roamed, waiting for victims.

The pile of the theatre hugged the northeast corner of the square, the back walls marked here and there with small windows. The theatre's entrance and grand piazza were on its other side in Hart and Bow Streets.

I saw a Mayfair gentleman near the back of the theatre, conspicuous in fine suit and tailed frock coat, a tall hat on his head. A dark carriage with a matched team waited not far from him. He was speaking to a game girl, the lady bold in a feathered hat and scarlet dress, answering him with laughter.

After a time, he held his hand out to her, offering. She took it, and together they went to the carriage and climbed inside. The coachman gave office to the horses and drove on at a snail's pace. I stepped aside to let the carriage pass, thoughts racing.

I'd recognized the gentleman, a man I'd met at White's with Grenville, by name of Stacy. He was a husband and a father; likely his wife and daughter were behind the wall in the theatre, enjoying the performance, while Stacy entertained himself elsewhere.

I knew that rich men often slummed, picking up game girls without discretion. I wondered as I watched the carriage recede into the darkness of King Street how often Stacy visited Covent Garden, and whose company he enjoyed there.

* * *

I walked north on James Street. The intersection between it and Hart Street was busy with people leaving the theatre between performances. A few enterprising acrobats had set up on the corner opposite me, two men and a girl tumbling and dancing while a little boy wove through the crowd with an upturned hat.

The acrobats were quite good and had drawn a small crowd. The girl scrambled up one man's back to stand on his shoulders, then he tossed her high in the air. The other man caught her with ease and set her on her feet again. The audience applauded.

I crossed the street, letting a threepenny bit drop into the boy's hat. He said, "Thankee, sir," before moving along.

A carriage rattled to a halt behind me, and I looked around to see a window drop down and a white face topped with an odd lace and feather headdress appear. A pair of shrewd eyes observed me, then the face left the window.

A footman swarmed from the back of the coach and opened the door for me. He assisted me in and closed the door, shutting me into an opulent, stuffy, and dark box with the lady who'd stopped for me.

"Whatever are you doing wandering the streets?" Lady Breckenridge asked, sending me a smile. Her headdress swayed somewhat with the carriage, but stayed in place. Female fashions were heading down the avenue of the ridiculous these days, with stiff lace and many flounced ribbons decorating hems, the skirts almost like canvases for layers of decoration. Headdresses weren't much better. I preferred the simplicity of a bandeau woven through locks, but women, especially in the aristocracy, had to follow fashion. Lady Breckenridge managed to look pretty even with the baglike lace hood covering her hair and the peacock feathers that drooped to either side of her face and stood straight up at her brow. Gloves covered her arms past her elbows, her short-sleeved, summer garment shimmering gold with silver and yellow adornments.

I'd come to prefer her in little but a peignoir, her black hair cascading, or better still wrapped only in her sheets. I raised her hand and pressed a kiss to her palm.

Her eyes darkened. "Come with me to South Audley Street?" she asked.

I'd been her lover only a few months, and every moment spent with her was a delight, but I lowered her hand and shook my head. "Donata, the most terrible thing has happened."

I meant to say the words calmly, but my voice broke, and I could not continue. I sat mutely in the carriage while it bumped its way God knew where, holding her hand and staring straight in front of me.

"What is it?" She sent me a worried look. "Tell me."

I had explained it to so many people today, to Pomeroy and Thompson, to Auberge, to Nancy and Felicity. The words grew more difficult to say, not less, as I repeated them. "My daughter has disappeared."

Her eyes widened. "Disappeared?"

I pressed my hand to my face. "Oh, God, Donata, we've looked all afternoon and all night, and she is nowhere to be found. And someone is killing game girls in Covent Garden, and what if he took her, too?"

I breathed heavily, my voice a dry rasp. I hated to break down in front of her, the woman whom I wanted to think nothing but high things of me. Most Englishmen and Englishwomen hated displays of emotion—cool sangfroid was the rule, unless it was cold anger. I'd lived too long in hot countries, where rage or grief was let loose under the merciless sun.

She chose neither to cling to me and pat my shoulder

nor bathe me in scorn. Instead she waited until my emotion had run its course, saying nothing while the carriage creaked and swayed through the warm streets.

I drew a long breath and wiped my eyes, my hands shaking. She sat calmly, a drooping peacock feather brushing her cheekbone.

In a low voice that threatened to crack again, I told her of the events of the day, starting with the meeting with James Denis. She turned away as I described speaking with my wife, and Denis suggesting I bring a suit of criminal conversation against her and Auberge. Then I told her of seeing Gabriella while I talked with Nancy and Felicity, how I'd sent her home, and how Carlotta had come looking for her later.

"We searched," I finished. "We took streets between us and we looked and looked. Auberge and I walked every street, every lane, we looked in every suspect house. She is nowhere to be found."

I finished, my elbows on my knees, my face in my hands. I could not afford to give in to despair. I had to remained clearheaded, to *think*.

Donata put her hand on my arm. "Gabriel, stay with me tonight."

I shook my head. "I have to return to Grimpen Lane. She might come back there."

Her hand moved, stroking my arm, soothing and firm. "There is no reason she would try to find her way to Grimpen Lane. If she is free, she will go back to King Street, where her mother is."

A swift pain darted through me, but I realized she was right. Gabriella knew little about me and was not certain she trusted me. She'd try to find her mother, and Auberge, much as I hated to admit it.

"Still, I must continue looking."

"You are all in, Gabriel. A wreck. Come home with me and let Barnstable give you a drop of laudanum and put you to bed. You need to rest and clear your thoughts."

"I cannot. Anything can happen in the few hours I am asleep. I want to be out searching."

She rested her head on my shoulder, the spice of her perfume touching me. "I will spread the word. All of London will turn out and hunt for her, every servant, every coachman, every errand boy. I know kind people. We will turn London upside down and shake it until she drops out again."

Part of me was touched at her concern and generosity, but that part was buried under a blanket of fear. "She might have been taken to a bawdy house. Or even out of London. A fast carriage could get far by this time."

She squeezed my hand. "I have many connections. I will use every one I can. I promise you that."

I turned, my view of her rather obscured by her peacock feathers. I touched the headdress. "Take this off."

She smiled and complied, as though knowing how ridiculous it looked but waiting for me to say so. She unpinned the headgear and dropped it to the seat opposite, where it lay like a fallen bird.

"I prefer your tresses long and loose," I said, touching them.

"That is a bold thing to say."

I slid my arms around her waist and pulled her close. "It is only the truth."

She held me quietly. I had grown to care for her deeply, my feelings a far cry from the day I first met her, when she'd directed cigarillo smoke and sardonic comments at me in the home of a rather tasteless baron in Kent.

Since then I'd come to know her as a fond mother, witty observer, steadfast friend, and even a vulnerable woman whose hopes for happiness had been dashed early in life.

She was a comfortable person to talk with, even when she was cutting a member of the *ton* to ribbons with her pointed humor. She was my lover without drama, taking and giving without rancor. I wanted to do nothing to lose what I had with her.

We reached her house in South Audley Street not long later, and I managed to enter the very modern, very monochrome dwelling without breaking down. She called Barnstable, her butler, who seemed to live to administer to my hurts. He had massaged balm into my injured leg when I'd hurt it deeply and helped heal my wounds after I'd fought with a French officer during the Berkeley Square affair.

This time, he smiled and led me upstairs to the spare bedroom in which I'd slept before, bustling about to fetch me a nightshirt and tea and laudanum.

I let him light the fire and warm the blankets for me—or rather, he gave sharp orders to Lady Breckenridge's maids and footmen to do so—but after he departed, I poured the laudanum-laced tea into the fire. I did not want to risk that Gabriella would turn up hurt or dead while I slumbered too deeply to easily wake.

I did realize that I needed to rest. I could only push myself so far, and I had to be ready to take up the hunt for her again. I also knew that Donata would be as good as her word. If she said she'd stir her friends and neighbors to join the search, she would.

I decided to rest a few hours in the bed Barnstable had prepared for me, the same one I'd lain in months ago, when I'd strained my knee. The room was small, but elegant, in pale green with tasteful plaster medallions on the walls and a candelabra lending a warm glow to the night. I lay down in the bed, pulling the blankets over me because the night had cooled, and closed my eyes.

I was still awake a few hours later when Lady Breckenridge joined me. She snuggled under the blankets next to me, as though perfectly prepared to stay with me all night, and said, "I sent word to Lady Aline, who promised to pass the news along. She knows even more people than I do. She is sending word to Sir Gideon Derwent, who will know some likely places to look, being a reformer. I also sent word to your Mrs. Brandon, though she has already retired for the night."

"Louisa. Dear God, I forgot all about her."

Donata rose up on her elbow and sent me a speculative look. "Surely not."

I scrubbed my face, noting the stiff bristles on my jaw. "She was to have come to my rooms this afternoon, so that I could take her to meet Gabriella. She never turned up. She might have missed us when we went out searching, but she would have waited."

"Perhaps she simply could not come," Donata suggested.

"She would have sent word."

"Well, she is home now and in any case will know what has happened. Call on her when you wake up."

"I will never sleep. I poured away the laudanum."

She lay down again, draping her arm across my chest. "You will break Barnstable's heart, you know. But you must sleep. I will stay until you do."

I knew what she meant. Felicity had offered me the same thing, only Lady Breckenridge did not offer out of pity.

I laced my hand through her hair, wanting to tell her no, but instead I found myself pulling her to me. In the darkness, she slid her body over mine and kissed me. She gave me comfort in that high tester bed, and much to my surprise, when she lay down again, I fell quickly asleep.

As morning brightened, I made ready to visit Louisa. Barnstable shaved me as well as any valet; he'd procured a razor to have ready for my visits, seemingly delighted that his mistress had taken a paramour. Barnstable approved of me, perhaps, I thought with wry humor, because I gave him a chance to practice his remedies. My humor wronged him, however; he was an excellent butler and took fine care of Lady Breckenridge.

Lady Breckenridge, awake and dressed in a morning gown of ecru silk, her hair covered by a small cap, announced her intention of accompanying me to the Brandons'.

"You hate rising early," I said, surprised. And yet, she was on her feet, her eyes bright as though she'd slept all night instead of snatching a few hours between dawn and full light.

She gave me a faint smile as her maid draped a thin shawl over her shoulders. "I am a jealous woman, Gabriel, and I know how fond you are of Louisa Brandon. I will go with you."

I could have argued, but I saw no purpose in it. I was grateful for Donata's help. She could have had many reactions to my daughter's disappearance, but she'd chosen worry and compassion. And further, she'd chosen action. Not for Donata Breckenridge a fit of the vapors and retiring to the country until it was all over.

She had her carriage readied to take us the journey from South Audley Street to Brook Street. As we rolled through clean morning sunshine and cool air, the streets rather empty except for servants on errands, I said, "You have no need to be jealous of Louisa Brandon, you know. We have always been friends, but nothing more, and since Brandon's troubles this spring, she has been quite attendant on him."

She chuckled. "You are so very literal, Gabriel. I know you are not slipping off to her bed under the colonel's nose, but you have known her for so very long. You and she share a deep friendship, and you exchange secret smiles when any subject is mentioned about which you and she have a shared memory. I feel a bit left out."

"I beg your pardon," I said, heartfelt. "I had no idea I was being so rude."

"You cannot help it. I imagine my mother and I do the same thing." She raised a delicate brow. "But do not try to tell me that you regard her as you would a sister, because I will not believe you."

I stretched my game leg, moving the tendons so it would not stiffen up. I thought suddenly of the night Donata and I had just shared together and the scent and feel of her on me, and leaned down and nuzzled her cheek. "You have no need of jealousy," I repeated. "None whatsoever."

She turned her head and met my lips in a kiss. Then the carriage bumped hard over a stone, and we broke apart, smiling a little.

I had not quite banished the trepidation in her eyes. By nature of life in the army, Louisa and I had shared many circumstances both happy and dire, and had seen what a man or woman living sedately in London would never see. Louisa had been exposed to the full horrors of battle and death, the heat of India and Spain, bitter winters and roasting summers, disease, dysentery, dismemberment, and parasites. She had weathered it all with aplomb, the only thing destroying her peace being her marriage to her stubborn and turbulent husband.

Lady Breckenridge was right—Louisa and I had shared much and comforted each other when need be. She was also right that I would never regard Louisa as a sister. I had been half in love with her most of my life, needing her, at least, until I'd stumbled upon the compelling attraction of Donata Breckenridge.

We said nothing more until we reached the Brandon house in Brook Street. A startled Matthews said that the master and mistress were breakfasting, but if we cared to join them, he would take us up.

In the dining room, we found Louisa picking at her meal, looking troubled, Brandon just lifting his newspaper, his face red and his breathing quick. We'd interrupted a quarrel, I surmised.

Louisa looked up when Matthews announced us and started when she saw Lady Breckenridge. "Your ladyship." She rose hastily, tossing her napkin into her chair. "Might I offer you breakfast? We are eating simply today, but my cook would be happy to prepare anything you like."

Brandon, too, had risen, his veil of politeness descending. He pulled a chair from the table and swept a gesture at it. "Please, sit here, your ladyship. You may have coffee, or chocolate, as you prefer. Matthews, get a footman up here, her ladyship is hungry."

"No, indeed." Lady Breckenridge gracefully slid into the seat and rested her hands on its arms. "I could not eat a thing at this appalling hour, but I am craving coffee. Fetch some very strong for me, Matthews, if you please." She flicked her gaze to Louisa. "I would never dream of calling on you this early, Mrs. Brandon, and it is horribly rude to interrupt your breakfast, but Gabriel is in trouble, and we must help him."

Brandon and Louisa exchanged a glance. I sat down, nodding at Matthews that I, too, wanted coffee.

"We have heard the news," Brandon said stiffly. "My wife insists that it is her fault. Please talk her out of this nonsense."

Chapter 11

LOUISA did indeed look haggard. Her face was gray-white except for spots of color burning in her cheeks.

"How on earth is this your fault, Louisa?" I asked. "Gabriella walked away from the rooms in King Street and either has lost herself or someone sinister has her. Or someone benevolent," I added, praying that this was the case. The benevolent person might even now be returning Gabriella to her mother. I wanted that circumstance so much that it put a sharp taste in my mouth.

Louisa lifted her gaze, and the shame in her eyes startled me. "I went to see her," she said.

I blinked. "Did you? When? You and I were to go together."

"I know." Her voice strengthened. "I was too impatient, for which I will berate myself for the rest of my life. I did not want you with me, you see, because I did not want you to hear what I said to Carlotta."

I grew still. "I never gave you the direction to the boardinghouse."

"You said King Street, Covent Garden. It was easy, once there, to ask for the house in which the two people from France and their daughter stayed. I boldly asked the landlady if I could see Gabriella."

I gripped the arms of my chair. "And did you see her?"

"Yes."

Her eyes moistened. She must have felt what I had, wonder that Gabriella had grown to such a beautiful young woman, pride in her intelligence and sweetness, and sadness that she had missed watching her blossom.

"You spoke to her," I said.

Louisa nodded. At that moment, a footman bustled in balancing a tray with a coffeepot and cups. The wonderful aroma of coffee filled the room. Louisa wiped her eyes while the footman set down the tray, arranged the cups, then laid out the sugar bowl and silver tongs and a small pot of thick cream. He took the tray and slid from the room, trying to pretend he did not exist.

Donata took up the pot and poured coffee into my cup. She knew I liked it black and strong, so while she dropped sugar and cream into her own liquid, she offered me none. She stirred her coffee and cream until it became the color of Felicity's skin.

She tapped her spoon lightly on the edge of the cup and set it down, her movements elegant and economical, the training of governesses and nannies who had polished her all her life shining through. "What did you say that upset her, Mrs. Brandon?"

Louisa's cheeks burned red. Brandon looked on, brows lowered.

"I told her that her mother had deserted Gabriel. I told her exactly what Carlotta had done—cuckolded him and left him for no good reason. I told Gabriella she'd been taken away and lied to because Carlotta did not want her returning to her true father. I told her what Carlotta's actions had done to him, how wretched he'd been to learn that his daughter was gone forever."

"Louisa," I whispered. "Dear God."

"I know it was utterly stupid," she said in an anguished voice. "But Gabriella deserved to know the truth. I know that Carlotta will paint you a villain to Gabriella and say that she had to run away from you and your cruelty. Carlotta wants her little nest in France with her lover and her children, and you know she will not risk losing Gabriella to you."

I fell silent, having no idea what to say. Louisa liked to be my champion, but I could imagine the effects of her words on Gabriella, who had just learned, to her enormous shock, that the man she'd always thought of as her father was no such thing.

Donata sipped her coffee thoughtfully. "And Gabriella was visibly upset?"

"Yes." Louisa bit her lip, not wanting to look at either of us. "She cried. I tried to comfort her, but she would not have me. She told me very clearly to leave. It broke my heart, but I did."

"You did not see—er, Mrs. Lacey?" Donata prodded.

"No. I left Gabriella in the downstairs parlor. By that time I was crying, too, and I knew I could not face Carlotta. I decided to go home." Silent tears trickled from her eyes. "It must have been after that interview that she left the house. I upset her, and she ran away. She might have been coming to see you, or perhaps she simply wanted to walk and think, I do not know." She wiped her cheeks with the heel of her hand. "I will not ask your forgiveness, Gabriel, because I do not deserve it."

I sat in stunned silence, trying to take in what she had told me.

Brandon noisily gulped his morning chocolate, leaving a dark stain above his upper lip, which he wiped away with a napkin. "You are not to blame, Louisa. She might have walked out of the house because you upset her, but if she got lost, it is not your fault." He shrugged his broad shoulders. "Who knows? She might have gone straight upstairs and had a row with her mother, and then decided to run away. Carlotta Lacey, as I recall, could try a saint's patience."

He flicked a glance at me, but did not apologize. He had thought Carlotta a flighty woman from the first, and had never been overly friendly to her.

"The point upon which we must focus," Lady Breckenridge cut in crisply, "is not why she left the house, but where she went."

"I have been over that in my head," I said. I felt relief and gratitude toward Donata for insisting she join me. She could watch from an outsider's perspective and tell us to stop the dramatics and start thinking. "If she tried to go back to Grimpen Lane, she'd walk through Covent Garden to Russel Street. That is a straightforward route, no reason to go any other way."

"Perhaps she stopped to shop in the market and got turned around," Donata suggested. "She thought she was heading toward Grimpen Lane when, in fact, she was walking down Southampton Street. This is her first time in London—England even—and she might easily have become confused."

"St. Paul's Chapel is distinctive. She would have known that Grimpen Lane was in the opposite direction."

"*You* know that," Donata said. "She might not remember, in her agitation."

Louisa had said nothing, remaining with her head bowed, not wanting to look at us. The golden curls at her forehead trembled. So worried I was over Gabriella's disappearance that I did blame her at present. She'd had no right to tell Gabriella those things, no right to interfere. She said she'd acted for my sake, but had she? I had told her to leave Gabriella and Carlotta alone, and she had not listened.

Colonel Brandon broke in. "It seems to me, Lacey, that you are predicting dire events before the fact. Perhaps the girl simply made her way back to France. She was upset and wanted to go home. If she had money and was resourceful, she could buy a coach ticket to Dover. Or she could have stolen whatever tickets and money her parents had put aside for their return. Or sold gewgaws or some such, in her determination to go home."

"Alone?" I asked. "A young woman does not travel alone, and no maid went with her."

"My reasoning takes in the fact that she is your daughter," Brandon said. "And you are the most bloody stubborn man I know. If she decided to return by herself to France, I am certain she would try to do it no matter what she had to do to get there. I know you have done more than a few damn fool things in your past, and you succeeded only by dint of your refusal to see reason. Young girl or no, she is a Lacey."

I sat still, torn between pride and irritation. "You do have a point," I said tightly. "I will check the coaching inns in and around London to see if she boarded a mail coach." Another thought struck me. "Auberge told me that they'd brought Gabriella to London with them because an unsuitable young man was pursuing her. We might be making a mare's nest of this, when all she's done is elope."

"As you did," Brandon said.

"As I did. And as her mother did with Auberge."

"We'll find her, Lacey," Brandon went on. He sat back in his chair, sipping his chocolate as though it was the finest brandy. "I know a commander whose soldiers sadly need something to do, and drilling is making them soft. I'll have him put them on to hunting down your daughter."

I stared at him, touched that he would want to help. "Thank you," I said.

He scowled at me. "You did save my neck from the noose, damn you."

"If you find my daughter, sir, we will be more than even."

"Thank God," Brandon said, and fervently drank his chocolate.

"WHERE to now?" Lady Breckenridge asked as we settled ourselves in her carriage again.

"You do not have to do this," I told her. "Have your coachman set you down at home, though I would be grateful for a ride back to Grimpen Lane. I must find Pomeroy and check in with Auberge."

She looked at me without expression. "Of course I must do this. She is your daughter, and I will do everything I can to help you find her." She leaned out of her window. "John, take us to Russel Street in Covent Garden."

I heard her coachman's terse, "Yes, my lady," then his chirrup to the horses as we clopped off down Davies Street toward Berkeley Square and south.

We rode through awakening London, neither of us speaking much, then Lady Breckenridge's coachman stopped in Russel Street to let us descend. I expected Lady Breckenridge would want to wait for me in the comfort of her coach, but she bade her footman help her down after me. Donata had never seen my rooms, and I hoped she had no intention of coming to them now. But she walked with me serenely down the lane, her skirt looped to keep out of the mud, her hand resting on my arm.

Mrs. Beltan's bake shop was open, and business was

thriving. I suggested that Lady Breckenridge wait there for me and enjoy Mrs. Beltan's yeasty bread.

"Not a bit of it, Gabriel," Donata said. "Let us be scandalous and ascend to your rooms."

I stopped her. "I live rather meagerly."

"I gathered that. Do not be vulgar; I care nothing for your money, or lack of it. Worrying about money is only for the parvenu. We of breeding shrug it from our shoulders."

"It is a very convenient thing to have, on the other hand," I said in a low voice.

"Gabriel, I have fountains of money, if you wish to continue on this vulgar footing. Let us please cease speaking of it; it is making me a bit queasy."

Her sardonic smile was firmly in place, and again, I felt gratitude. She was trying to put me at my ease in a potentially embarrassing situation.

I led her into the stairwell. She looked around in curiosity, taking in the faded murals with the shepherdesses and shepherds of old chasing each other in idyllic bliss. Halfway up, I handed her to a stair above me and kissed her.

She eased away when we finished, looking pleased. "Donata," I began.

A door above us opened and Grenville's weary tones floated down to us. "Lacey, is that you?" He stepped out onto the dark landing and looked down. "Oh, I do beg your pardon. I am a gooseberry, am I?"

To hear the most fashionable man in England describe himself as a gooseberry made me laugh, the first amusement I'd felt since Gabriella had gone missing.

"I stayed the night," he said, ushering us into the sitting room. "I hope you do not mind. Matthias and Bartholomew fixed me up well."

The two young footmen were sitting on either side of

my table, going at a repast that looked like all my breakfasts for the past week combined. The tray that Grenville must have eaten from, the plate scraped clean of food, reposed next to the wing chair.

Matthias and Bartholomew sprang to their feet when they saw Lady Breckenridge, Bartholomew hastily chewing a buttered slab of bread.

"Steady, lads, finish your meal," I said. "Any news?"

Grenville sent me a grim look. "I hoped you would bring some. No, we searched until we could not keep our eyes open, then I returned here for a few hours' sleep. Pomeroy's lads are still at is, as is my coachman, and Matthias and Bartholomew have been in and out. I succumbed to sleep; I am sorry."

"I did as well, but we may start fresh. Have you heard from Auberge this morning?"

"Yes. He came as I was getting out of bed. No, she did not return."

I took the news unhappily, but deep inside, I had thought that would be the outcome. I told Grenville Brandon's idea that Gabriella had tried to journey back to France, and he agreed that was a possibility.

And so the second day of the search for Gabriella began. Jackson returned with a fresh set of patrollers, five of them this time. Lady Breckenridge's servants joined in, two footmen and a coachman, and before long, servants from the households that Lady Breckenridge and Lady Aline had notified turned up, ready to look. Nancy and Felicity came in, too, with a couple of girls in tow.

At the last came Colonel Brandon. He turned an uncomfortable shade of red as Grenville, neat and fresh and shaved despite making do with my bed, stared at him in surprise. Brandon brought four others with him, lieutenants of the regiment whose commander had said needed something to do. We could not, of course, all crowd into my rooms, and so we spread out among Grimpen Lane while Grenville and I gave orders. A few urchins who generally hung about looking for handouts or odd jobs also said they'd join, for appropriate pay, of course.

I outlined the task: Comb London and find Gabriella or find out where she went. I sent a contingent to check the coaching inns, the urchins to check the bawdy houses, for which some of them already did jobs. A few of the patrollers were to make their way up and down the river, asking the watermen if they'd found her in the night.

I sent Brandon's soldiers farther afield, to check the roads that led from London, especially those toward France. They were to ask at every inn and every posting point if anyone had seen a young girl, either alone or with a young man. Colonel Brandon joined them, riding out with them on their cavalry-trained horses.

They dispersed, and Grenville walked with me back upstairs. "What shall I do, Lacey? You did not give me an assignment."

"I need you to be my field general, to set up a post where others can report back to you and you to me." We entered the sitting room, where Lady Breckenridge had been watching out of the window. She joined us when we came in. "I also need the two of you for inside information in Mayfair," I went on. "I am not completely convinced that searching alone will be the answer, either for Gabriella or for Black Bess."

Grenville cocked a brow. "Inside information?"

"Yes." I described seeing the coach last night stopped in Covent Garden, while the gentleman fetched himself a girl. "I met him once with you, I believe. Mr. Stacy?"

"Jeremiah Stacy?" Grenville looked taken aback, then thoughtful. "I cannot see him doing such a thing; he is a shy gentleman. If you had said his friend Brian McAdams, I could believe it. He enjoys erotic novels and etchings from

France and talking rather crudely about the act." He caught Lady Breckenridge's eye and blushed. "Oh, I beg your pardon."

She waved away his apology. "Do not be reticent on my account. My husband knew every crudity invented and openly boasted of doing them. I think I can no longer be disgusted."

Grenville looked embarrassed, but anger for the dead Lord Breckenridge burned inside me once again.

"You could not have mistaken McAdams for Stacy, could you?" Grenville asked me. "If it were dark, and Stacy lent him the coach?"

I shook my head. "No, it was Stacy. I remember him distinctly. He has the very long nose and lanky build, correct?"

"Yes," Grenville said. "I never thought he'd slum. Not the type, I should think."

"I mean to ask him. I'll send around my card and pay a call." Because Grenville had introduced me to him, I could presume to call on the man, or at least meet him somewhere.

"He won't be at home. He'll be at Tatt's. That's his passion, horseflesh. At least, I would have said so before you told me this. I'll go with you, and we'll quiz him."

Lady Breckenridge leaned against the writing table and crossed her ankles. "You think he might have something to do with Gabriella?"

"I have no thoughts one way or the other," I responded. "He might have seen something while he was busy chatting up game girls. He might know something about Mary Chester and Black Bess. He might know something about Gabriella. Then again, he might know nothing at all and simply enjoys having it off with girls from Covent Garden."

"Well, we can quiz him at any rate," Grenville said. "I'll

take you to Tatt's this afternoon. What else do you want us to do to storm Mayfair?"

"If you know of any other gentleman with a fixation on street girls, please tell me," I said. "I will quiz every one of them if I have to."

"My husband certainly knew gentlemen of odd tastes," Lady Breckenridge mused. "I could see what some of them have been getting up to lately."

"Thinking of you even speaking to them is repugnant to me," I said.

She shrugged. "I am not overly fond of them, but I can find out what they know. I can use Barnstable to invade their servants' halls and refresh himself on gossip. He'll enjoy it."

I had no doubt that Lady Breckenridge's somewhat young and energetic butler would be delighted to help with covert investigation.

"What will you do?" Grenville asked. "While we're hard at it?"

I had thought of it last night before Lady Breckenridge found me. "I want to pay a visit to a nearby house, one Marianne showed me during the Hanover Square investigation. It's possible that Gabriella or Black Bess went there."

Grenville looked dubious. "Are you definitely connecting the two—or the three, rather—disappearances?"

"I do not *know* whether to connect them. But two game girls vanish from Covent Garden, and then my daughter goes, all in the space of a few weeks. I hardly think it coincidence. Brandon reminded me that Gabriella was my daughter—but that is only another point toward her being kidnapped. I go off half-cocked, but I am also resourceful. Unless her mother has trained that quality completely from her, I doubt she'd have run off without preparing. Everything points to her having meant to return to the boardinghouse quickly. No bundle of clothing missing, none of her personal possessions gone. I will ask Auberge whether she took anything from him or Carlotta, but I feel in my bones that she did not."

"If she eloped," Lady Breckenridge mused, "she might have gone with the clothes on her back and trusted the young man to provide for her. Perhaps this unsuitable man is quite rich."

"In that case, why is he unsuitable?" Grenville asked.

Lady Breckenridge looked thoughtful. "He might be a bounder, he might have a reputation for ruining young women, he might have a gambling addiction—so many things can attract a young woman and upset her parents at the same time."

I wondered which scenario disturbed me more, the thought of Gabriella snatched as she innocently walked through the square, or the thought of her willingly running off with a rakehell.

"I will certainly ask Auberge all about him," I said. I looked at them, my friends so ready to drop their appointments for the day to help me. Grenville, the great man of fashion, had turned his back on a social engagement the night before to keep searching for Gabriella. I could not help but be touched by their generosity.

"Thank you," I said. "To the pair of you."

True to their upbringing, both looked slightly embarrassed at being caught out doing good deeds.

"My dear friend," Grenville said. "I would a hundred times rather help you solve a case than be at home to the dozens of dandies and aristocrats who want to call on me or speak to me at White's, coffeehouses, or gaming hells. Most of them are half-drunk before they meet me and only want my approval on their cravat knots and the cut of their coats. Their company, quite frankly, has palled. Far more interesting things happen around you."

"I am happy I can provide entertainment," I began, but I did not mean it harshly. I'd said it so many times that it had become rather a joke between us.

"More than just entertainment. You soothe my vanity by making me think I can actually do some good in the world."

I smiled. "It must be difficult being one of the wealthiest, most influential men in England."

He gave me a withering glance, but let it go.

Lady Breckenridge came to me and placed her hand on my arm. "I am quite fond of you, of course, Gabriel, but I also very much enjoy prying into the affairs of my Mayfair neighbors. The veneer of discretion hides such sordid secrets, I have always found. I may dig through the dirt for you and feel virtuous at the same time." She laughed softly, self-deprecating.

"In other words, we don't help entirely for your sake," Grenville said. "We are selfish and pleasure-loving."

"Precisely," Donata said.

"Well, no matter your motives, I do need you. Go home and rest, Grenville, then we'll meet for Tatt's." I touched Donata's shoulder. "You gossip to your heart's content and ask Barnstable to visit servants' halls. Send for me anytime you like."

She slanted me a smile, telling me without words what time she'd like to send for me. Donata Breckenridge was not a fainting flower with false modesty. She enjoyed desire and saw no reason to hide the fact.

Grenville rubbed his chin as though his makeshift shave in my rooms hadn't suited him. "I'll take a hackney home. I'll hunt up Jackson and have him take you where you need to go in my carriage."

"Generous of you."

"Jackson needs the exercise. And if you're determined

to go alone, I want someone with you who will report to me when you forget to."

I acknowledged the hint. Often, when I was in the heat of an investigation, I pursued things on my own without calling Grenville in, and this offended him.

"I will not be alone. I plan to take Major Auberge with me."

"Will you?" Grenville asked. "Why?"

"Because I need to know about my daughter. And much as it pains me, he knows her far better than I do."

He acknowledged this with a sympathetic glance, but he said nothing. Lady Breckenridge rose on her tiptoes, pressed a kiss to my cheek, and with her back to Grenville, gave my forearm a surreptitious and suggestive stroke. Then she turned away, as though she'd done nothing untoward. "You will ride back in my carriage, Grenville," she said, "and we shall talk about people."

"An excellent idea," Grenville responded.

He offered her his arm, and the two strolled out. Grenville's cool sardonic tones floated up the stairs. "By the bye, did you notice Rafe Godwin's fantastic ballooning pantaloons at Lady Woodward's musicale Tuesday night?"

"Ghastly," Lady Breckenridge agreed. "I quite expected him to float to the ceiling." Grenville's laugh answered her, and then they were gone.

I smiled faintly as I closed the door. The two of them occupied a world I did not understand. It would never occur to me to made witty comments on a gentleman's pantaloons, no matter how ridiculous I found them. Lady Breckenridge and Grenville delighted in such things, yet when serious matters occurred, they were resilient and ready for them.

With these thoughts, I gathered what I wanted and went downstairs to walk to King Street.

Auberge proved willing to resume the hunt with me. As we left the boardinghouse, Jackson stopped Grenville's carriage in front of us and said laconically that he would drive us about.

I gave him the direction to a house in a lane off High Holborn, and climbed inside with Auberge. Auberge's face was chalk white, his eyes sunken, and I realized that he probably had not slept at all.

I never saw Carlotta at the boardinghouse. Auberge had come down alone, and quickly, though I heard a door bang as he descended the stairs. He thanked me for looking him up, then said nothing as we left King Street and went north toward Long Acre, not even asking our intended destination.

As we pulled up in front of the house I'd directed Jackson to, he finally bestirred himself. "I hoped when I saw you coming you brought good news with you."

"I wanted to," I answered.

"My wife . . ." He flinched, then went past the awkwardness. "She wants to return to France after we find Gabriella. She has always hated England. But if we do, I do not know how to do the divorce, then."

"The solicitors will find a way if they suspect a hefty fee," I said. "Why do you say she hates England? She had everything here, friends, a come-out, a country home. Her father was a squire. He was enraged that I'd married her, but that was to be expected, since we'd eloped without permission. Then I dragged her off to India, where she was miserable."

"She went to get away from her father." His voice held more emphasis, as though surprised he had to tell me this. "She disliked India, but she hated England more." He studied me. "You did not know this?"

"She never mentioned it." Or at least, not that I remembered. If Carlotta had ever tried to talk to me, I likely had not listened very hard. I had been young and brash and full of myself.

I wanted to ask him why she had wanted to flee her father, but the coach had stopped and we needed to descend.

It had been a year since I knocked on the door of the small, quiet-looking house, but the same maid answered it and she looked me up and down with the same belligerence. "It's you, is it? What'yer want?"

"Does the woman called Lady still live here? I would like to see her."

"Maybe she does, maybe she don't." She switched her black gaze to Auberge. "Who's he when he's at home?"

"Major Auberge."

The belligerence increased. "Is he a Frog? What's he want to come here for?"

I wasn't certain if she meant this house or England altogether. "If Lady is here, I would be obliged if you'd take her my card."

The maid gave me another once-over, and her expression changed to mere sullenness. "She liked you last time. Said you were a gentleman, and not many like you about." She snatched the ivory rectangle of card I held out to her. "I'll see if she's receiving." She backed up and slammed the door in my face.

I leaned against the brick of the house, settling in to wait.

"What is this place?" Auberge asked, gazing up at it. He saw what I saw—gray-brown brick, a brown-painted door, windows blank with no one looking out of them, some of them shuttered.

"A lying-in place for game girls and courtesans. Some benevolent person set it up, I still do not know who, but the girls pay their bed and board. It is a sort of place for them to go when they can go nowhere else. I found it a year ago when I was searching for another missing girl."

He looked at me. "Did you find this girl?"

"Not in time."

His gaze held mine a moment, then he turned away, though not before I'd caught the despair in his moist eyes. I think I realized at that moment how much he loved Gabriella, notwithstanding she was not his natural daughter.

The door opened again, and the maid reappeared. "Come on, then."

She took us to the small, rather shabby sitting room where I'd waited the last time I'd been here. Marianne Simmons had brought me to this place, thinking that perhaps the girl I sought had come here to give birth. She had been wrong, but I'd met a woman called "Lady," a young lady of the gentry by her accent and manner, who had come here for her own lying-in and then stayed to help the other girls.

Lady would not tell me her real name nor the name of the man who'd impregnated her. I had thought of her off and on over the last year, but had made no inquiry, fearing to destroy the haven she had found here. If the young woman had wanted to or had been able to go home, no doubt she would have. She seemed competent and intelligent and resourceful, the sort of young woman who knew what she wanted.

When she entered the room, I saw that the year had changed her little. She still moved with confidence and grace, and her face was unlined and serene. A small linen cap covered her dark hair, and she wore a dark serge gown with a raised waistline and no adornment. She looked much like a servant, but her manners made it plain that she was not.

She dropped a curtsy to me and then extended her hand. "Captain Lacey. It is a pleasure to see you again."

"And a pleasure to see you. Is all well?"

"Indeed. You may not believe me, but I enjoy staying here and helping the girls. Some of them dislike me for interfering, others are grateful, it is of no matter."

"And you have not changed your mind about giving me your real name?"

She shook her head slightly. "I will not. On the other hand, I have read much about you in the newspapers, stories about how cleverly you have helped the magistrates find murderers. I read them with interest."

"Thank you," I said with some dismay. The newspapers either exaggerated or got things blatantly wrong. "This is Major Henri Auberge, from France. We would like to ask you a few questions, about girls who have gone missing."

Her expression became troubled. "Missing? Street girls, you mean?"

"Yes. And one other." I gestured for her to sit, which she did, again gracefully. I moved to shut the door to the sitting room against the noise of female shouting upstairs. The maid, who had stationed herself near the open door, flashed a disappointed glance at me as I closed it.

I took a seat facing Lady, and Auberge sat rather awkwardly on a tattered Sheridan sofa.

"Do you know of girls named Black Bess and Mary Chester?" I asked Lady.

"Goodness, yes," she said at once. "Both of them have come here, Mary to have a baby, and Black Bess ill because she rid herself of one."

My interest was piqued. "When did these events happen?"

"With Black Bess it was a year ago. She's managed to keep herself from increasing since then, but that may be because the abortionist damaged her. She was quite ill."

"Damn all quacks," I muttered. "I beg your pardon. What about Mary Chester?"

"She had a baby not long ago, April, I believe. She was

relieved it had come because she didn't want to face her man, a sailor who was supposed to come in on a merchantman in early May. She had the baby and gave it up. I believe the ship was late in returning as well, and she was happy she would be able to face him without him being the wiser. Broke her heart, though. She is rather a simple girl, but a good one, at least as good as she can be living the life of a street girl. Her father sold her to a brothel when she was twelve and she has been struggling ever since. She is fond of Mr. Chester—calls herself Mrs. Chester—but she still plies her trade when he's gone; she knows how to do nothing else. He leaves her money, but it runs out, of course." She twined her long-fingered hands together. Her nails were white and clean and trimmed. "Why do you ask about her, Captain?"

"I fear I have to tell you that Mary Chester is dead."

She stared at me, her lips parted. "Oh dear. I hadn't known she was ill. Why didn't she come here?"

"She was not ill. She was killed."

Her gentle face whitened with shock. "Killed?"

"I do not know how she died, but it looked to be murder." I described how she'd been found in a back lane between the Strand and the river. "Mr. Thompson of the Thames River patrol is investigating, but I do not know what he has turned up."

"How terrible," Lady said. She straightened her skirt with a shaking hand, trying to remain composed. "Poor Sam Chester."

"Thompson must have broken it to him by now. I am afraid he will be suspected—motive, jealousy. You have just bolstered that motive. Perhaps he discovered that she'd been pregnant with another man's baby and grew angry. He seemed understanding of her profession when I interviewed him, but perhaps he was hiding his true feelings. And she had mentioned to her friends that she was to meet a wealthy gentleman in Covent Garden. His jealousy might have gotten the better of him."

Lady shook her head. "Not Sam Chester. I have met him a few times. He is gentle, even though he is a sailor. I doubt he could ever hurt Mary."

I rested my hand on the cool brass handle of my walking stick. "I agree with you. I liked him and was sorry for him. He seemed genuinely worried. The magistrate, however, will want an easy solution to a sordid case unless the true culprit is discovered. Do you know who was the father of her child?"

"No, she never said. She might not have known—he might have been one of her customers. Likewise, I do not know who is this wealthy gentleman you mention. The only man she ever talked about to me was Sam Chester. She loved him."

"Black Bess—who did she talk about?"

"Oh, heavens, never tell me she has been killed, too?"

"I do not know. She has disappeared as well. She, too, has a young man, a laborer who lives near Drury Lane. I have not spoken to him yet, but it seems she had the same sort of understanding with him that Mary Chester did with Sam. And she mentioned meeting a wealthy man in Covent Garden, same as Mary."

"I truly wish I could help, Captain," Lady said, distress in her eyes. "But I cannot. I have not heard from the others of a wealthy man in Covent Garden, and if I may say it, Captain, more than one highborn gentleman has had his way with street girls." Her cheeks burned red.

"I know. I have my eye on one, whom I will shake about, but I know of no others. This is an imposition, but could you ask the other girls? If a wealthy man has been preying on girls in Covent Garden, I want to find him. They might confide in you more than they would in me."

She inclined her head. "Of course. Anything I can do to

help." She looked curiously at Auberge, who had followed the discussion without a word.

"Now to the more difficult question," I said. "My own daughter has gone missing. She is seventeen, the same age as the game girls, and she has quite vanished." I swallowed hard as I said the last word. Auberge bowed his head, not protesting that I called her my daughter. "Her name is Gabriella. Do you know anything, *anything,* about her?"

Lady's eyes softened with compassion. "Captain, I am so sorry. I am afraid I have heard nothing about it, although I will ask the girls who come in. She was not a . . ." She left the question hanging, and all at once, I saw her as a refined young lady sitting in her parlor, pouring tea and talking of her charitable works with her father's friends. She did not belong here, and yet, she seemed to fit here, the benevolent young mother to troubled children.

"She was not a game girl. She lived most of her life in France and knows nothing of London and its ways."

She leaned forward. "I am sorry. I will certainly keep my eyes open and ask the girls to also. If they know anything at all—where may I send word?"

"Any number of places." I withdrew one of my cards and a stub of pencil and began scribbling. "My rooms in Grimpen Lane or the bake shop below it. Grenville's house in Grosvenor Street. The Bow Street Public Office, or number 31, King Street, a boardinghouse there. Ask for Madame or Major Auberge."

She took the card, and her brown gaze flicked again to Auberge, clearly wondering how he fit into all this. He stirred and offered his hand. "I, too, am Gabriella's father. Her—how do you say in English?—stepfather."

I saw the flash of confusion on Lady's face while she struggled to remain politely impassive. It was highly unusual for a father and a stepfather to be alive at the same time. That we were suggested scandal, but she was far too well bred to inquire into it, or even betray that she was interested.

I rose, ready to return to the search. Lady got to her feet with us. "I will do what I can, Captain. I promise."

She shook our hands prettily, again reminding me of the gentleman's daughter in her sitting room.

I did not withdraw my hand, but held hers hard and said in a low voice, "Tell me who you are. I can restore you to your family, I swear to you. I know people who could arrange a marriage for you, a good one, either with the man who put you here or with another who would not be prejudiced by your past." I felt confident that between Grenville, Louisa, Lady Aline, and the Derwents, we could find a kind man happy to have such a pretty and compassionate wife, no matter what had happened in her unfortunate past.

Her smile deepened, and amusement twinkled in her eyes. "You do not understand, Captain Lacey. I am happy here. This is my family, as odd as they are. My own family, I am afraid, are in no hurry to see me restored."

"A marriage then. Let me do something."

She shook her head and gently but firmly loosened her hand from my grasp. "It is difficult to explain. At home, I did little besides look pretty in a frock and play at the harp and paint insipid watercolors. I was nothing, and I did not even know it. If I marry, I will be nothing again, a wife in a cap who arranges fetes and paints more insipid watercolors." She spread her hands to indicate the room, and beyond. "Here, I found myself. After my initial distress, I realized that, at last, I could be useful. I can help a girl who is in despair, I can try to make her life better. They need someone like that, even if some of them hate me for it. The midwives and doctors will come here because of me, the apothecary will let me have medicines for little or nothing. They need me. I *want* to stay here. Please, Captain, do not inform my family, do not find me a husband. Let me stay and do what I was meant to do."

Her eyes glowed fervently, and I thought I understood. I bowed to her. "I will keep your secret. But if you ever change your mind, you know you have only to come to me."

She smiled, dimples appearing at the corners of her mouth. "You are a kind man. I will help you all I can, and keep your offer in mind. Good day, Captain."

"Good day to you, Lady." I bowed again and left the room, joining Auberge, who waited, under the scrutiny of the curious maid, in the foyer.

We traveled back down High Holborn in near silence. As the carriage rolled down Drury Lane toward Long Acre, Auberge lifted his head and said, "I am in near despair, Lacey. What do I do if she is truly gone?"

Chapter 12

I clenched the handle of my walking stick. "Not despair. Not yet. We must not give in yet."

As he continued to watch me in anguish, I drew a long breath. "Good God, man, how do you think I feel knowing she fled into the street after discovering my existence?" I demanded. "I plunged her into confusion, and if I had only kept my mouth closed, she would be happily at home with you and Carlotta. How do you think that makes me feel?"

He only watched me stonily. "We were caught up in our own worries about this divorce, and we neglected her. If I had been more careful—if I had left her home in France—"

"We can flog ourselves until we bleed," I broke in. "You said you brought her with you because of a young man. Tell me about him. Is he the sort of blackguard who'd follow her and convince her to elope?"

He switched to French, letting his words flow more easily. "I would not say so. Emile is no worse than any other young man, I think. He is a few years older than Gabriella and will come into his own money when he is age twenty-five. We wished them to wait until then, but Gabriella is impetuous." His look turned ironic. "I love Gabriella so dearly, but she is stubborn. My God, but she is stubborn."

I smiled grimly. "That sounds about right. She comes from a long line of stubborn men and women. I eloped with her mother, and so did you, and I am afraid now that Gabriella knows that, she will use it as leverage in her argument to marry him."

His eyes crinkled, his despair lightening a little. "No doubt."

"What is it about Carlotta that made us both run off with her?" I mused. "Her air of distressed innocence, I suppose."

To my surprise, Auberge smiled. "She had *her* way, you know, even as we thought we were having ours. She is stubborn, too."

"So I learned." I paused. "And you are—fond—of her?"

"I love her deeply." He answered with a French lack of shame about serious emotion. "I know we wronged you, I knew even when I carried her to my home. But you never came after her."

"I gave up, I suppose," I said. "I'd tried to be a good husband, and failed. I knew in my heart that she was better off with you. Happier. I am not surprised she ran away with you. She must have hated me."

He gave me a bemused look. "She never hated you. She was upset when we ran away, saying you were a good man. She cried to think on what you would feel when you discovered her gone."

I stared, astonished. "Did she? She left a letter for Louisa. Not even a note for me," I finished bitterly.

"She could not bring herself to write it. She knew she

wronged you. She would not have written at all, but I persuaded her to leave a letter at least for Madame Brandon."

"I nearly went off my head," I said. "Poor Louisa had to break the news to me, and then stop me from violence. I was sore angry."

He reddened. "I know it was a terrible thing. But not only was Carlotta unhappy as an army wife, but she had just learned you were returning to England, and she was frantic not to. She would do anything not to go to England, including run away with a French officer who had a farm near Lyon. She could disappear forever, become Madame Auberge, and none would know. I was the, as you call it, blackguard. I was in love with her, and did not try too much to persuade her to stay with you."

I looked at him in faint puzzlement. "You said that before, that she wanted to leave England forever. The eagerness with which she accepted my proposal astonished me, and I flattered myself that she loved me madly. But your words paint a different picture. She wanted to leave England, and India was as far away from England as anything can be."

Auberge nodded. "Her father wanted her to marry a certain man with a vast fortune, she told me. Her father needed the money to get himself out of a very nasty debt. But the man was repugnant to Carlotta. He was much older than she, and lecherous. He wanted only to get his hands on a young girl, if you see. When she refused him, her father beat her quite harshly, and threatened to force the marriage." He paused. "She said that as a good Church of England young woman, she did not believe in miracles and magic, but she thought that God must have sent you to her to save her from misery. What she suffered following the drum, she said, was nothing to what she would have suffered as this man's wife."

I stared in astonishment. "Why the devil did she not tell me this?"

"I do not know. She was young and afraid. Perhaps when you discovered she was so disobedient, you would take her back to her father? It is not Carlotta's way to think clearly, sometimes. I suppose she decided to simply be happy with you and far from her father."

"If she had told me . . ." I sat back, awash in regret for the past and what had not been. "I would have been kinder. I would have told her she need have no fear of her father ever again. She was, and is, a Lacey. We are not known for giving back what we have." I frowned. "But why did she fear returning to England later, when she was safely married to me? She was out of her father's reach, then."

"I do not know," Auberge replied. "I know only that she was afraid and wanted to run away with me. I did not question her too closely, and I have let it lie ever since. I must admit that I was pleased she wanted to leave you for me, and I did not want her to change her mind. And so I took her away." He gazed at me, his look slightly defiant.

"And as you say," I said lightly, "she had her way."

He gave me a faint smile. "She had her way coming to London this time as well. When we received the letter from Mr. Denis, I wanted to refuse. But Carlotta wanted to come. Her father is dead now, and she wants the divorce from you so she can marry me in truth. We live in a Catholic country, although I am not devout, and divorce is almost impossible there. She does not care at all about the Catholic Church, she wants only the divorce and then a quick English marriage to me. That way, in her mind, it will all be fair. We long ago began the fiction that Madame and Major Auberge had married in England, so that our neighbors would not wonder that our parish had no record of it, and she wants it to be true."

"I see. That sounds like Carlotta." I thought a moment. "And if Denis had not put the idea into her head, she likely would still be there with you on your little French farm."

"Possibly. I confess to you that she had to argue a long time before I agreed. I feared, you see, that when she saw you again, and you still her husband, well . . ." He lifted his hands in a shrug.

"You thought she would want to come back to me? And you profess to know Carlotta."

"I thought that you would claim your rights to her. You are her true husband, you have the English law behind you. I am only the Frog roué who stole your wife."

"My life with Carlotta finished years ago," I said, "and she is not my possession, whatever the law says. I, too, want this divorce, so that I can marry another."

He looked relieved. "When I met you, I knew you no longer wanted her, which I confess, pleased me. You wish to marry a woman called Lady Breckenridge?"

"Yes. I suppose I should not be so surprised it's common knowledge."

The corners of his mouth creased. "The English servants of the boardinghouse gossip. They know you are a friend of Mr. Grenville, who seems to be more worshipped than royalty, and that you are paramour of Lady Breckenridge, a widow of some means."

I grimaced. "I ought to post a notice outside my door."

"It is the same in a small French town. The women in the market square, they know everyone's business but their own. They are curious about Carlotta, but dismiss her past because she is English, and they are fond of her. They look after her, and my children."

"Which is how she wants it," I observed.

"Yes."

I fell silent as the coach bumped to a halt in Russel Street. Carlotta, the sweet, innocent slip of a girl, certainly had manipulated me into carrying her off, and then Auberge, and used that same sweet innocence to make a home for herself in a provincial French village. Auberge and I thought ourselves strong and masterful, but Carlotta in the end always had what she wanted. She possessed strength masquerading as weakness. I had to admit her success.

However, I would not let her have her way in the matter of Gabriella. I wanted my daughter, and I would fight for her.

When we reached the bake shop, a man pushed himself from the wall where he'd been waiting and approached us. I did not recognize him, but his pugilist build and stoic patience implied that he worked for Denis.

"Captain," he greeted me, as though he knew me. "Major. Mr. Denis, he sent me to find you."

I stopped, and Major Auberge looked on, curious. "I had meant to send a message to him," I said, "but I suppose he already knows what has happened?"

"That your daughter done a bunk? He knows. 'Swhy he sent me." He straightened his rather battered hat. "You need to come with me, Captain. Something I need to show you."

My heart squeezed with fear. Auberge went white, anticipating terrible news.

"Gabriella?" I asked abruptly.

He shook his head. "Naw. A man. Come on."

He gestured us to follow, and set off at a lumbering gate back toward Russel Street. Auberge and I strode after him, I in some relief.

The man led us to a carriage that had pulled up at the end of Russel Street where it ended at Covent Garden. The coach was opulent, but not Denis's usual conveyance, which I would have noticed. A coachman sat on his perch, holding the horses in a bored manner.

The pugilist opened the carriage door. I looked in and stopped in amazement.

Huddled against one of the seats, holding his arms

around his body and regarding me fearfully, was the pathetic figure of Bottle Bill, the habitual drunken man I saw most days at the Bow Street house.

"He has something to tell you," Denis's man said. He gestured for me to enter the carriage. I glanced at Auberge, who returned the look blankly, then I hoisted myself into the coach, the pugilist assisting me.

I sat down opposite Bottle Bill and waited for Auberge to take the seat beside me. Bill watched me warily with bloodshot eyes, his usually amiable face pale with fear.

"What's all this about, Bill?" I asked him.

"You tell him now." The pugilist leaned in the door. He did not speak threateningly or even glare with his small, dark eyes, but Bill cringed back.

"I didn't mean nuffing. Leave me alone."

"Bill," I said sharply. He swiveled his gaze back to me. "Tell me what you know."

"I didn't mean to, did I? I don't know what I'm doing when I've drunk a bottle or two. That's why the bills always haul me in, inn't it?"

I was in no mood to placate the man. "What the devil did you do?"

"Tell him," the pugilist said, his tone still bland.

"I found her, didn't I? The girl with the yellow hair. She were dead, weren't she?" His eyes moistened.

"Mary Chester?" I asked.

"Never knew her name. I found her. In me lodgings, all dead and cold. Right in front of the door, so I tripped over her when I went in. I never meant nuffing, I swear to you."

I leaned forward. "Did you kill her?" When he only began to weep, I shook him. "Bill, did you kill her?"

"I don't know," he wailed. "I were drunk, weren't I? I'm always drunk."

"Where are your lodgings?" I asked.

"Down Strand way. Back of beyond. I had to move her,

didn't I? Had to get her out of me doorway. He helped me. We wrapped her up tight, carried her to a lane, and buried her there. Out of sight. No one to find her. Rest in peace." He pressed his hands to his face and sobbed.

Auberge looked bewildered, likely unable to follow Bill's garbled speech.

"You said *he* helped you," I prompted. "Who?"

"Don't know 'im. Said he'd help me, and I wasn't to tell, 'cause I'd swing."

"Bill, for God's sake. You have to tell me who it was."

"Don't know, do I? Had a posh carriage. But it were dark and I were drunk, and I don't remember."

I believed him. Bill sober was a weak, gentle man, Bill drunk was mean and violent. Two Bills, one in a bottle.

"What did he look like?" I asked impatiently. "Tall, short? You must remember *something*."

"I don't. Don't hurt me, Cap'n, I swear I don't remember nuffing."

I tried another tack. "Why did you bury her under debris?"

"Don't know. Seemed decent. Gent said no one would think I did it if she were streets away."

"What I mean is, there are better ways of disposing of a corpse. Throw her in the river, take her out into the country and bury her, sell her to a resurrectionist."

Bill blinked. "Never thought of that."

"Of course you didn't. It was the gentleman's idea to hide her, was it not?"

He nodded fervently. "He helped me. He helped me 'cause he said I'd swing."

Auberge frowned, clearly trying to work out what we were talking about. "What is this resurrectionist?"

"Grave robbers," I answered. "They prey on corpses of the indigent and sell them to quacks who teach other quacks. Some of the more unscrupulous stoop to murder to further their trade. Who is going to miss one more shiftless man or woman from the streets?"

"Ah," Auberge said. "In France, we have a similar thing."

"Why did this man help you?" I asked Bill. "Why should he not shout for the Watch when he saw you with a dead young woman?"

"Don't know. I were drunk, Cap'n. I don't remember nuffing, I said."

"I know you do not, because I do not believe you killed her."

He opened his red eyes wide. "She were on me doorstep. And I were drunk as anything."

"Likely you were. And this posh gent, knowing Bottle Bill can't control himself when he's in his cups, places the body of a young woman on his doorstep to shove the blame onto you. When you come home too soon, he's happy to help you hide her, because, he says, he feels sorry for you. But instead of disposing of her body in a way that she won't be found for some time, he helps you hide her in a nearby lane, where someone is certain to find her very soon. Perhaps someone will even see you covering her up. That will scream your guilt, and you will pay for a crime you did not commit."

Bill looked confused. "I didn't kill her?"

"I'll wager you did not. I wish you could tell me who this gent with the posh carriage was."

"I didn't kill the poor thing?" Bill asked hopefully. "You sure?"

"Almost sure. I will be completely certain when I find him. Now, Bill, I want to ask you something else. Did you know a girl called Black Bess?"

He looked surprised. "Bessie? Sure, I know her. She laughs at me, but sometimes gives me a penny when I've drunk away all me coins."

"She went missing about the same time Mary did."

His eyes widened. "Cor."

"When was the last time you saw her?"

He considered. "Don't remember. Not long. Days are all the same to me."

"When you saw her last, did she talk about having a wealthy protector? Or that she soon would have one?"

"No," he answered doubtfully. "But then, she did say she'd come into some money. Maybe she meant a rich flat."

"Maybe she did." I sat back, not satisfied, but my mind turned over several ideas. "If you remember anything, anything at all, about Bess or Mary or the gentleman who helped you, you come and tell me right away. If I'm not about, tell Denis's man. Understand?"

"Aye, Cap'n." He fumbled a salute. "I don't want to swing," he added in a trembling voice. "I truly don't."

I left him huddled in the carriage. Outside, I addressed Denis's man. "Watch him. Both because he might be lying through his teeth, and because this other man might try to make certain he never remembers anything more. If Denis objects, he can speak to me."

"Planned to watch 'im, Captain," the pugilist said, sounding surprised. "We're looking out for your daughter, too, sir. Mr. Denis said to."

"Well, tell him I am grateful." I was, at that moment.

"He'll want to see you, sir."

"No doubt. I have an appointment at Tattersall's that I must not miss, and I might be able to call upon him after that."

The pugilist's face never changed expression, but I saw skepticism in his eyes. "He likes gents to make an appointment or come when they're called."

"I know he does. He will simply have to make do."

I set my hat straight. The clear blue sky was beginning

to cloud over, England's rainy climate tired of giving us sunshine. The pugilist watched me disparagingly as I nodded to Auberge, and we started back for my rooms.

I left Auberge behind when I kept my appointment at Tatt's. He rejoined the search with Bartholomew and Matthias, who, to my knowledge, still hadn't slept, but they looked none the worse for wear.

Black Nancy wandered in before I left in my best frock coat and riding breeches, and flopped into the wing chair.

"Goodness, but I'm wrung dry," she bleated. "I ain't run this hard carrying ale at the inn. It's heartbreaking, too, Captain. No sign of her."

"I know," I said, trying to keep the dejection from my voice.

"Most likely she's fetched up in a bawdy house. That Mr. Thompson says his watermen haven't reported finding anybody in the river. Me pals is checking the houses, but so far, nothing." She stuck her feet out and pointed her toes, swiveling her ankles. "I'll be out again soon as I rest a bit, don't you fret."

"Rest as long as you want, Nance," I said. "You are kind to help, but I fear very much that it will all be in vain."

I had not wanted to express that fear in front of Grenville, or Auberge, or even Bottle Bill. But with Nancy, for some reason, it came out of me.

Her eyes darkened, and she rose from the chair to come to me. "Take heart, love. I didn't mean to sound like I was giving up."

"I simply . . ." I swallowed, wet my lips, and tried again. "I know too much about London and what happens to girls let loose in it. They can be ruined, or lost, or dead, in the wink of an eye. It has happened many times. I've seen it happen. You know that."

"Maybe, but most girls don't have someone like you looking out for them." She rubbed her hand along my shoulder. "Don't give up, Captain. We'll bring her in."

I smiled into her dark eyes, truly grateful for her help. With effort, I mastered myself. "What can you tell me about Felicity?"

Nancy did not expect the question. She blinked. "Felicity? She's a good sort, I suppose. Not mean-spirited, like some game girls can be."

"Where did she come from? She intrigues me—I want to know about her."

"Well, all right, if you say so." She looked a bit annoyed at my interest. "Her mother was a maid, brought over from Jamaica, her father, who knows? A white gent, by the looks of her, but she don't know. She was downstairs maid in a Mayfair house, but she legged it because the master kept trying to have his way with her. She said if that were going on, she might as well get some coin for it, and so she took to the streets. Gentlemen like her 'cause she's fine spoken and pretty, in a foreign-looking way."

"Exotic," I suggested.

"That's the word. That's all I know about her, Captain. What do you want to know for?" She looked slightly jealous.

I smiled. "Do not worry, she has not replaced you in my affection. I merely wondered. She is shrewder than most, and I wonder if she doesn't know more about this than she lets on. A wealthy gentleman picking up girls in Covent Garden would surely be interested in Felicity with, as you say, her fine speech and her exotic looks. So why has he not taken her up?"

"Who? You meant the gent what Black Bess and Mary were talking about?"

"Possibly. I might be meeting this very gent today."

"Oo, are you going to shake a confession out of him?" she asked, delighted. "Can I watch?"

"I will try to find out all he knows, certainly. And no, you cannot come with me, because I am going to Tatter-sall's, which is a haven for gentlemen. No women."

She looked disappointed. "I will have to console my-self. Ah, well, as long as you tell me all about it if you pummel him."

"I assure you, you will have the entire story." I began to leave, then turned back. "By the bye, why is she called Black Bess?"

Nancy tugged at a lock of her own richly dark hair. "Same reason I'm called Black Nancy. 'Cause of our tresses."

"Why isn't Felicity called Black Felicity?"

Nancy looked blank. "Don't know. Never thought of it. Don't sound as good, though, does it, like Black Nancy."

"No, I admit, the cadence is not there."

Nancy grinned. "Well, I don't know what *cadence* is, but I'm glad I got it. You go off and shake up the gentleman. As long as you like me best, I'll overlook your interest in Felicity."

"You are too kind." I snatched up my hat and prepared to go. "Rest here as long as you like. You have been at it all day and night. Lie on the bed if you like."

She laughed suddenly and twirled around, skirts swirling about her plump ankles. "Thought you'd never ask, Captain. I'll take you up on that. And brag to me pals I was flat on me back in your bed." She blew a kiss to me, and I went out the door, certain I'd regret my sudden charity.

Jackson waited for me at the carriage, checking over the harness. He looked up when he saw me coming. "Ready, sir? Mr. Grenville said I was to deliver you to Tatt's safe and sound."

Jackson was a typical coachman, broad of shoulder
and of hand, used to working around horses. Like other
coachmen, he'd filed his incisors to points, giving him a
rakish look when he smiled, which was seldom. In his red
livery and black hat with brush, he looked well turned out
but just a but savage, a man more at home with beasts
than men.

I knew he must be one of the best coachmen in the business, because Grenville employed only the best. I also
noted that Grenville let him use his real name rather than
calling him generically "John Coachman" as most people
did their drivers so they wouldn't have to bother remembering their names.

Jackson held the door open for me, and I thanked him. I
settled into the leather squabs, and the coach listed as Jackson hauled himself to his perch. I heard him shout to the
horses and crack his whip, and we jolted through traffic toward Mayfair.

TATTERSALL'S lay near Hyde Park Corner. It was the
demesne of the Jockey Club and an auction block for the
very best in horseflesh. Here upper-class gentlemen and
the aristocracy bought and sold horses, placed bets on
races important and unimportant, and talked horse, sport,
and hunting.

I did not own horses, but came here often with Grenville
to look them over and lend my opinion when he wanted to
buy or sell. As a cavalryman, I knew horses, and could in-
stinctively discern whether their conformation was correct
or not, whether they were sound or sickly, whether they'd
have the spirit for racing or were better suited for country
hacks. Best of all, I could ride whatever horse interested
Grenville, whether he purchased or not, and in the saddle, I
was the equal or better of any man.

When I reached the place, and Jackson stopped the coach and helped me down, a number of gentlemen had drifted in to spend the summer afternoon. In the enclosure, with its small rotunda in the center, I saw Lord Alvanley and a few of his cronies watching two grooms put mounts through their paces. Leland Derwent and the friend who was his shadow, Gareth Travers, stood nearby—although, since Travers was the more robust of the pair, I should say Leland shadowed him.

Grenville, resplendent in pristine riding garb, cutaway frock coat, immaculate buff breeches, and polished high boots, saw me, broke away from the group of gentlemen speaking with him, and strode toward me. "Lacey, what news?"

"None, I am afraid. Is Mr. Stacy here?"

"Not yet. I told him three o'clock—if he does not arrive, we will hunt him down. In the meantime, there's a horse I want you to look at."

So saying, he led me along the columned walkway that surrounded the green. Leland Derwent hailed me. "Well met, Captain." He shook my hand, staring at me with admiration that a year of my acquaintance had not diminished. In Leland's eyes, I was a war hero, and he loved to hear me tell endless stories about the hardships of the army. "I am so sorry about your daughter," he said. "My father is doing all he can."

I withdrew from his grasp and shook Travers's hand as well. "Thank you. I very much appreciate his assistance."

"He knows all the reform houses and the workhouses, where she may have turned to if she found herself lost," Leland said. "He'll look through them all."

"Thank you," I repeated.

"He is using the opportunity to put another reform bill before the House of Commons. He will call it the Lacey Bill if he can."

I blenched. "God help me. Grenville, where is this horse?"

The horse in question proved to be a bay stallion, five years old, which Grenville wanted to use as a hunter. I handed Grenville my walking stick and let a groom hoist me into the saddle.

I walked the horse to the rotunda, casting a wry glance at the bust of the Prince of Wales within it, then squeezed my lower legs against the horse's sides. He smartly picked up his pace, trotting smoothly where I guided him. Well trained. His trot was so smooth I barely had to rise and fall in the saddle with it.

I tapped the horse with the crop and leaned into my left leg, and he flowed into a canter. I took him around at this gait, not letting him move too fast, collecting him if he extended too much. He responded well, although I was not too surprised at his ease of pace. Grenville always asked my opinion, but in truth, he was a fine judge of horses, and could pick out the best. Richard Tattersall liked Grenville's attendance, because any horse he showed interest in automatically jumped in price, whether Grenville bought it or not. Everyone wanted a horse that had caught Grenville's eye.

I cantered the stallion around again, letting him pick up speed, so that Grenville could see what he'd be like at full tilt. A few gentlemen applauded. I trotted him out, then walked him, and at last returned to where Grenville stood.

"He is a wonderful horse." I patted his neck. "Who wants to part with him?"

"Lord Featherstone. He doesn't ride much anymore, and decided yesterday that he had no reason to keep the horses he did. So they all went on the block." He grimaced. "I had better get my bid in before the price goes up. I always pay a mint for my horseflesh, having to outbid every gentleman who wants a horse of which I approve."

I slid to the ground, reminded once more that I was not sound the moment my left foot touched the ground. The groom handed me my walking stick and I leaned on it, flexing my leg. "Another difficulty of being the most fashionable man in London," I told him, amused.

"Yes, do not rub it in. Ah, here's Stacy, come at last."

I looked to where a tall, thin man walked into the enclosure, his riding coat and breeches as well made as Grenville's. When Grenville inclined his head at him, he started over, looking a bit smug that Grenville had singled him out.

"Stacy," he said, shaking his hand. "You remember Captain Lacey. Chat with him a moment, will you, and I will snatch up this horse while I can still afford it." He strode off, and Stacy chuckled at his back.

"He makes a good joke," he said.

I studied the man beside me, remembering meeting him at White's. Jeremiah Stacy was a few inches taller than me, with long, thin limbs, very much as though someone had taken a normal man and stretched him. He had dark hair and blue eyes and a reasonably handsome face. He looked down at me without concern, genially wondering why Grenville had left me in his care.

"Will you walk with me, Mr. Stacy?" I asked. "I would like to speak with you privately."

He looked surprised. "Very well." He gestured toward the corner of the enclosure nearest the loose boxes. "There?"

"That will do." I fell into step beside him, waiting until we were out of earshot before I began. "I asked Grenville to bring you here today on purpose to speak to me."

"Oh? What about?"

He bore no trace of trepidation, as though his conscience was clear. I felt a hint of doubt, but I plunged on. "I saw you last night. In Covent Garden."

He shrugged. "I attended the theatre with my wife."

"Not at the theatre. You left it early."

"Yes, to meet friends for cards." He studied me. "What are you getting at, Captain Lacey?"

Grenville reached us before I could expound. He looked satisfied. "Excellent. Featherstone was in a hurry to sell, so I got close to my price, only a little inflated because Alvanley decided to stick his oar in. Alvanley used to attempt to emulate Brummell, now he wants to emulate me. Such a tragedy he cannot have his own personality."

Stacy smiled slightly. "Congratulations, Grenville."

"Thank you. Carry on, Lacey."

"You left your wife and daughter at the theatre," I said to Stacy, "and went off to play cards."

"I have said so. My wife and daughter were to attend a soiree afterward. We often arrange our evenings this way."

I nodded, as though satisfied. "On your way, your carriage rolled through Covent Garden. You stopped. You descended. You spoke to a game girl and invited her into your carriage."

Stacy stopped, his cheeks burning a sudden red. "Why do you say so?"

"Because I saw you."

He lost his congenial expression. "What business is it of yours?"

"Then you agree that you did this."

Stacy looked at Grenville, who pinned him with a remorseless black stare. "Always thought you marched the straight and narrow, Stacy."

Stacy shot a fearful glance at the crowd of aristocrats and dandies under the colonnade. "For God's sake, keep your voice down. I couldn't—I do not want anyone to know."

"Least of all your wife," I said.

He paled. "Oh, you would not be so much of a bounder to *tell* her, would you? She would die of shame."

"Your secret is safe," Grenville assured him. "At least for now. As long as you tell us what you did."

Color flooded his face. "What the devil do you think I did?" He regarded Grenville with some distaste. "Why should you want to know?"

"We are not voyeurs, do not worry," Grenville said smoothly. "What I mean is, where did you go? How long did you stay with her, and where is she now?"

"What business is it of yours?" He repeated.

I leaned on my walking stick, giving him a cold stare worthy of any of Denis's pugilists. "Tell us, Stacy."

His eyes glittered in sudden worry. "How should I know where the devil she is now? I did what I always do. My coachman drove through the quietest streets he could find while . . ." He broke off. "And then returned me to Covent Garden. I set her down there and went on. To play cards, as I said."

"Do you do this often?" I asked sharply.

"Yes." His eyes shifted. "Rather too often."

Grenville adjusted his hat and gave a sniff, his way of showing disapproval without saying so. "I was surprised when Lacey mentioned that he'd seen you. I would not have pegged you for it."

"It really is my business, Grenville," he said desperately.

I cleared my throat. "For myself, I do not care for your reasons. I want to know whether you enjoyed yourself with a girl called Black Bess or a girl called Mary Chester."

"Black Bess?" he gasped.

"Specifically, I want to know whether you promised either of them a good sum of money to take up with you."

His mouth hung open. "Dear God. What has Bess been telling you?"

"Bess has told me nothing." My voice went harsh. "She has disappeared, and Mary Chester has been murdered, and I want to know what you had to do with it."

Chapter 13

❦

STACY made choking noises, as though I'd begun to strangle him. "Murdered? Bloody hell."

"You knew Bess and Mary, then?"

He looked up at me, his face going gray. "I do not always know their names. Black Bess told me hers. I don't remember a Mary."

"Blond hair, dyed, pretty. Came from Wapping."

He drew a ragged breath. "You don't have a flask on you, do you, Grenville?"

Grenville produced a silver flask of brandy from his pocket and handed it to Stacy. Stacy opened it and drank deeply. "Thank you."

"Mary Chester," I prodded. "Had you been with her?"

He looked shaken. "Possibly, several weeks ago, if she is the same girl. I haven't seen her since. That is the truth. I certainly did not murder her. What do you take me for?"

"I take you for a man who goes trawling for game girls,"

I remarked. "Why you choose to is your own business, as you say. They likely appreciate your coin, and your fine carriage on a rainy night. But Bess and Mary went missing, and you were with them both."

His face was white, the brandy clearly not helping. "Coincidence."

Grenville drew out his quizzing glass and peered at Stacy through it. Stacy flinched. Grenville examining a man thusly was the preliminary to said man being dismissed as a vulgarian. Grenville doing so in front of a large crowd at Tatt's could ruin a man socially, forever.

"You know, Stacy," Grenville said in a cool, rather bored manner. "Slumming can be a recipe for the clap."

Stacy reddened again, a vein pulsing in his neck.

I recognized that Grenville was very angry. While I generally blustered and threatened when enraged, Grenville turned ice cold. He was distressed at the death of Mary and the disappearances of Bess and Gabriella. The thought that Stacy, one of his own crowd and a member of White's, could have anything to do with it had his blood boiling.

"Damnation, Grenville," Stacy wheezed. "I am not the only one who does so."

The quizzing glass didn't move. "Yes, but you are the only slummer who has drunk from my flask. Keep it, there's a good fellow. I hardly want it back."

Stacy's mouth opened and closed, but before he could respond, a new voice broke in. "Extolling your own virtues, are you, Grenville?"

Another man strolled to us, one of a height between mine and Grenville's, his tailed coat hanging from broad shoulders. His breeches and boots hugged legs muscled from riding, but although his garb was fashionable, he wore it as though he cared nothing for fashion and had bought it because that was all his tailor would make for him. He had dark hair and eyes, a square jaw, and a chin blue with whiskers. He spoke with the faintest of Scottish accents, as though he wanted to speak Glaswegian but strained himself while in London to speak like a Londoner.

"Not got a leg to stand on, I should think," he finished. He looked pointedly at my walking stick and my stiff leg.

I did not rise to the bait, but Stacy looked uncomfortable. "McAdams, this is a private conversation."

"But I am here to rescue you, my friend. Is Mr. Grenville berating you because you like to spend time in Covent Garden?" He made a tut-tut noise. "While he parades around with an actress who's little better than a whore? The captain, now, he's caught himself a viscountess. Very well done, I must say, Captain. Although I'd say the Breckenridge came after you with all guns ready and flags flying, wanting to snare herself a cicisbeo. A feather in your cap, that is."

Grenville twirled his quizzing glass in his fingers, his eyes flat. "Crudely done, McAdams. Insults ought to be subtle."

"What?" McAdams's eyes widened in mock surprise. "You will not slap my face and call for your seconds? After I have spoken so of your lady?"

Grenville hid a yawn behind his gloved hand. "You are hardly worth the effort of rising early and traveling all the way to Hyde Park green. Waste of gunpowder as well. My lady, as you call her, has far better manners than you, albeit that she's an actress from the gutter. As for Lady Breckenridge, she could flatten you with a single barb at twenty paces. She has a command of language and true wit that you will never achieve in your lifetime, no matter how you strive. Ah, perhaps she *has* disparaged you at some time, so that you feel it your right to speak so slightingly of a lady who is well beyond your reach."

McAdams smiled coldly. "Grenville, my friend, I do not fear your censure."

"You are a fool then." Grenville shook his head in frank disbelief. "I can make certain you never set foot in a respectable parlor again, let alone White's or any other club, just by putting about that you are a bounder."

The lines around McAdams's mouth tightened, but he would not back down. My own anger was up, but I took a step back and let Grenville fight. This was his world, with its own rules, and here, Grenville was master. It was a marvel simply to watch him.

Stacy clenched the flask still in his hand. "McAdams, I have no need of rescue. Please go."

"But you looked so distressed, my friend. If Mr. Stacy wishes to invite a girl to his carriage, that is nothing to do with you. Why do you harp at him for it?"

"Tell me, McAdams," Grenville said, "were you the one who put him on to it? Dragged him from the respectability of Mayfair to the dark of Covent Garden?"

"Perhaps." McAdams looked smug. "He wanted a bit of diversion, and I gave it to him."

"And I am sorry you ever did," Stacy said under his breath.

McAdams looked at us in disbelief. "Good lord, can three Englishmen be any more stuffy? What is the matter with passing an hour with a gutter girl? That's what they're for. They don't expect you to give them houses and expensive presents like a courtesan, and they don't cry when you beat 'em a little. They expect it."

I made a noise of disgust. Grenville's brows rose in cold hauteur. "Well, that has torn it for you, McAdams. You're out."

"Over game girls?" McAdams laughed. "I've always thought you a bit touched."

"It is not funny," Stacy interrupted. "Some of them have gone missing and one is dead. They think I had something to do with it."

McAdams laughed again. "Oh, good lord, what if he did? They're not worth bothering about, gentlemen. Go look at the horses. They're far more important."

I broke in. "Murder is murder, Mr. McAdams. The law states that it is a capital offense, whether you be convicted of killing a game girl or your own brother."

McAdams paled slightly but lost none of his bravado. "A jury might not think so. Girls no better than they ought to be. They'd die soon enough anyway, of some disgusting disease."

"Perhaps you are right about a jury, but the kidnapping and murder of a respectable young woman is a different matter altogether," I said.

"A respectable young woman?" Stacy repeated. "What are you talking about?"

"My daughter has gone missing as well," I said stiffly. "She left a boardinghouse in King Street and presumably walked through Covent Garden and has not been seen since."

Stacy stilled. McAdams hooted a laugh. "Better keep a rein on your offspring, Lacey. Such a comedown for a gentleman of standing, to have his daughter become one of the demimonde."

"Now, for that, I will call you out," I said. "After I conclude this business, my seconds will make an appointment with you."

"We duel over whores now?"

"McAdams, for God's sake, shut your mouth," Stacy cried. Gentlemen under the colonnade turned to stare at us. Alvanley brought out his quizzing glass. Stacy lowered his voice to a frantic hiss. "Shut up, I tell you. This is serious business."

"For you perhaps," McAdams drawled, though he shot me a wary look. "I have nothing to do with it."

"Yes, you do. You told me to look up Black Bess in the

first place. And now she's missing. It is bad for the both of us."

McAdams raised his brows. "Not for me. I have not been to Covent Garden in weeks."

I turned to Stacy. "Both Bess and Mary spoke of a wealthy gentleman who'd soon do well by them. They went specially to Covent Garden to meet him, each of them, a week ago. Did they have an appointment with you?"

Stacy blenched. "No. I've spoken to neither of them in some time."

"You never promised them money? Or to set them up?"

"No, indeed, why would I? Spending an hour with them is one thing, taking them as a mistress is something else entirely. No, I never promised them anything."

"Then who was the wealthy gentleman they so looked forward to meeting?" I mused. "Would settle them for life, they thought. McAdams?"

McAdams barked a laugh. "Good God, no. Why would I spend more than a crown on a street whore? They wouldn't know what to do with it."

I gave him a steady look. "I look forward to shooting you."

He returned my look with mock dismay, but the wary light in his eye grew deeper. Grenville, on the other hand, ignored him altogether. Grenville was already cutting him, but the man was too self-important to notice.

Stacy glanced at me in trepidation. "The thing is, Captain, I believe I might have seen your daughter."

My disgust at McAdams vanished in an instant. I brushed him away as if he was a fly and advanced on Stacy. "Did you? Where? When?"

"Was it yesterday? I was in Covent Garden in the evening, on my way to the theatre to meet my wife. I drove through to, um, decide . . ."

I understood. He'd probably gone to survey the girls for his later visit.

"At any rate, I'd descended, because I fancied an orange, and I wanted to get it myself from the orange girl. After I purchased it and, er, chatted with her a few moments, I saw a young woman pushing through the crowd, looking a bit lost. I thought, you know, that she seemed out of place, and I asked if I could help her. She stopped, grateful, and asked the way to Russel Street. We were near to it, so I pointed it out. She thanked me and walked on, more cheerfully. I got back into my coach and drove away."

"Did she reach Russel Street?" I asked.

"Have no idea. I was in the coach, and my coachman drove away."

"Busy eating your orange, no doubt," Grenville remarked.

"Yes, getting dratted peel everywhere and knowing my coachman would cut up rough. He's fond of the conveyances, treats them like they were his children. Anyway, he dropped me in front of the theatre, I met my wife and daughter, and I never saw the girl again. That is all I know."

"What did she look like?" I demanded.

Stacy considered, his eyes flickering nervously. "Pretty, in a girlish sort of way. Brown hair, cannot remember the color of her eyes. Wearing a nice enough frock, nothing that caught my eye. Definitely not a street girl, I could see. Daughter of respectable parents, I thought."

"And she spoke like a respectable English girl?"

"She did, though I detected a faint accent. Prussian maybe, or French."

I felt hotness rush through me, followed by tingling in my fingers, like I was growing dizzy. "That was her. It must have been." I gave him a hard stare. "If you harmed her in any way . . ."

Stacy's eyes widened. "I did not. I promise you, Captain, I directed her to Russel Street and left her alone. I do know the difference between a street girl and a young lady. Good lord, she was the age of my own daughter."

His words rang with sincerity, but I would not take them at face value. "I hope you are right," I said softly.

Grenville looked him up and down with his quizzing glass again. "So do I. You are our primary suspect, Stacy. Mind what you do in Covent Garden. There is a massive search going on for Lacey's daughter, which includes Bow Street Runners and men who work for James Denis. I should be careful, were I you."

McAdams clapped Stacy on the shoulder. "I advise you to inform your solicitor, my friend. He may be able to bring a case of defamation of character."

Stacy gave McAdams a cold look. "I will be fine." He stalked off, but instead of joining the group watching the next horses to be exercised, he wheeled away, departed through the walkway, and was gone.

I handed one of my cards to McAdams. "So that your seconds may call on mine. Good day." I inclined my head and walked away under the curious stares of those not looking at the horses.

Grenville, on the other hand, cut McAdams dead. I watched from the colonnade as he turned his back, removed his snuffbox, and took a pinch, blatantly ignoring McAdams. Every man turned to stare as Grenville calmly replaced his snuffbox and walked away from McAdams without acknowledging him.

As I joined him to seek out Tattersall and arrange delivery of Grenville's stallion, the assembled dandies and earls and barons began to gabble like a mad flock of geese. Not one of them spoke to McAdams.

GRENVILLE invited me back to his home in Grosvenor Street so that he could change his suit before resuming the search for Gabriella with me. Ensconced in his dressing room while his valet, Gautier, re-dressed him, I sipped a much-needed brandy.

"Do you think any of what Stacy told us was the truth?" Grenville asked, cranking his head back so Gautier could tie his neckcloth. "Or was it all rubbish?"

"He admitted he saw the girls and was with them," I replied. "But after that, who knows? I'd like to borrow your coachman, Jackson, and have him help me talk to Stacy's coachman. He'd be an eyewitness to everything his master does. Whether he's a loyal servant or loves to gossip about his betters remains to be seen."

"Take him." Grenville waved a hand at me, causing his valet to cluck in disapproval. "As for McAdams, he is certainly worth investigating, far more likely to lure girls to their doom. You heard what he said about beating them. The man is disgusting." He lowered his head and held out his arms for his coat. "I dislike duels, but I will gladly hold the pistol box for you on this one. Although he may not last long enough to meet you, now that I've cut him. He might flee England altogether."

"He seems resilient to opinion," I observed.

"Well, he will not be for long. If I cut him dead, then other men will follow suit. They know I only cut for a good reason. Alvanley muttered to me as I left that it was time the boor got his comeuppance. Alvanley is an imitator, but he has a great deal of power really."

"Perhaps we will get McAdams for murder, and there will be no need to continue to cut him."

I liked the idea of McAdams as murderer, because watching him stand in the dock would satisfy me. I felt a little sorry for Stacy—not too sorry—and hoped McAdams proved to be the culprit.

McAdams could have done it; after all, it was he who'd introduced Stacy to the concept of slumming in Covent

Garden, and by his own admission, he was not in any way gentle with the girls.

I would check with Thompson to see how Mary Chester had actually died. Perhaps McAdams began his violent ways and went a bit too far. Perhaps the prior bruises on her throat had come from him, indicating that he'd already enjoyed being rough with her. Perhaps this time, she had died, and in panic, he'd hidden the body on Bottle Bill's doorstep. If McAdams went often to Covent Garden, he'd have become familiar with Bottle Bill and his habits as we all were. The magistrate would easily believe that Bill had become violent under the influence of drink and killed Mary, intentionally or no.

"I will pot him one way or another," I said. "I'd like to speak to Marianne as well. She might know Stacy if he haunts Covent Garden. I'd like her opinion of him."

Marianne, like Lady Breckenridge, was a shrewd observer, and as an actress, she'd seen the seamier side of the upper classes and had often been privy to the gossip that gentlemen kept from their wives, daughters, and sisters.

Grenville looked uncomfortable. "I am afraid you cannot. I meant to tell you, but hadn't a chance at Tatt's. Marianne's gone missing as well."

I grew alarmed. "Good lord, has she?"

"Yes, but she went as she usually does, taking her best hat and a handful of guineas and telling my footman she'd be back when she was ready."

"Damn and blast her," I said feelingly. "Why did she decide to disappear just now, when girls are going missing left and right?"

"I really could not say," Grenville answered. His lips were white. He told Gautier, who busily brushed the coat he'd helped Grenville don, to run off somewhere. The valet nodded, laid down the brush, and discreetly departed.

Grenville faced me and threw open his hands. "You

warned me from the very beginning about her. I wish to God I'd heeded you, but the woman intrigued me. I gave her clothes and money and jewels and a house and servants and then my carriage, and even her freedom. I've made a grand fool of myself, haven't I? If it ever comes out that she runs off to another man whenever she pleases, I'll be a laughingstock."

He exhaled slowly. "I have decided, Lacey. I will not see her again. When she returns, will you please tell her for me that I am finished chasing her? She may keep the money and jewelry and do whatever she likes with them. I no longer care."

His hands fell to his sides, and his cool mask slipped. I'd never seen him so dejected.

"You would break her heart," I said. "She truly cares for you."

He gave a bitter laugh. "She has a damn odd way of showing it. I wish she hadn't chosen now of all times to go, because I am worried, she, too, has become a victim. I believe I'd rather hear that she is in the arms of her lover than that she is dead under a pile of rubbish near the Strand."

I eased back in the chair and made my decision. Marianne had asked me to tell him, and as much as I did not want any part of this business, they'd both fully dragged me into it. Besides, I counted Grenville a friend and was fond of Marianne, in a way. I hated to see them at cross-purposes like this.

"She is not cuckolding you, Grenville," I said. "She's gone to Berkshire."

He stilled. "Berkshire?"

"A small house near Hungerford, to be exact."

Color flooded his face, then he pointed a long finger at me. "You knew why she went last time, and never told me, blast you."

"She begged me to keep her secret. Two days ago, I saw

her in Covent Garden, where she told me she was thinking of making her way to Berkshire again. This time, however, she wanted me to tell you why. I tried to talk her out of it, but you know how well Marianne listens."

"Indeed," Grenville said in a cool voice. "Pray go on."

He was angry again, at me this time, and I felt the full weight of his cold wrath, just as McAdams must have.

"Marianne has a son."

He stared at me a moment as though waiting for me to go on, then his black eyes focused sharply. "A son?"

"He is about seven years old, and he is a half-wit."

"A half-wit . . ." He frowned suddenly. "Lacey, you had better not be inventing this. Is *she* inventing it?"

"His name is David. I met him. She keeps him in a little house near Hungerford, and pays a woman to look after him. That is where all the money you give her goes, to buy his food and his clothes and to pay for his upkeep. She would not tell me who the father was, only that he'd died years ago. I believe her."

I lifted my brandy to my lips and drank, but for the first time since I'd been allowed to partake of Grenville's fine stock of brandies, I barely tasted the liquid.

His face was utterly still, his gaze fixed, his lips parted. He remained thus for a long time, watching me while I watched him.

An ornate gold clock in the corner sweetly chimed the quarter hour. Grenville passed a shaking hand through his hair. "Why in God's name didn't she tell me?" He fastened his glare on me. "Why didn't *you* tell me?"

"She feared your reaction."

"My reaction?" he spluttered. "She would rather let me think she had a lover she could not give up than she was taking care of a child by herself?"

I held up a hand. "Consider. Your money is going to another man's child, a half-wit child at that. When you learn the truth, will you withdraw the gifts in disgust? If so, what is Marianne to do for the money? Return to the theatre? Look for another protector who won't scrutinize her so closely?"

He stared in amazement. "Is that what you think I would do?"

"It is what Marianne fears."

Grenville swung away and paced across the small space of the dressing room. He suddenly turned back and brought his fists down on the dressing table, setting the mirror and Gautier's various brushes dancing.

His face was red, his eyes black agates, hard and glittering. "God damn the pair of you. Is this what you think of me, that I'd beggar a child? That I'd throw Marianne out to grub her living on the stage, so she can hang about in hopes that some disgusting man like McAdams takes her home? Is that what you have thought all this time, that I am the sort of man who could do that?"

I remained quiet. "You must admit that you are difficult to predict."

"For God's sake, Lacey. Have I ever behaved anything but generously to you—to her? I have offered you both everything I have, damnation, I offered you my friendship, and her my love and both of you stare at me as though you cannot deign to accept it. I have taken her among my friends; I have given you the stamp of my approval. You know you would have been nothing without it, and I gladly gave it, because I saw the worth of you." He ran out of breath.

"I know what you have done for me," I said. "You have always told me that it was because I interested you."

"Yes, and you puff up with pride because you believe it an insult. Selfish of me to expect gratitude, I suppose. From either of you. But consider, if the bloody girl had told me, what do you think I could have done for this David? I can give him the best care money can buy. I can give him his own house, a string of attendants if he wants them. I can do this, Lacey, I am damn powerful. Why the devil doesn't she understand that?"

I said calmly, "This is the other reaction she feared. That you'd smother him with generosity and take him away from where he is happy."

He stared at me in shock. "You agree with her."

I set aside the brandy with reluctance and rose. "Yes," I said, "I do."

"Devil take you, Lacey."

"She does not want you to overmaster her. She wants David left in peace."

He scrutinized me a moment longer, his face sheet white except for red that stained his cheekbones. I watched him try to contain himself, to draw his cool poise about himself, in much the same manner as Gautier had eased on his coat.

His next words were quiet, but spoken with finality. "Tell Marianne I will continue the money to help her son, but I no longer want to see her. And I believe I no longer want to see you either. I will allow my servants to help carry on the search for your daughter, but that will be all." His eyes were filled with suppressed anger and hurt. "I gave you my implicit trust, Lacey. I was a fool to expect it in return, I suppose."

I bowed in silence. "I am sorry to have angered you." I turned without further word and strolled to the door. I half expected him to call me back, to say in good-natured exasperation, "For God's sake, Lacey, let us sort this out," but he did not. Both Marianne and I had wronged him, and he had cuffed us, and I, for one, felt I deserved the blow.

I quietly closed the door behind me and made my way down the polished staircase, the satinwood rail gleaming as deeply as gold. With some regret, I took my hat and gloves from the underfootman at the door, and went back out into the London afternoon. It had clouded over, and the first drops of rain fell as I made my way to the hackney stand at the corner of Grosvenor Street.

I decided to pay a call on Denis, notwithstanding his lackey's suggestion that I should not arrive without an appointment. If Denis was indisposed, he would not admit me, and I would go on. I had plenty to do without this aside.

Denis's butler, as cold as his master, took me upstairs and bade me wait in the austere reception room in which I'd awaited his attention before. Not long after that, the butler returned and ushered me to Denis's study. Denis flicked his dark blue glance from his correspondence, curtly told me to take a chair, and asked what I wanted.

"Only to know if you have heard anything about my daughter," I said.

"If I had, I would have sent word, or already restored her to you."

"Yes." I remained seated, uncertain how to explain what I wanted. Reassurance? I would not get it from Denis. Or maybe I wanted truth, which was what Denis gave in abundance—real, brutal, unromanticized truth.

He seemed to sense my need. He carefully set his correspondence aside and twitched his fingers at the lackey who stood at the window. "Fetch the captain port," he said. The lackey moved to the door and summoned another footman. I noticed he did not leave the room, which would put me alone with James Denis.

"Tell me what you learned," he said. "And perhaps I can aid you."

I hesitated. "You are heavy-handed with your aid."

"Perhaps. But heavy-handedness is often effective. The

trick is to know when to employ it and when to be re-strained. You have learned something. What is it?"

I told him about Stacy and McAdams. I was worried enough and angry enough that I did not care whether Denis and his ruffians paid a call on Mr. Stacy. If Stacy had hurt my daughter, Denis could do his worst.

"I have met McAdams," Denis said, twining his fingers on the desk. "A man who does not know when to be re-strained, I would say. He is crude and ill-mannered. You think him a better candidate for the crime than Stacy?"

"He is the sort who would hurt a girl for the pleasure of it. Stacy might do the same, I do not know. The only differ-ence between the two is that Stacy is ashamed of his pro-clivities while McAdams boasts of them. But either of them could have killed Mary Chester."

"You mean that either of them are *capable* of it. You are not being as rational as you could be, Captain." He gave me an admonishing look. "Think of it this way. Did either gentle-man have the opportunity to kill her? Where do they say they were on the night—or day—she died? Do they have wit-nesses? Could Bottle Bill have killed Mary Chester and be in-venting the 'gentleman' who assisted him to throw you off the scent? You certainly believe him capable of murder, when he is drunk. He is often arrested, I understand, for being violent." He spread his hands. "Many possibilities, Captain."

The butler entered, placed a table at my elbow, and laid a round white cloth in its precise center. In the center of that he set a crystal goblet full to one-quarter of an inch of the brim with dusky amber port. The rich scent of it reached me as the butler bowed and walked softly away.

I ignored the glass for now. "You mean I need to stop frantically running about, and begin to investigate. I have been searching, not thinking."

"You have plenty of people going through London for you," he said. "Sit back and think."

I was not sure he meant for me to literally do so at the moment, but I leaned back in his comfortable chair, lifted the goblet of port, and drank deeply. Like Grenville, Denis kept the best in wines, and this was one of the finest I'd tasted.

"I will closely quiz Stacy's coachman," I said. "The man drove him everywhere; he would know what day Stacy picked up Mary Chester and where he took her. He would know when Stacy was last with Black Bess, he would know whether he is telling the truth about seeing Gabriella. I should question McAdams's servants as well, and find out about his visits to Covent Garden."

Denis gave me a slight nod. "Reason and thoroughness. That is what will find Miss Lacey."

"That is what you do, is it not?" I asked. "You sit in this house and reason, then you send hirelings out to do your bidding."

"I employ many, that is true. Some do well running about the streets bringing me small bits of information, others do well sitting back and reasoning in their own right."

I swallowed another draught of port, then set the goblet down, off center, on the cloth. "You want to employ me. Which do you see me as, a runner or a reasoner?"

A small smile lifted the corners of his mouth. "I see you as unique, Captain. You have an interesting perception of society—you are one of them, but also on the fringes, and you can observe them both as an insider and an outsider." He lifted his hand to tick off points as he spoke. "You were reared at Harrow and Cambridge, yet you forsook that life to fight in the heat of India and the mess of the Peninsula. You were an officer among officers, yet you achieved your rank through merit instead of money, which gives you a perception of what merit truly is. You are trusted by the demimonde, yet you choose your lovers from the very loftiest of women. You can see what a man truly is, and yet be blindly loyal to him for all his faults. You were befriended by Grenville, a severely cautious man who befriends very, very few, and you are equally befriended by people in the gutter. Even my own servants express admiration for you."

"I had no idea I was such a paragon," I said dryly.

"You are not. You are evil-tempered and too ready to give in to your passions. You are too curious for your own good, and you have allowed past hurts to fester. These are minor flaws common to many." He fixed me with a keen look. "What I can obtain from you is a unique perspective on events and your peculiar way of reasoning through a problem. Also, you can win people's trust and regard, which could be quite useful to me."

"Useful to you," I repeated. "An interesting way of putting it."

"I intend to own you, as I once told you. I still consider you a threat, exactly because of your unique perspective and the fact that the people I do not own rally to your side."

"I inconvenience you."

"An interesting way of putting it." He tossed my words back to me. "I am making quite an investment, looking for your daughter and funding your divorce, and I intend to collect."

"Do not bother with the divorce," I said. "I will look elsewhere for help."

His eyes flickered. "Where? Of your acquaintance, only Grenville and I can fund such an endeavor. Lady Breckenridge could, but she would draw herself into deep scandal should anyone discover it. Sir Gideon Derwent could, but he would be more likely to encourage you to reconcile with your wife, which I know to be impossible. You and Grenville have had a falling-out, so I am much afraid, Captain, that you are stuck with me."

I had reached for the port during this speech, but at his last sentence, my fingers froze upon touching the glass. "Good lord, I've just come from there." I let go of the goblet and shot him an ironic look. "I suppose every time I visit the privy, it goes into a report."

He smiled thinly. "You exaggerate. One of my men saw you leave Grenville's very soon after you went in, and from the look on your face, you were upset and angry. You went away to find a hackney, and my man came straight back here, arriving before you did. I simply guessed the rest, and you confirmed it."

"I must learn to control my expressions," I said.

"You never will. You convey your exact thoughts, which is a reason people trust you. You never say one thing and think another."

"Many would call that rudeness." I got to my feet. "Do you have any other useful information for me, or shall I sit here while you tell me exactly what I do every day?"

He did not even blink at my abruptness. "Question the young woman called Felicity. She, too, had the privilege, if you can call it that, of entering Mr. Stacy's coach."

I stopped. "Did she? How do you know?"

"When you began an interest in Mr. Stacy this morning, I called in all information about him. He has often been seen in Covent Garden by my men. They cannot give me a list of names of which girls he has taken up, as it was casual observation only, but one man saw Felicity with you and remembered she had been one of them."

"I wondered myself," I admitted. "She is a beautiful young woman and stands out from the others. I doubt Stacy could resist her."

"You have," Denis observed with a quirk of his brow.

I touched the head of the cane that Lady Breckenridge had given me after the Glass House affair, a gift that had sealed our friendship.

"I am satisfied with what I have," I answered. "Stacy, obviously, is not."

"Perhaps not. I have also asked my men to start following Stacy and his friend McAdams about to see what they get up to. We will soon see if they lead us to the lost young women."

"Thank you," I said.

Whether he appreciated my gratitude or not, I did not know, because he drew his correspondence in front of him and returned his focus to it. He was finished with me. I was just as happy to depart.

Chapter 14

I returned home to a written message from Thompson of the Thames River patrol. Like his speeches, the note was laconic.

> *Mary Chester suffocated—likely deliberate. She'd been dead two days when we found her. From the dirt stains on her frock, she'd lain in or rolled in soil before she died for whatever reason. Coroner is convinced it's unnatural death and has called an inquest for three days hence. Sam Chester is beside himself with grief. Thompson.*

At least we knew how Mary had died. Suffocated. The word implied a pillow pressed against a mouth or some such thing. I had a sudden fear that the soil stains meant someone had buried her alive, but if the coroner had thought such a thing, Thompson would have said so. I set down the letter, making a note to attend the inquest on Monday.

Grenville kept his word that he'd continue to help, not withstanding his disgust with me. Later that evening, his coachman, Jackson, came to fetch me.

"Mr. Grenville says you want to talk to Stacy's coachman," he said. He filled my doorway, a strong, broadshouldered man who looked capable of handling unruly horses or ruffians. If he ever stopped coaching, he could work for James Denis. "I know the tavern where he drinks. I'll take you there."

I snatched up my coat, ready. Bartholomew, even with his searching, had found time to bring me beefsteak for supper and brush my clothes. "Will I be allowed into this hallowed hall of coachmen?" I asked.

Jackson smiled slightly, revealing his pointed teeth. "We'll make an exception, sir. Just mind your manners."

The tavern he took me to was near where the Strand ended at Charing Cross. The Church of St. Martin-in-the-Fields loomed above the rooftops, but on this Friday night, the tavern was full to bursting with noise while the church sat silently.

The regulars of the tavern eyed me askance as I entered, but the landlord looked at my fine frock coat, courtesy of Grenville's tailor, and his eyes brightened.

"My lord," he said, on the off chance that I was one. "A private room?"

"No, thank you," I said. "But three tankards of your best ale, please."

The landlord nodded, took the crown I offered him, and scuttled away. Jackson led me to a table where another man in coachman's livery waited. The long table was occupied by other drinkers, but the end Stacy's coachman had chosen was relatively empty.

Jackson hooked his foot around a stool and pulled it out,

popping himself down at the end of the table. I seated my-self on the bench opposite Stacy's coachman. The landlord obligingly plunked three tankards of ale in front of us.

"Captain Lacey, this here is Payne. He's been coaching for Mr. Stacy for eleven years."

Payne offered a work-roughened hand across the table. "Obliged, Captain." He raised his tankard to me and drained at least a third of it.

He was a bit older than Jackson, with hair going gray at the temples and gray scattered through the darker hair on top of his head. His face was weathered, with whitish lines about his eyes. His square-tailed coat was of fine green serge, his dark waistcoat of serviceable wool. The brass buttons on the coat gleamed with polish, and a polished brass chain hung across his chest. His coachman's tall hat with brush lay on the table next to him. He, like Jackson, had a master who wanted his coachman well turned out.

"Mr. Stacy is a good man to work for?" I asked.

Payne lowered his tankard and wiped his mouth. "It's a good position, fine coaches to look after, and I'm fond of the beasts."

I noted he'd said nothing directly about Stacy. "I am afraid that I came here to pry into your master's habits. But there's been murder done, and I want to know by who and why."

Payne jerked his thumb at Jackson. "So he said. I told Mr. Stacy I was coming here tonight—thought it would be fair. He told me to tell you straight-up truth."

I nodded. "I appreciate that, both from you and Stacy. You know, in that case, I wish to ask you about the girls Mr. Stacy invites into his coach in Covent Garden."

"In Covent Garden, in Haymarket, in the Strand." Payne looked mildly disgusted. "He can't resist a tart swishing about in her skirts. He likes to watch them—from inside the coach, mind you—getting to know them all. You know, some gentry-coves like to know all about butterflies and the like, some go into the country and pick up rocks and old bones. Mr. Stacy likes game girls."

"His collection, so to speak."

"A good way of putting it, sir. He has me dawdle the carriage along while he looks out of the window and watches where they go and who they talk to and what they buy in the markets at Covent Garden. He learns when they come out and when they go home, and even where they live. And then, once he's decided who he wants to meet, he gets out of the coach, chats to the girl, and invites her up. That's usually in the dead of night, although sometimes he'll get down in the evening, just to talk to them. Maybe make an appointment to meet him later."

I turned my tankard absently on the table. "Once he invites one into the coach, he asks you to drive slowly about the streets?"

"Aye. He says I am to drive for one hour, very slowly, any route I choose, as long as I return to where I started at the stroke of the clock."

Jackson offered, "While he gets to know them even better, eh?"

Payne took another pull of ale. "Do you know, sir, I could not tell you what he gets up to with them. They might chat about bonnets for all I know. I looks after the carriage, both inside and out, and I never find anything you might call disgusting."

"Perhaps he is very careful," I suggested.

"Oh, aye, he must be. Else he'd have the clap or something else nasty, wouldn't he? But Mr. Stacy is always clean as can be."

I considered this as I drank my own ale. The brew was good, a mixture of malt taste and a touch of tartness. "Now, I must ask you about Black Bess and Mary Chester.

Will you describe what he did on the nights he took up with them? You know which girls I mean?"

Payne nodded. "He told me you'd ask about them. See, I knew their names and habits, too, as I always had to drive him about while he watched. I never noticed special, but you look at people, you know, to break the tediousness, when not keeping an eye on the horses."

I assured him I understood. "Start with Mary Chester, as she is the one who's turned up dead."

"Poor girl, eh? Well, he meets this Mary about a week and a half ago, I'd say. He'd seen her when he had business over Wapping way. He invests in ships, betting his money that they won't go down or be stolen by pirates. Sometimes he loses, mostly he wins. He likes to look at the ships, sometimes, so we go to London docks or Wapping.

"On one journey, he sees the girl, who looks half-respectable, but smiles like one of them game girls. He wants her, so it's nothing for it that he talks to her and fixes it up to come back after dark and have at her. I found him a public house that didn't look too down at mouth—which ain't easy near the docks, mind you—and he had wine in a private parlor, reading a book, nice as you please, until time. Then he goes, meets her, we have the hour drive, and sets her down again. We went back to Mayfair then, thank the lord."

"And after that?"

Payne looked puzzled. "How do you mean, exactly?"

"Did he ask her to meet him again, in Covent Garden perhaps?"

"Well, if he did, sir, he never told me."

"Did he often tell you?" I asked. "What he meant to do, and with whom?"

"Not in so many words. But I saw who he got down to talk with and who he invited in later. He never talked to me about it at all, 'cept to tell me where to go and when to do the slow drive."

"Now for Black Bess," I went on. "When did he meet her?"

Payne grinned, showing that he, too, had filed his teeth. "I remember her. Black-haired wench, a taking thing. He met her about a day or so after Wapping. Had his eye on her for a long time, and it wasn't the first time he had her in the coach, if you take my meaning. He liked Black Bess. Had her twice. But he set her down again as usual, and we went off home. Didn't see her after that."

"Again, did he make an appointment to meet her in Covent Garden later?"

Payne shook his head. "Not that I knew about."

It looked more and more like McAdams could be the wealthy gentleman who promised to meet the girls. Stacy might have made the appointments for him, perhaps recommending girls he liked the best.

I halted that thought. Stacy was urbane and polished, McAdams crude, despite their similarities in station. I remembered Stacy's embarrassment at McAdams's boorish comments when Grenville and I interviewed him at Tatt's. Would Stacy wish McAdams's company on a girl he liked?

Then again, I had no idea how Stacy thought about things. The man had a wife and a daughter, but preferred to hunt and capture game girls for his sport.

"I have to ask a distasteful question," I said. "Does Stacy hurt the girls?"

Payne looked surprised. "Naw. Leastwise I never saw such a thing. They like him, smile when the carriage stops and all. If they were afraid of him, they'd melt away when they saw him coming, wouldn't they? They must tell each other all about it, wouldn't you think?"

"True," I conceded. If Stacy had the habit of beating girls, word would get around, and only the most desperate would go with him. The others would look for easier marks. "Now, I must come to yesterday afternoon. Mr. Stacy was in Covent Garden?"

"That he was. I drove him, not through the market, it was too crowded, but down Russel Street, thinking to skirt round it to Southampton Street. He was looking again, you know, for who he wanted to take up with next. At the edge of the market, he signals me to stop, and he gets down. There's an orange girl he talks to, and he saw her and makes his way to her. He paused to talk to another game girl on the way, but he left her pretty soon. He talks to the orange girl, buys an orange, and walks back to the carriage. He tells me to drive on, gets in, and we're on our way."

"Did you see a young lady stop him, seemingly to ask directions?"

Payne looked shame-faced. "I have to admit I didn't notice, sir. The crowd was big, and people kept pushing by the horses, like. A few boys tweaked the harness and I had to clear them off before they spooked the beasts. So he might have talked to her, but I wasn't looking at him all the time. Sorry, sir."

"The game girl he paused to speak to—she could not have been my daughter? Gabriella has dark hair, and she might have seemed agitated and in a hurry."

"No, this were a game girl. Don't know what she's called and didn't see her face. But my master knows the difference."

No doubt he did. That was one point in Stacy's favor—at least he regulated his proclivities to girls who were used to such things.

I recalled Thompson's note about Mary. "What was Mr. Stacy doing Wednesday night?" I asked abruptly.

Payne blinked. "Wednesday?"

"This Wednesday just gone. Did he come to Covent Garden?"

"No, sir." His voice held more confidence. "He went to Almack's to meet his wife and daughter. They go every Wednesday."

Almack's, that bastion of respectability, where all the *ton* paraded. Young ladies making their debut waited in some anxiety for the approval of the patronesses, in the form of vouchers for tickets, before they could attend. The most blue-blooded went to Almack's Assembly Rooms to parade their eligible daughters, drink lemonade, and dance on the roped-off dance floor.

Lady Breckenridge had described it to me. "The lemonade is insipid, the talk is insipid, the orchestra is insipid, and the patronesses rule over it like it was the kingdom come. I longed to go as a debutante, and wondered why I had the moment I entered the place. I begged my mother to take me home, and she did, to my surprise. She hated it, too." She'd rolled her eyes. "But lord, a young lady must go, and lord, she mustn't dance the waltz until one of the biddies says she can. Is it any wonder I am so scandalous? I had to be, for the relief."

Almack's one night and Covent Garden game girls in his coach the next. I knew that many respectably married gentlemen kept mistresses, but I wondered how many lived such a double life as Stacy. "Did he go to Covent Garden Wednesday at all?"

"No, sir. Dinner at Lord Featherstone's, Almack's Assembly Rooms at eleven o'clock, and home again at two. That was all. Why do you want to know?"

"Because that was the night Mary Chester died, apparently."

Payne's graying brows lifted. "Was it now? Well, it couldn't have been my gentleman. He never went near the place all that day."

"What about his friend, Mr. McAdams? Did Stacy ever take McAdams to Covent Garden with him?"

"Naw. This is something my master did alone." He drained his tankard and swiped the last of the ale from his mouth. "It were Mr. McAdams got my master started in that way, though, about three years ago. I overheard them—Mr. McAdams telling Mr. Stacy that he could find good sport right here in London without having to go out to the country. Kind of shoved him in the direction, like. I've never seen Mr. McAdams in Covent Garden, but that don't mean he don't go."

"True." I signaled the landlord to bring him another ale. "I do appreciate you answering my questions so frankly, but I must ask why you continue to work for Stacy. You seem to find his activities a bit repulsive."

Payne shrugged. "Well, he ain't no worse than any other master, I'm thinking. The wages is good, and he buys the livery. I don't much like his 'sport,' but then, all gentry-coves are a little mad for wenches, ain't they? He likes the game girls, but it's what they're for. He don't push his attentions on those he should not, if you take my meaning. And they don't seem to mind him."

I nodded and lifted my tankard, which was still half-full. "In other words, he treats ladies like ladies and game girls like game girls. I suppose most gentlemen do."

"Exactly, sir. So, I shake my head and drive on as I'm told. Even if he does write it all down in a book."

I stopped, my tankard halfway to my mouth. "A book?"

"I almost forgot."

As the landlord deposited another tankard in front of Payne and took up the empty, Payne reached into his coat and drew out a leather-bound book, one made for keeping a journal. He slid it across the table to me. "He told me to give you this. He's that embarrassed, like, but he wants you to see that there is no entry for your daughter."

I waited until the landlord was well away, then, with some trepidation, I peeled open the book and scanned a page.

Stacy wrote in a clear, flowing script, the kind perfected by tutors in such public schools as Eton and Harrow. I still could feel the sting of the cane across my knuckles when my fumbling fingers could not shape the loops and curls to the tutor's satisfaction.

"October 3," ran the entry. "Brown, blue, good teeth, round. Haymarket. SnT2n."

"What does that mean?" I asked, pointing to the letters and numbers.

"Don't know, sir. Never asked."

"Something about the girls he don't want no one to know?" Jackson suggested. "In case someone else reads the book?"

"Quite," I said. I wondered why the devil Stacy would let me see this, but if I could understand only half of it, perhaps he saw no harm. "Even so, he wrote his observations in a book? Good lord, what if his wife found it?"

"She won't, sir," Payne said. "He has me keep it for him, and I give it to him only when we make our outings, if you see. He's not written his name anywhere in it, so if someone finds it, they won't know it's his, unless they recognize the writing."

"They might think it yours," I pointed out.

"Makes no difference. It's mostly nonsense, isn't it? He wants you to read the entries for yesterday."

I flipped to Thursday: "3 o'clock, CG, oranges, blonde, round. AySnTn."

Farther down the page was another entry: "Midnight, oranges, T2yC3."

From this I surmised that the orange girl had made him happy at midnight, but nothing more. It coincided with me seeing Stacy's carriage in Covent Garden that night. I flipped back to the entry for Wednesday and found none. Either Stacy had gone to Almack's in truth, or he'd removed the page for that day. I lifted the book and peered down the length of its spine, but could see no evidence of pages cut from the binding.

"May I keep this?" I asked. "I will return it tomorrow."

Payne's brows twitched. "Mr. Stacy would not be happy."

"If Mr. Stacy has nothing to hide but this little peccadillo, there will be no harm. I do not intend to share it with my friends. I will return it with my own hands to your master tomorrow."

Payne did not look pleased, but he nodded.

I tucked the book into my own coat. "Thank you, Payne. Enjoy the ale." Nodding, I rose. Payne stood up and bowed to me, and thanked me nicely for the drink.

Jackson followed me outside into the deepening night. He clapped on his hat against the rain and straightened it. "Nasty goings-on, ain't there?"

"A bit." I pressed the book in my pocket against my chest, and we started down the tiny lane to the Strand, where a groom watched after Grenville's horses and rig.

"At least I have no cause to be ashamed of my master," Jackson said. "Never catch Mr. Grenville doing anything so sordid."

"Indeed," I agreed.

"And writing it down. The man must be daft." He shrugged. "Ah, well, there ain't many like Mr. Grenville." He opened the carriage door. Rain streamed down the windows and the polished wood, but Jackson was as poised as though it were a clear afternoon. "Where to now, sir?"

I elected to return home. I saw candles glowing in my front windows above the dark bakery and concluded that Bartholomew had returned and was waiting for me. I quickened my pace, hoping there was news.

When I entered my sitting room, I found Bartholomew

nowhere in evidence. Instead, Lady Breckenridge was curled up in my wing chair, her eyes closed.

When the door shut, she awakened and smiled. "There you are," she said. "You've been ages."

I had held myself upright too long. Seeing her brought of flood of healing warmth to my limbs, and I had to press my walking stick against the carpet in order to remain standing.

A faint crease appeared between her brows. "Gabriel? Has something else happened?"

She rose and came to me. I dropped the walking stick and gathered her up, much preferring to lean against her. She smelled fine, as she always did, and I buried my face in her neck, inhaling her fragrance.

I felt her soft chuckle. "Well," she murmured. "That's all right, then."

DONATA slept with me all night and said hang the scandal. "They know," she observed in the early hours of the morning as she lay next to me, tracing patterns on my chest. "Everyone knows. They can make of it what they will. I no longer care."

"Bold lady." I touched her cheek. "I like you being bold."

"You were not made for a timid woman. It does not suit you." She sent me a smile. "Did you know? It is my birthday."

"Is it? Good lord, why did you choose to spend it with a wreck like me?"

"Well, I usually spend it at home in Oxfordshire, but I did not want to leave London while you were in the midst of troubles." Her fingertips moved to my lips. "I am thirty."

"Ancient," I said, amused.

"I am certainly ten times wiser than at twenty. What an astounding innocent I was."

"I am sorry you had to face so much," I said with sincerity.

"One must hurt to learn," she answered, with a stoicism I knew she did not feel. "I have my little lad; I in no way regret that. And I trounced you at billiards. I in no way regret that."

"I paid up that five pounds," I reminded her with mock severity.

She remained silent, studying me, her eyes a mystery. "What do you in no way regret?"

"Losing to you at billiards," I said.

"You knew I wanted you to say that."

"Perhaps." I drew her close and kissed the dark line of her hair. "I in no way regret falling in love with you."

She looked at me, startled. "In love?"

I nodded. "The feeling came unlooked for, but I have grown to cherish it. I love you, Donata."

Her answer came without words, and it satisfied me very much.

BRILLIANT sunlight and the sound of curtains drawing back awoke me. I pried open my eyes. Donata lay in a nest of linen next to me, sleeping the deep sleep of a late riser. Bartholomew hovered in the room at a respectful distance, holding a tray heaped with dishes.

"Good morning, sir. I brought breakfast for yourself and her ladyship, along with your morning correspondence."

I brushed hair out of my eyes and sat up carefully, so as not to disturb Lady Breckenridge. "Thank you, Bartholomew. It was good of you."

Bartholomew set the tray on the bedside table. The aroma of sausage wafted to me, and my stomach rumbled.

"And Miss Simmons has come to see you."

I half groaned, torn between relief that Marianne was all right and annoyance that she had chosen to call just now. "Marianne on an empty stomach is not to be borne. Tell her to come back later if it has nothing to do with the search."

Bartholomew hesitated. "The thing is, sir, she arrived in London early this morning and went to the Clarges Street house. The servants there were instructed to deny her admittance, and she is most distressed."

"Yes, she would be. Very well, hand me my dressing gown, I'll see her."

I looked regretfully at the beckoning sausages, took a quick sip of the coffee that steamed in its cup, then climbed from the bed. Bartholomew helped me don the dressing gown, then I went out to explain things to Marianne. Through it all, Donata never woke.

Chapter 15

MARIANNE wore a chocolate brown traveling gown with a cherry red sash and a brown-and-green-plaid shawl that matched the trim on the bonnet she dangled from its cherry red ribbons. She was well turned out and looked quite smart, her childlike looks and golden curls complemented by the ensemble.

Her face, however, was white and strained, her eyes red with weeping. "Lacey, what in God's name happened?" She threw the bonnet to the floor as I stepped out of my bedchamber. "I went to Clarges Street and that pious maid Alicia refused me the door. When I argued with her, she said it was *his* orders, and then Dickon pressed forward, sweet as you please, and said I had to leave. They would not tell me why. They would not let me in even to get my things. Damnation, what happened?"

Skirts swirling, she fell into the wing chair, where she sat with arms folded like a petulant child.

"I told him about David," I said.

She grabbed the chair's arms and sat up straight. "You did, did you? Well, I suppose I told you to. You were supposed to have sent word to me, so that I could stay with David if he cut up rough."

"There was not time to send word. I told him the entire story late afternoon yesterday."

"I expect he was disgusted, knowing his money went to the by-blow of another man, never mind he's dead and gone seven years now. I knew he would. Catch me taking your advice again, Lacey, you lost me a soft billet."

She spoke offhand, but her fingers whitened where they gripped the chair, and she struggled to calm her breathing.

"He was not angry because of David," I said. "As I suspected, he was all sympathy, and even said he'd keep the money going to him. No, he was incensed because we did not trust him."

She looked startled. "What do you mean?"

"We believed he'd either refuse to have anything to do with David or that he would take complete control of David's life. He decided to do neither. But the fact that we did not trust him to be good-hearted upset him a great deal." I paused. "He is a man slow to anger, but we managed it between us."

"He grew angry at you, too?" she asked.

"He asked me to explain that he would continue your allowance so that you could care for David, but requested that he never see you again. Or me."

"You? Why not you?"

I sighed. "Because I doubted him, just as you did. Because he has unbent a great deal for us, and we repay him by suspecting everything he does. Both of us are cautious by nature, but with Grenville, we went too far. He was trying to do good by us, and we threw it back in his face."

Her throat worked. "I ruined your friendship as well?"

"I ruined it." I touched my chest. "With my pride. Hence all the pithy warnings about pride going before a fall."

She turned her head and stared at the cold fireplace. "It does not matter. I was ready to give him the push, at any rate. So dull living in his house and being paraded about when he likes."

"Stop," I said.

She jerked her head up, her eyes bright with tears. "It is true."

"No, it is not." I spread my hands on my worn dressing gown. "I planned to pen him a letter of abject apology, and I believe you should as well. If we throw ourselves at his feet, he might just condescend to acknowledge us again. I believe it worth a try."

She hesitated. "Throw myself at his feet?"

"Whyever not? What have you to lose that you have not already lost?"

Marianne tried to hold her bravado, but for the first time since I'd known her, she let her entire mask fall away. Even seeing her with David hadn't revealed what she showed me now. I saw a woman desperately lonely and frightened of her coming life, a woman who had found one straw to cling to, and even that straw was being ripped from her grasp.

She cared for Grenville. I had known that before, but I had not realized how much. Tears spilled from her eyes, not tears of self-pity. She pressed the heels of her hands to her face and let the tears flow. "God help me, Lacey, what have I done?"

I drew a handkerchief from the dressing gown's pocket and went to her. Crouching before her, I dabbed at the tears that smeared her face. "You fell in love and did not know what to do."

"Fell in love," she repeated bitterly. "What kind of idiot am I?"

I stroked her hair. "He cares for you as well, I know he does. Go to him and grovel—on your knees if you have to. Tell him what you feel for him."

She gave a short laugh. "So he can kick me, and then have his footmen drag me from the house? I am already in pain enough, thank you very much."

"You must trust him. He might not take you back, or me either, but we have to tell him what he means to us. For me, he means a deep, loyal friendship, better than I ever thought I'd have. For you, a man who can make you happy."

"Can he?" She wiped tears from her eyes. "I have never been happy, Lacey, I cannot imagine what it is like."

"Do you think it worth a little groveling to find out?"

She gave a shaky laugh. "Oh, why not? I don't suppose he can make me feel any worse than I do now. You are right, you know, I love the bloody man. I love everything about him, damn him."

"I know you do." I stroked her hair again, trying to look hopeful, but in truth I did not know what Grenville would do. He'd been deeply angry and deeply hurt, and I had the feeling he wished the both of us at the bottom of the river.

"I vow," came Lady Breckenridge's voice. "I really ought to send someone ahead before I enter rooms."

Marianne jumped. I rose carefully, knowing that Donata could not be pleased to see me, clad in only my dressing gown, kneeling before Marianne and touching her tenderly.

Donata herself had dressed, her long-skirted, half-sleeved gown looking as fresh as it had when she'd arrived. Her hair was bundled into a long velvet hood, and a fine chain dangled from her wrist. She looked ready for a brisk walk in Hyde Park, not as though she'd just come from the bed of her lover.

Marianne heaved herself from the chair. "I'll go down

and get Ma Beltan to give me coffee," she said wearily. "What time do you think his nibs pries himself out of bed?"

"I really have no idea," I said. "He rises at a fashionable hour, but might get up earlier today, because of our current problem."

Marianne's face softened. "Bartholomew told me what happened. I am sorry, Lacey."

I nodded my thanks. "Come back after you've found coffee. I have a few things I need to ask you while you're waiting."

She wiped away more tears. "If I must." She moved past Lady Breckenridge, who watched her coolly. "You needn't worry, my lady. I am not after stealing him; I only borrowed his shoulder to cry on."

Donata's brows arched as Marianne went on out the door. A lady of the demimonde such as Marianne should not have presumed to speak to a lady of the *ton*. They both should pretend the other did not exist, and in their worlds, they did not.

The door closed with a click, and Donata turned to me. "That creature is Grenville's Marianne Simmons, is she not?"

I smiled faintly. "She is."

Her face softened to understanding. "You told me you were forever smoothing the waters between them."

"Yes, but these waters now might be too rough for me to steer. I will have to let them flounder for a time."

"Hmm." Her eyes narrowed, and from behind her back, she drew out Stacy's crisp leather-bound book. "I came out to tell you that this makes for interesting reading, I must say. What the devil is it?"

I started. I had taken the book from my pocket when I'd undressed the night before, and I supposed I'd left it on the bedside table. I reached for it. "Nothing for your eyes."

She lifted it away. "But it is quite intriguing. 'March fifteen, the Strand, blonde, brown eyes, innocent expression, quite pretty.' I do not imagine you mean a horse. I cannot make out the rest, 'SnTy2y.' What on earth is that?"

"The book does not belong to me," I said quickly. I held out my hand for it, but she turned away, leafing through the pages.

"Whom does it belong to, then? And what are all these numbers and letters? Is it code for races this gentleman will bet on?" She looked back at me. "I think not."

"I did not mean for you to find that," I said, rubbing my hands on my suddenly cold arms. "It belongs to Jeremiah Stacy and might contain evidence as to whether or not he murdered Mary Chester."

Her look of suspicion was replaced by one of interest. "Really? Why?"

"I hesitate to tell you. It is rather sordid."

She brightened. "Excellent, then it will not be dull. Do tell me, Lacey. I am a bored widow in need of excitement."

I smiled to myself at the description, then launched into an abbreviated version of my discussion with Payne. She listened avidly, glancing at the book from time to time. When I had finished, she grimaced. "Goodness, and I thought I knew everything about my neighbors. Patrice Stacy is a vapid thing, but I do not think she deserves a husband with an obsession with prostitutes. Are all men so disgusting?"

I was saved from having to answer by Marianne reentering the room, carrying a mug of coffee and a hard roll. "I believe they are," she said, "with a few exceptions." She plopped down comfortably at my writing table and took a noisy sip of coffee. "I heard you mention Mr. Stacy. What's he done?"

I leaned against my chest-on-frame and folded my arms, giving up trying to pry the book from Donata's interested hands. "I wanted to ask you about him. If you ever met him, what you thought of him, anything you've heard of him. He might have murdered a game girl and kidnapped another."

Marianne raised her brows. "Really? I wouldn't have pegged him for it, but he is an odd cove." She tore off a bite of bread with white teeth and chewed thoughtfully. "I haven't seen him in some time, but he used to linger at the theatre in Drury Lane, waiting for opera dancers and girls in the chorus to emerge. He liked to talk to them; sometimes he'd single one out, sometimes another. Some of the girls hoped he'd set them up as their protector, because he has plenty of blunt, but he never did."

"He was never rough or threatening?" I asked. "No one was afraid of him?"

She shrugged. "He seemed harmless. He liked to talk and jest, liked to pretend he was friends to all the girls, though in truth they only wanted his money. Some gentlemen are like that. For them, talking to low women and getting to know them is a thrill, even if they never touch any of them."

Lady Breckenridge continued leafing through the journal. "I see now. He went one better, and wrote of his encounters in this book. Rather like a man who describes sightings of exotic birds. Vulgar," she said dismissively. "His name is rarely on my guest lists, but it will be nonexistent now."

"He wrote it down?" Marianne asked. "May I see?"

Wordlessly, and before I could stop her, Lady Breckenridge held the book out to Marianne. Marianne took it, wiped her buttery fingers on the bread, and began leafing through the pages. "I wonder what the letters and numbers mean."

"I have no idea," I said. "His coachman did not know either. Stacey's personal code, I suppose, for whatever he wanted to note without being obvious."

"A point in Stacy's favor that he let you see this," Lady Breckenridge remarked.

"Yes, his coachman answered my questions readily, apparently with Stacy's blessing. Stacy seems quite eager to be open and aboveboard, as though he has nothing to hide among gentlemen. The coachman could be a very loyal servant, however, and help Stacy cover anything he might have done."

"The smaller letters are all *y* and *n*," Marianne murmured. "Probably for *yes* and *no*. So the larger letters are a question or a quality, and the answer is yes or no."

"You might very well have hit on it," I said.

"What are the numbers then?" Lady Breckenridge mused. "If *2y* is *2 yes,* I wonder what that means?"

The fact that the two of them, my lady and Marianne Simmons, were clinically discussing sordid notes made by a gentleman about street girls made me shudder. I could only stand by and watch.

"I wonder if *S* stands for syphilis," Marianne speculated. "All entries are marked with an *S*. That would be a concern to a Mayfair gentleman with a family. Perhaps one reason he walks among the street girls and gets to know them is to discover what diseases they have. *Sn* means they are healthy, and therefore acceptable."

Lady Breckenridge nodded. "Yes, I can see the fastidious Stacy making certain they have no disease." She sniffed and opened the reticule that she'd left on the writing table, from which she withdrew a thin cigarillo. "Rather like purchasing horseflesh. Does he check their teeth?"

"Perhaps that's what *T* stands for," Marianne said, scanning an entry.

"*Teeth, yes,* I suppose that makes a sort of sense."

"Unless it means something more sordid."

Lady Breckenridge lit the cigarillo with a candle. She

filled her mouth with smoke, then let it trickle out with her words. "Goodness, I can think of several sordid things that begin with the letter *T.*"

"So can I," Marianne agreed.

I lifted the book from Marianne's hands. "That will be enough of that."

She gave me a sullen frown. "I am trying to help, Lacey. If Stacy offed this girl, I shall be very angry with him. Grenville will have to cut him dead."

Lady Breckenridge had sunk gracefully into the wing chair, a little smile on her face at my discomfiture. There were no other seats in the room, so I remained standing. "Grenville has already cut Brian McAdams, another possibility for the murderer."

Lady Breckenridge wrinkled her nose. "McAdams was a friend of my late husband. I have been cutting him for years, but Grenville's gesture will blackball him. I am pleased to hear it."

I mused. "Even if Stacy did not kill Mary Chester, do you think, Marianne, that he could kidnap a girl and hold her against her will? Do you think he is the sort who would do that?"

She frowned. "I do not know. He was always friendly and chatty, but as I said, a bit odd. His good nature could mask cunning, but as you know, I never trust a gentleman." She finished with a bitter twist to her lips.

"My thought was that perhaps Stacy did kidnap Mary Chester and Black Bess, and very possibly my daughter. Perhaps he did not mean to kill Mary, or perhaps someone else did that—McAdams with his rough ways. When Stacy discovered that either he or McAdams had killed her, he panicked and carried her to Bottle Bill's doorstep, knowing about Bottle Bill's violent drunken spells—having learned this either from the girls or from his own observation."

"You could always ask him," Lady Breckenridge said. "You and the sword in your walking stick."

"I intend to." I ran my hand through my unruly hair. "I would like to have Pomeroy arrest him while we continue to look for Bess and Gabriella, although I am afraid that if Stacy is taken, McAdams might harm them so they will say nothing against him. Pomeroy could arrest both, but moving against two upper-class Mayfair gentlemen is risky for him."

"You could have Pomeroy arrest Stacy and then follow McAdams to see what he does," Lady Breckenridge suggested.

"I thought of that as well. Denis has already put men to follow Stacy and McAdams, so we may see what they do, and I will certainly grab Stacy and shake him again. What I want most of all"—I stopped and drew a breath—"is the return of my daughter."

Both ladies looked at me, true sympathy in their faces. Each of them had a son, and they knew what they would feel if they were lost.

"And of course, Stacy and McAdams might be innocent of this crime," I said after a time. "Bottle Bill is a panicked and pathetic man. He will say what he needs to say to keep himself from Newgate, so he, too, might have killed her accidentally and be lying through his teeth about it."

"Then what do we do?" Marianne asked.

"Keep searching," I said. "I'll not stop until she's found."

"Neither will we," Lady Breckenridge said. She did not come to me; she remained seated with her cigarillo, but her eyes told me more than words what she felt.

THE search continued that morning, through the afternoon, and on into evening, with various contingents reporting to me, and Pomeroy sending messages from Bow Street.

Coaching inns had been searched and landlords questioned, to no avail. None remembered seeing a girl fitting Gabriella's description at their inn, either alone or with a young man. Sir Gideon Derwent persuaded a few magistrates to invade and close down several known bawdy houses, but Gabriella was not found in any of them. Neither was Black Bess.

Colonel Brandon came to report to me himself around eight o'clock that the inns they had checked along the road to Dover had yielded nothing. If Gabriella had fled to France, none saw her. He had sent the soldiers farther, to check Dover itself and any ships leaving for Calais.

"Thank you," I said sincerely. "Your help has made much difference."

"I would feel better if I had some news to report," Brandon said.

"Even knowledge that she has not been somewhere helps. We can narrow the search, concentrate effort elsewhere."

We stood in the bake shop, where I had returned for coffee and bread for supper. Brandon lowered his voice so that the lady who had come in to purchase a loaf would not overhear. "How long do you plan to search?"

"As long as it takes," I responded. "The rest of my life if necessary."

He scrutinized me with his piercing blue eyes. "You do know that she might never be found. I dislike to tell you that, but it happens. We saw it all the time in Spain and Portugal, where families would be separated and sons and daughters lost."

"I know." I remembered the despair and grief of people searching for one another in the Spanish towns we had taken and the sickening feeling that I could do nothing to help them. French soldiers dragged off daughters for their pleasure, or sons to recruit against their will. The English, there to drive out the French, had not always been kinder.

"I know you will not stop," Brandon said. "I will help as I can."

"Tell Louisa it was not her fault."

"I know it was not. She is apt to take the blame, especially in matters where you are concerned."

"Whatever happened to us?" I murmured.

"Eh?" He gave me a sharp look. "How do you mean?"

"We used to be fast friends, in the first days, in India. You got me my commission. You pinned the rank on me yourself, smiling like a proud papa. And then . . ."

He scowled. "And then, I realized that you were a stubborn, arrogant, hotheaded pain in the fundament."

I had to smile. "If you thought so, why did you not cut me? Why help me rise through the ranks? You risked your money and your good name."

He looked uncomfortable. "Because you were a damn fine officer, that is why. We needed good officers, and much as I hate to praise you to your face, you were one of the best." He loosened his collar. "Besides, if I had dropped you, Louisa would have killed me."

I wanted to take offense at his words, but there was nothing for it. I laughed out loud. The bread-buying lady stared at us on her way out. "You are a poor specimen, Brandon."

"You were not married long enough to understand." He gave me a superior look. "When your Lady Breckenridge gets her fingers into you, it is I who will laugh." He nodded to me, then to Mrs. Beltan behind her counter. "I'll be going, Lacey. I will help you search as long as you need me."

His face a bit redder than usual, he ducked out of the bake shop, slapping on his hat. Any conversation that hinted of sentimentality or reconciliation embarrassed him.

I finished my dinner and went out in search of Felicity. I quickly found her in Covent Garden, talking to another game girl in the shadow of the theatre. I didn't know the girl's name, but she had often called out to me as I walked in the area, teasing me with her friends.

"Any good news, Captain?" Felicity asked as I walked away with her after a short exchange of banter with the other girl. "Lela there hasn't seen Black Bess in ages, or anyone who looks like your daughter, I'm sorry to say."

"Thank you for trying. But I do want to speak to you about something else. May we?"

She flashed a smile as I gestured her onward as if she were a society lady at a garden party. As she walked with me toward where an ale seller had made makeshift benches by laying boards across empty ale kegs, I reflected that "exotic" described her well. Her deep brown eyes and bone structure conjured visions of harems of the East, complemented by dark skin and glossy black hair that enticed a man's touch.

She showed off each advantage, wearing a gown of striking blue that accented her skin, and dressing her hair in heavy braids looped against her head. She could smile with a combination of red lips and white teeth to entrance a man's gaze to her mouth. She did not dress immodestly, but any gentleman looking at her would find his thoughts instantly turning to desire.

I seated her on a relatively empty bench and sat down next to her. I removed Stacy's journal from my pocket, opened it to a page I'd marked, and held it in front of us both.

"'Great happiness,'" I read in a low voice. "'Black beauty. Sn2y3y. Pleasure untold.' I have not quite worked out what all the twos and threes mean, but I do understand what he means by *great happiness*. It's another way of saying Felicity."

Her eyes were still, but I sensed thoughts whirling behind them. "What is this, Captain?"

"The notes of a man called Stacy. You know him."

She shrugged. "What if I do?"

I closed the book and tucked it back into my pocket. "I noticed this entry when I read through it this morning. Strange that I have been looking for a wealthy gentleman who could have lured Black Bess and Mary Chester to Covent Garden, and yet, you have never mentioned Mr. Stacy, a wealthy man of Mayfair who likes to talk to game girls and make appointments with them."

She avoided my gaze. "Maybe I did not want to get him into trouble?"

"Why should Mr. Stacy get into trouble if he has nothing to do with this?"

She shrugged again. "I would not like to see him arrested, Captain. He is *very* rich." She ended with a suggestive smile that did not reach her eyes.

"He might have kidnapped and killed Mary Chester, and the same fate might await Bess. Not to mention my daughter."

She laughed, a sultry, seductive sound. Anyone watching us would believe that she was busy seducing me. "He wouldn't hurt a fly."

"Mary Chester is dead."

"Her hard luck."

I raised my brows. "You do not care that Stacy, a man you let bed you, might have killed a woman, even accidentally?"

"And I tell you, he could not have," she said.

"Why not?" I set my mouth in a hard line. "Explain it to me. Why should I not have Pomeroy arrest him for murdering a game girl? He is the most likely person to have done the crime—both girls went to meet a wealthy gentleman, and Stacy has admitted a passion for girls he meets in

Covent Garden. An obsession, more like, from his journal entries."

"Maybe," Felicity said. "But I tell you, he's a gentle sort. Wouldn't hurt a fly, like I said."

"But what if a girl refused him? Might he cut up rough? Force her?"

To my surprise, she laughed again. "You do not understand, Captain. Of course he would not. He never did the job with any of us. He couldn't."

Chapter 16

I blinked. "You mean Stacy is impotent?"

"That is exactly what I mean. His wick won't stand up long enough. Poor man."

I stared at her. "Then why on earth does he take all these girls into his carriage? According to his coachman, they stay with him for an hour, while Payne drives through the streets, dead slow."

She gave me a pitying look. "You are obviously a man with no fear in that regard. He dandles them on his knee and talks to them. He touches, they touch him. But there is never consummation."

"But perhaps, in his frustration . . ."

"Naw. He likes the touching, and the girls don't mind him pawing. He doesn't hurt us, he's never going to give us a by-blow, and he pays good money. And he's friendly, doesn't treat a girl like she's gutter trash and then expect her to give him what he wants even when it's clear he hates her."

At this last her eyes flashed anger, rage so incandescent I could not believe it contained in one human being. She shielded her gaze a moment later, but I had seen.

"This has happened to you?" I asked quietly.

She tried to sound offhand. "It happens to all girls who ply a particular trade."

"You are thinking of a certain instance."

She shook her head. "It does not matter. When you do what I do, you learn to expect it. There's gentlemen, Captain, that hate women. Perhaps their mothers beat them or their wives scorn them, I do not know, but they hate them with fury. And so they find a woman who must sit still while he despises her. She has to let him unleash every ounce of anger and frustration and hatred onto her, and she has to take it, because that's what she's for."

Her dark eyes swam with tears. She did not cry, as Carlotta might, wanting pity and soothing words. She fought her own demons and did so on her own.

"That is not what you are for," I said.

She brushed moisture from the corners of her eyes. "Don't talk like a reformer, Captain. They come round telling me I can be 'useful.' As what, I'd like to know."

"My friend Mrs. Brandon found Nancy a position at an inn. Perhaps she can do the same for you."

Felicity laughed again, in true mirth. "Nance is different from me. She's a cheerful soul, and I am no fool. Any man who employs me wants me in his bed, and that is all. Women dislike me on sight. Maybe it won't be so when I'm old and wrinkled, but it is now." She gave me a knowing look. "And Nance adores you. If you told her to climb up into the church spire yonder and cluck like a chicken, she'd do it. For you."

"You exaggerate. And I cannot help but notice you also have led me a long way from my original questions. If you think Stacy could not have harmed Mary or Bess or Gabriella, who could have? If you are protecting someone, I will have the law on you as hard as I will on him. I want my daughter back."

"I know." She laid her hand on my arm. "I really do not know where she is, Captain. I wish I did, 'cause I'd love to see the look on your face if I brought her home to you. You'd be that grateful. You might even forget about that pretty gentry-mort you have as your ladybird long enough to thank me."

I slanted her an ironic glance. "You will have to make do with only my gratitude." I stood up and pulled her to her feet. I gave the ale seller a coin and had him draw a cup, which I handed to Felicity. "Take some refreshment, then keep searching, if you will. And if you know anything, *anything,* I want you to tell me. All right?"

She took the cup. "All right. I'll do my best for you, Captain, promise." She drank the ale, but gave me such a smoldering look over the rim of the goblet that I flinched and strode away as quickly as I could. Her low laughter floated behind me.

MAJOR Auberge had come to my rooms in my absence. He waited uncomfortably for me in the bake shop and, at my invitation, ascended with me to my rooms.

He looked unhappier than ever, his face aged and tired. "Please tell me you have discovered things," he said. "I cannot bear this much longer."

"I have been questioning people, but no, I have not found her."

He covered his face and was silent for a time. I left him

alone, moving about my rooms reading messages and scribbling answers.

When at last Auberge lowered his hands, his lashes were wet. "What are we to do? Carlotta is grieving deeply. She has begun to worry about our other children in France, though I assure her that my brother can look after them especially well. Better than we can, it seems."

"Do not give up," I said savagely. "We owe it to Gabriella not to give up."

He shook his head. "This is perhaps why France was pushed aside by England in the war. We feel things so, and we cannot go on."

I tossed down my pen, sending ink spattering over my clean paper. "Do not talk like a fool. We feel things as much, but I refuse to give up. And I will not let you either."

"I am an old man, and tired. I have not slept since she went, no matter how I have tried." He gave me a look of naked misery. "I know she is not my daughter. I know she belongs to you. But I love her, and I cherish her."

"Tell me about her," I said suddenly. "Tell me what she was like when she was young, how she grew, what she learned." I hooked my arm over the back of the chair. "Tell me everything."

He looked surprised, then reluctant, as though he did not want to sift through memories that were now painful. After a few moments, however, he sank to the wing chair, and began to tell me. He spoke haltingly, sometimes groping for the words in English, but as he spun the narrative, my daughter came alive for me.

He described how he'd had difficulty adjusting to living with a small girl in his house, how she wanted to see everything and explore everything and overturn everything. She'd taken eagerly to riding, with Auberge leading the little horse and her perched on a tiny saddle. She'd grown swiftly, her pudgy arms and legs lengthening to coltish limbs, as she ran and played and rode across the hills of their French home.

She had great affection for her younger brothers and sisters and helped her mother look after them all. She was a quick learner, reading both French and English and writing in a good hand before she was six years old. She had lessons with her brothers under their tutor, and declared she wanted to be a teacher or a governess. Everyone had laughed, because of course, she would marry well and hire governesses of her own. She blossomed into a young woman and had already caught the eyes of many young men, although she had not yet made her debut.

I listened intently, picturing what he told me, my chest tight with envy. I laughed when he described how she'd told the parish priest that she refused to say rosaries because she wanted to worship the English God, like her mother. Though she had grown up far from me, some of her antics put her much in mind of me as a child, and I smiled with pride at her putting on her brother's clothes at twelve and climbing a fence to steal apples.

"She is a Lacey," I said. "Carlotta must grind her teeth over it."

Auberge nodded. "She is apt to blame Gabriella's wilder escapades on you. In my hearing only, of course."

Of course. I imagined that Carlotta had wanted never to tell Gabriella her true origins because the girl might have wanted to hie off to England to find me. She might want to become a Lacey in truth, and learn of her English background. Carlotta, on the other hand, obviously wanted nothing to do with me.

Once more, in the continuing litany in my head, I prayed to God that Gabriella was alive and well.

Bartholomew marched upstairs to interrupt our reminiscences. "Mr. Grenville has arrived, sir."

I looked up in surprise. I had been selfishly relieved that he had not called Bartholomew home last night as a result of our falling-out, and I wondered if he'd come here to fetch him now.

I heard his step, and then Grenville, resplendent in afternoon riding clothes, appeared. He hesitated at the sight of Auberge, but nodded cordially. "Major."

Auberge seemed to sense his wariness. He rose. "Mr. Grenville. I will go."

"No need," Grenville said. "I have come to continue assisting you. Jackson, too, is keen to have another go."

I got to my feet. "I am grateful. There was no need to come yourself."

"There was need." He shifted. "Like to see a thing through myself, and all that."

I shrugged as though I did not care one way or another. "I was about to go down to the Strand, to the place Mary was found, and look near there. I know Denis's men and Pomeroy's have scoured the place, but I want to look again. Whoever carried the body to Bottle Bill's would not have wanted to take it far."

"Excellent. I will have Jackson drive you."

"That is not necessary, but good of you to offer. Perhaps you and he can join Colonel Brandon, who has started searching points farther east, into the City and beyond."

"Dash it, Lacey." Grenville shifted again, his eyes dark and troubled. "I am trying to eat humble pie. I am not good at it, never having to do it before."

I blinked. "You are apologizing?"

"Yes, do not sound so devilish shocked. I know it is a strange endeavor for Lucius Grenville, but you might let me get through it."

"I am surprised only because I had thought to write an apology to you," I said. "I behaved badly, and I know it."

"No, I behaved badly." Red crept into his cheeks.

"Throwing a tantrum because neither you nor Marianne would think and speak as I wanted you to. I expected you to fall down and worship me because I condescended to befriend you. You ought to have struck me with that walking stick and told me what a prig I was."

I gave him a faint smile. "Why, when you are striking yourself so well?"

"Do not laugh at me, Lacey, I beg you." He squared his shoulders and held out his hand. "We could both go on and on about who is the worst, but shall we shake and settle it? My stomach will certainly feel better."

I took his hand, suddenly feeling better myself. I had feared my friendship with him at a true end.

He grinned at me as we clasped hands, hard, then he assumed his air of nonchalance. It would never do for the great Grenville to be seen having an emotion.

"What about Marianne?" I asked as I stepped back.

He looked pained. "I will cross the Marianne bridge when I come to it. I am certain that she will step on me when I grovel to her, but I will do it."

"She said much the same thing about you."

His brows rose. "Did she?"

"Yes," I said. "She returned from Berkshire very early this morning and was most upset to be turned away from the Clarges Street house."

"Hmm." He straightened his already straight neckcloth. "Well, this will be an interesting reconciliation. Shall we go out and search, gentlemen? The air around the Thames might not be as cloying as it is here."

The sun had set by the time Jackson let the three of us out on the Strand. Jackson stayed with the carriage while we found the lane near Bottle Bill's lodgings where Mary's body had lain. In the approaching night, a few rats scuttled there, but no one else. One of Denis's men went past on the cross street, noticed us, and came, with his lantern, to see who we were, then went back to searching when I told him what we were doing.

The lane was cluttered with debris, old boards, part of a door, rusting basins. Bottle Bill and his helper had brought Mary here from his lodgings two streets over. Once the sun fully set, the lane would be inky black. Already the blank walls of the houses to either side cast deep shadows.

"Let us return to Bottle Bill's rooms," I said, "and widen the search from there."

Grenville and Auberge agreed, probably because we each felt there was little else we could do, and we walked in silence to the house were Bottle Bill eked out his existence.

The door to Bill's lodgings was gray with age, the paint peeling until only a few streaks of black were left to tell us the door's original color. I had wondered how the murderer managed to get the body inside Bill's lodgings, but I saw that the door did not latch correctly. Bill probably never bothered to lock it. Indeed, the door was ajar even now, and I knocked on it as I pushed it inward.

I found an empty room, fairly large, but stuffy, the only air coming from the cracked window near the door. A pallet of blankets lay against the wall near a fireplace, which was cold. Across the room sat a table with the remains of a meal.

The room led to no other. Where I would expect to find a door to a stair that would take me to the upper rooms, a blank brick wall stood instead. As Auberge and Grenville listlessly looked about, I went outside and noted a second window next to Bill's and a door beyond that, which looked much newer than Bill's door. I concluded that this had once been one house, and Bill's part of the downstairs partitioned into one room, which could then be let.

I wondered if the landlord lived next door, or whether the rest of the house was let to someone else. I stepped up to the second door, which had a little more paint than Bill's, and lifted my walking stick to tap on it.

Just then, I heard shouting in the street beyond. "Nab 'im! Come back here, you!"

Bottle Bill himself hurtled down the lane, arms pumping, head down. I stepped in front of him, and he rammed into me full force.

I dropped my walking stick and seized him hard. He fought furiously. Auberge and Grenville emerged from Bill's lodgings, and two of Denis's men ran up behind me.

"Let me go," Bill screamed. "I didn't do it."

I shook him. "Didn't do what?"

"Let me go," he moaned.

"There you are, you little bugger," Denis's man, who'd looked in on us earlier, said. "Let me have him, Captain. I'll thrash him for you."

"What did he do?"

"Didn't stop when we said. He's got something hidden, he does, but he runned away when he saw us coming."

My grip tightened on Bill's bony shoulder. "Bill? What are you hiding?"

"Nuffing. It ain't nuffing. I didn't do it. Let me go." He began to weep.

I shook him again, but he only cried in gasping sobs, and I knew I'd get nothing coherent from him. "Show me where he was running from."

Denis's man hoisted his lantern. "This way, sir."

I dragged Bill along, though he did not want to go. He tried to twist away from me, but Grenville caught his other arm, and together we half carried him back down the lane. Denis's lackeys, whose names I had never learned, led us down a street.

The name plaque on the nearest wall was so worn that I could not read it, but I had a vague idea where we were from my searching this morning. The narrow street led us along in a meandering course then ended in a flight of stairs that went down to the river. Another plaque, this one more legible, assured us that these stairs had once been used by Elizabeth the Queen, more than two hundred years before. A house stood at the top of the stairs, worn and crumbling.

"Not in there, sir," the man with the lantern said. "Over here."

He led me to a triangle of space between the house and the top of the stairs. The triangle was about two feet on a side, the remains of someone's attempt at a tiny garden. The earth had been turned up here, as though someone had been digging. On the stair side, the bank tumbled away to the roiling Thames, and the house pressed its other side. Nothing the size of a girl could be buried here.

Bottle Bill whimpered. I let go of him, and he sank to the stones in front of the house, pulling his knees to his chest.

"Why were you digging here, Bill?" I asked, but not forcefully; I knew he would not answer.

"He was burying something." The lackey with the lantern swung it over the patch, and the second one squatted down and started digging with a flat knife.

I pulled a clod of earth away and saw the glint of glass. Denis's man slammed his knife into the earth in disgust. "It's gin. Bottles of gin. Bloody son of a bitch was burying bottles of gin."

Behind me, Bill twitched. "I didn't do it."

I sighed in exasperation. I pulled out three bottles, green glass and heavy, and clinked them to the cobbles. "Damn you, Bill."

Denis's man with the lantern yanked one more bottle out, which I had missed, and smashed it to the ground. Bill winced, cringing from the broken glass.

"Sorry, sir," Denis's lackey said. "It's for nothing." He started to turn away.

"Wait," I commanded. "Bring the light back. Shine it just there."

I pointed to where he'd pulled out the last bottle. I'd seen something when the dirt fell away, but I was not quite certain what. I scrabbled in the mud, disliking the cold ooze on my gloves, but I was beyond caring. I scraped away earth and mud from what I'd seen. The others crowded in behind me.

"It's a board," I said. I started to lift it away, then I realized it was nailed in place. I wrenched it, hard, and the rotted thing gave way.

I almost slithered forward into a hole about two feet in diameter. Denis's man grabbed me in time, but I shook him off. I lay down and inched forward until I could peer into the dark hole. Dank, fetid air washed over me, sickening and heavy.

"There was a covering here of some kind. It's mostly gone. Give me the lantern."

Denis's man nearly hit my face with it in his eagerness to hand it to me. I passed it down into the hole.

I recoiled as a small rat climbed up the dirt, scrambling to get away from the light. I waited, but none others followed. It was either alone, or its fellows were braver. I leaned in again.

"Careful, Lacey," Grenville said behind me.

Denis's man held my legs, his weight like a rock. I doubted I'd fall, unless the man suddenly decided to rid Denis of a problem called Captain Lacey for once and for all. I risked it, lowered the lantern inside, and shined the light about.

This must have been part of an old cellar, but it, like Bottle Bill's room, had been bricked off from the rest of the house. Perhaps the original wall had leaked, long ago, and the owner found it easier to seal it off. The brick wall to my right was infested with slime and mold. To the left, rotting timbers barely supported a wall that had crumbled to let in the dirt of the bank. About ten feet below me, or as near as I could judge, was an earthen floor, hard packed.

I withdrew. "Help me get down there."

Grenville had pressed a folded handkerchief to his nose. "Lacey, it cannot be healthy down there. It smells like a sewer."

"If rats can exist there, so can I." I turned to Denis's man. "Will you lower me until I can drop to the ground?"

He nodded stoically. I stripped off my coat and handed it to Grenville. He automatically shook it out and folded it carefully over his arm, like a good valet.

"I, too, will go down," Auberge announced.

"No," I said. "Let me see how safe it is first. I do not want us all plummeting down there and caving in a wall."

"You should let one of us go, sir," the man who'd held the lantern said. "Mr. Denis will be angry if something happens to you."

I eyed their broad, muscular bodies and shook my head. "You'll never fit. Now lower me until I tell you to let go."

So saying, I lay on my belly and swung my legs into the hole, letting my booted feet drop in first.

I had a sudden vivid flash of one of my soldiers lowering me into a similar hole on a Spanish summer night, to rescue a group of Spaniards who had gotten trapped when the building above them collapsed under canon fire. Their eyes had gleamed in the darkness, teeth flashing in grins as I came tumbling in with ropes. They'd hidden in a cellar full of wine and had seen no reason not to indulge while they waited, believing themselves buried forever.

That cellar had been dry and warm; this hole was foul with damp and rats and rot. Denis's man got on his knees and held me under the arms. He strained his weight against mine as he lowered me slowly. When I judged that I was about four feet from the floor, I told him to let go.

He removed his hands, and I slithered through mud and earth, a little farther than I'd thought, then my feet landed, *thud,* on the hard-packed floor.

"Lantern," I barked. My words fell flat on moist walls, close around me. The lackey lowered the lantern to me, and I reached up and grabbed its handle.

The light showed me little but a narrow tunnel, mildew-encrusted brick on one side, rotten boards and mud on the other. The air was fetid and, as Grenville had remarked, smelled of sewer, but as I stepped forward, the smell receded, as though it had been trapped here but released when we opened the hole.

I could clearly hear the voices of the men I'd left on top. "You all right, Lacey?" Grenville asked. "Please answer. I am the smallest man out here, and do not relish climbing in to pull you out."

I knew full well that Grenville would ruin his coat climbing down if necessary. He'd destroyed gloves, waistcoats, and fine suits in his adventures with me without a word, much to his valet's despair.

"I am fine," I said. "I am moving forward, following the house wall."

So saying, I took a few steps, hoping I did not come to a rotted part of the floor that would send me plunging into a far worse hole, or straight into the Thames.

I moved on carefully, wondering if anyone had truly been down here in recent times. The air was still, but breathable, and I reasoned that there must be more holes in the bank somewhere.

Darkness yawned before me. I took a few more steps, and then the brick wall angled sharply in front of me. "Damn," I muttered. I called back. "I've come to the end. There's nothing here."

"Do you want me to shake up old Bill, Captain?" Denis's more talkative man shouted. "Make him tell what he knows about this place?"

"No," I said, turning back. "Let him alone. He's terrified enough."

"Right, sir." He sounded disappointed.

"I'm coming back. You'll have to lift me out."

I started forward, and then I heard it. Distinct, and behind me, soft in the close air, I heard a faint whimper.

I hadn't imagined it. I *couldn't* imagine it down here in this horrible place with nightmare things crawling over my feet. I swung around, holding the lantern high.

The brick wall, I found, examining it, didn't reach all the way to the ruined wall. There was a space between it and the dirt bank, just large enough for me to squeeze around. Or rather, almost large enough. I got caught between brick and mud, and had to struggle and curse before I popped through.

Beyond was a dugout space, black and close, not four feet square, beaten against earth and shored up with old brick.

In this space two girls lay together. One sat against the wall, the other leaned on her, head on the older girl's breast. They wore dirty blindfolds tight against their eyes, their hands bound behind their backs.

I did not know the girl sitting upright, but I did know the other one—my own Gabriella.

The cry that tore from my throat echoed in the still air. Tears blurred my vision, and I dashed them away, needing desperately to see.

The girls lay motionless, not reacting to my presence at all. I banged the lantern to the floor, grabbed a knife from my pocket, and knelt, jerking the blindfold from Gabriella's eyes.

It must have been she who whimpered, because she did

it again, screwing her eyes shut tight at the glare of the lantern. I pulled her up from the other girl, who did not move, and sliced the bonds that held her hands.

I gathered her into my arms, holding her tight against me, kissing her hair and face, tears wetting my cheeks and smearing mud against hers.

"Gabriella," I whispered over and over. "I found you, I found you. My sweetest girl."

Chapter 17

"LACEY!" Grenville's cry rent the air. "Where are you? Answer, damn you."

I choked on sobs, rocking Gabriella against me. I could not tell if she knew who I was, but she relaxed against me, limp, and did not fight.

The other girl moaned and stirred. Alive, thank God. Holding Gabriella, I reached over and wrenched her blindfold away. Like Gabriella, she cringed from the light, making noises of panic.

"It's all right," I said hoarsely. "You're safe now. You're safe." I turned and shouted through the gap in the wall, "They're here. I found them."

My voice came out a croak. I could barely project it from here all the way to the hole in the roof.

"Lacey?" Grenville's voice sounded closer, as though he'd stuck his head through the opening. "Shout again."

"I found them," I said, tears in my voice. "Bring rope, for God's sake."

There was a stunned instant of silence, then Grenville scrambled up and began shouting orders. More noise at the entrance, argument, this time Auberge's voice, and then I heard someone scramble into the hole.

"You're safe," I whispered into Gabriella's hair. "Oh, my love, I found you."

She looked up at me, coherence reentering her eyes. "You," she whispered, sounding puzzled, her voice cracked.

"Sweetheart, I have been looking everywhere for you." I squeezed my eyes shut and simply held on to her.

"Gabriella," Auberge gasped on the other side of the gap.

Gabriella shoved me away. Joy lending her strength, she flew to her feet, flung her body through the gap, and threw her arms around Auberge. "Papa!"

The word struck through my heart at the same time I was flooded with happiness and relief. Auberge caught her hard against him, crying and kissing her.

The other girl was squinting at me through the lantern light. "Who the devil are you?" she said in a weak voice.

"Captain Gabriel Lacey," I said. "At your service, ma'am." I sliced the ropes from her wrists, and she sagged against the wall, her face twisted in pain. "Are you Black Bess?" I asked her.

"Aye, it's me." Her eyes were haggard rather than hopeful. "I'm that glad to see you, whoever you be. Lord, but I could murder a beefsteak." Then she fainted.

WE lifted the two girls from the foul hole with the aid of ropes Grenville had brought from his carriage. Gabriella was lifted out first, Auberge holding her until Grenville could hoist her safely free. She tried to hold on to the rope herself, but her grip slipped in her exhaustion. Grenville and one of Denis's men caught her and eased her out, moving as gently as could be.

I carried the recumbent form of Black Bess, limp in my arms, she having endured a longer burial than Gabriella. She opened her eyes again as we lifted her free, and reached for the brawny arms of Denis's men, who pulled her to the open air.

As I dragged myself from the hole, the last one up, I saw Grenville's carriage, his matched grays pale smudges in the night, pull up at the end of the street. The lane was too narrow to admit the coach, and Jackson climbed down from the top, ready to help.

Auberge cradled Gabriella in his arms, crooning something softly in French. She leaned her head on his shoulder, eyes closed, her body melding to his, as though it knew the source of safety. I laid my hand on her head, smoothing her hair, but she never responded to my touch.

Black Bess stood on her feet, leaning heavily against Grenville. "I can walk on me own," she insisted. She took a step, and her legs crumpled. "Devil take it."

Grenville lifted her without a word and began to carry her to the carriage. One of Denis's men grabbed Bottle Bill, who still rocked and wept against the house, and dragged him along with us.

At the end of the street, Jackson loped toward us, on his way to lend assistance. Black Bess raised her head and saw him. She gave a hoarse cry and a moan, and struggled to get away from Grenville.

"Stop," Grenville said. "You're all right."

Gabriella lifted her head to see what was the matter. Her eyes widened in fear, glittering in the light of the lantern, and she clung tight to Auberge. "No, Papa."

Jackson neared us, the lantern's light falling on his

weather-beaten features. He took in the two girls and grinned in relief. "You've got them, sir? Thank God Almighty."

Black Bess looked up at him, her eyes still round in fear.

"They're afraid of Jackson," Grenville said. He frowned at his coachman, his eyes going flat. "Why are they afraid of you?"

Jackson looked taken aback. "Couldn't say, sir."

Denis's men crowded him, belligerent. Gabriella buried her head in Auberge's shoulder.

"No," I said suddenly. "Not Jackson." I was looking hard at him, at his costly tailcoat with the gold braid and his tall hat with its brush, a costume distinct all over London. "They are not afraid of Jackson, they are afraid of his coachman's livery."

The others stared at me in surprise, including Jackson. "A coachman, sir?" he said. "I'll be damned."

"Yes," I said. "We were looking in the wrong direction. Not Stacy or McAdams. *Payne.*"

POMEROY was kind enough to allow me and Auberge and Grenville to accompany him when he went to arrest Payne, coachman to Mr. Jeremiah Stacy.

"Payne?" Stacy said in confusion. "I do not understand."

It was early morning, and Stacy received us in a sitting room in his house on Upper Grosvenor Street, his attire hastily donned, his hair still tousled with sleep. I imagine that when his valet announced to him that a Bow Street Runner had come to call, he had tumbled out of bed in tearing hurry.

The sitting room was pleasant enough, with white-painted paneling picked out in gold trim, chairs upholstered in rose damask, and paintings of pretty landscapes lending their colors to the scene. I saw the hand of Mrs.

Stacy here, feminine touches of beauty that soothed the eye.

Stacy faced us in the middle of this lovely room, his blue eyes slightly red from however many bottles of port he'd consumed the night before.

"Your coachman, one Lewis Payne, has kidnapped three young women and killed one," Pomeroy said with good humor. Pomeroy was always happy when he made an arrest, particularly one that would lead to certain conviction and reward. "We would like very much to speak to him."

Stacy turned to me. "These are the girls you quizzed me over at Tatt's? You are saying *Payne* did this?"

"I am afraid so," I answered. "Both of the young ladies we recovered have sworn that a coachman answering to the description of Payne waylaid and kidnapped them, held them hostage in a filthy hole, and killed Mary Chester. Mary's death seems to have been accidental, but he was responsible."

Stacy gaped. "Good God."

"Could not have pegged him without your evidence, Mr. Stacy," Pomeroy went on. "The Runners are always grateful for cooperation."

"My evidence?" Again Stacy looked to me for enlightenment.

I removed his journal from my pocket, the leather a little more thumbed than when I'd received it. "It makes interesting reading, Stacy. I'd keep it well hidden. But it made me understand why Payne did it."

His face whitened. "Where did you get that?" He snatched it from my hand. "This is a personal diary, Captain, how did you come by it?"

"Payne gave it to me." I paused. "You mean to say you did not tell him to?"

"No. Good lord, why would I?" He went red. "I suppose you and Grenville spent a merry evening over it."

Grenville gave him a wry look. "When Captain Lacey told me what its contents were, I admit that I did not wish to read it. What a gentleman does in his private life is his own affair. Lacey is a man of honor, I assure you. He will not breathe a word of it."

"No?"

"No," I said. "An odd hobbyhorse you have, but I have been assured by the young ladies of this book that you are harmless."

He held the journal close to his chest, as though protecting it from us. "But you say Payne is not?"

"You must remember that when you were riding through Covent Garden observing game girls like a naturalist observes newfound plants, Payne was observing them as well, from his perch atop the coach," I explained. "You like the girls because they amuse you, or perhaps you enjoy feeling a bit lofty, playing benevolent lord to them. The point is, you like them, and they are fond of you in an indulgent sort of way. But there are men, I was reminded by Felicity, who hate them, who see game girls as the outlet for their rage and disgust at women in general. Payne must be that sort of man."

Stacy stared at me in shock. "Mary and Bess were girls that I . . ." He bit his lip.

"You favored them. Perhaps Payne justified taking them because you'd been kind to them. I imagine he loathes you as much as he loathes them."

Auberge, who'd been very quiet since we'd returned Gabriella last night to her weeping mother, cleared his throat. "But my daughter, why did he take her?"

"I imagine Gabriella was a mistake," I said. "He saw you speaking to her in Covent Garden. That is what you usually did, spoke to the girls beforehand and set appointments with them for later. You were on your way to the theatre. Payne dropped you there, drove round the corner to

Russel Street, found Gabriella again, and took her." The anger in my voice heightened. "I do not know how he lured her away, but I mean to ask him, quite closely."

"Dear God," Stacy said, dazed. "Those poor girls. Are they all right?"

"Black Bess and my daughter are recovering. Mary Chester, of course, is already dead. Bess told me that Payne tried to rape Mary, she resisted, and she died when he wrestled her down. Probably suffocated in mud or earth; there were patches quite deep down there. I had wondered why Mary had soil stains on her gown, like she'd been buried, but I understood once I had a look in the place he'd kept them. It is almost like a grave. The bruises on Mary's neck, of course, were put there by Payne, likely when he took her in the first place."

Pomeroy broke in. "But then he sees he has a dead body on his hands, and he can swing for murder. He already knew that Bottle Bill liked to stash gin by the empty house. He sees his chance—he can dump the body on Bottle Bill, and then if the other girls are found, well, there's good old Bottle Bill with his pile of gin and his violent tempers when he's drunk. Poor old sod."

"Payne did his best to shift the blame to you as well, Stacy," I remarked. "Not only did he offer me your journal with all your secrets, he lured Bess and Mary away with the hint that you were willing to take them up and be their protector. With the temptation of a large amount of money dangling before them, they gladly agreed to meet him in Covent Garden—thinking, of course, that he would take them to you. All their friends would remember them chattering about a wealthy man who planned to do well by them, which pointed attention to you."

"The bloody man," Stacy said, his anger rising. "Well, by all means, Mr. Pomeroy, arrest him. This is the thanks I get for giving him good employment."

"He'll be in the mews, then, will he?" Pomeroy asked. "We'll have a walk round there and chat with Mr. Payne." He bowed. "Captain, Major, will you accompany me? But I must ask you not to murder the fellow. I won't get my reward money unless he stands more or less upright in the dock, and is still breathing."

GRENVILLE elected to stay inside with Stacy. "You are a man in sore need of brandy," he told Stacy. "And a bit of a convivial chat. We'll allow the army men to tend to the messy work."

Stacy looked grateful, and he and Grenville wandered away into Stacy's dining room, Grenville signaling to a footman to bring brandy on the way.

"He's a kind gentleman," Pomeroy observed. "Mr. Grenville, I mean. Shall we?"

Stacy's townhouse was located in Upper Grosvenor Street, an address that reflected his wealth, near Park Lane, which bordered Hyde Park. We went around the corner to the King Street Mews, a collection of stables and outbuildings nestled between the houses of Upper Brook and Upper Grosvenor Streets. In the coach house behind Stacy's home, we found Payne.

The man wore his livery coat unbuttoned, his coachman's hat hanging on a peg near the door. As we entered, he was busily inspecting the right front wheel of Stacy's elegant town coach, crouching to observe the lay of the axle.

"Good morning to you," Pomeroy sang out.

Payne started and rose, a shout ready for whoever had come unannounced into his master's coach house. He saw Pomeroy, he saw me, and he stopped.

After a moment of silence, he tugged his forelock. "Captain. What can I do for you this fine morning?"

"This is Milton Pomeroy," I said. "He was my sergeant

during the Peninsular War and is now a Bow Street Runner. He has come to arrest you."

"Bow Street," Payne said hesitantly, his lined face paling.

"For the murder of Mary Chester," Pomeroy broke in. "And for the kidnapping and assault of one Mademoiselle Gabriella Auberge and one Miss Bessie Morrow."

He stared as one amazed. "Not I, Mr. Pomeroy. Mr. Stacy did that."

"Not according to the witnesses, Mademoiselle Auberge and Miss Morrow. They give very—what you might call, vivid—descriptions of your build and your face and exactly how Mrs. Mary Chester died."

He scoffed. "The evidence of game girls. Which is no evidence at all."

"One game girl," Pomeroy corrected him, "and one very respectable daughter of a war hero, Captain Lacey here. I believe a jury will not like that one bit, since many of them'll likely have respectable daughters of their own."

"No," Payne said, puzzled. "She were a game girl. My master only touches the nastiest ones."

My sword stick came up. "That is *my* daughter you speak of, Payne. I have promised Pomeroy I will let you live to face your trial, but do not press me."

He spat. "You gentlemen and your pity for game girls disgusts me. They're dirty whores, full of the clap and ready to lay on their backs for any gent with a penny."

"Most of them are driven to earn their living as they can," I said tightly. "That does not give you permission to kidnap them and murder them. Their lives are miserable enough without men like you making things worse."

His lip curled. "That's what they're for, Captain. They want to be used and thrown off. They're like rats in the sewers, waiting to be flushed out like the filth they are."

"That's why you put them in that hole," I said, realizing. "Rats in a sewer."

"That's where they belong. Look what they did to my master, a respectable gent before he started wallowing in them and writing it all down in a book. They pulled him down and made him disgusting. If your daughter was waltzing about Covent Garden market on her own, she's no better than they are."

I had him pinned against the wall before Pomeroy could stop me, my walking stick hard across his throat. Auberge closed in beside me, but he in no way tried to hold me back. I heard Auberge's breathing, hoarse and tight with fury.

"Remember, Captain," Pomeroy warned. "He needs to be more or less upright."

"You stole my daughter," I said, ignoring Pomeroy. "You hurt her and you terrified her and you buried her. I'll give Pomeroy his conviction, but first you are going to learn exactly what you did to me."

Payne's eyes widened. My fist caught him on the jaw, and his head rocked back. He was a big man, and tried to fight, but Auberge held him fast. I sensed Pomeroy lurking beyond, ready to rescue Payne from us or cut off his escape, as need be.

Payne stared at me with a stunned expression, then his gaze shifted to Auberge. "Why are you doing this?" he bleated, as pathetic as Bottle Bill.

"I am Gabriella's father," I said, drawing back my hand.

"As am I," Auberge said quietly.

What entered Payne's eyes then was abject terror, and the sight of it pleased me very much.

Chapter 18

Several weeks later, as the Season wound to its conclusion and the *ton* began to drift to their country homes for the summer, Lady Breckenridge hosted a private supper party for an exclusive slate of guests. Present were Lucius Grenville, his odd friend Captain Gabriel Lacey, Colonel and Mrs. Aloysius Brandon, Sir Gideon Derwent, his wife and his son Leland, his son's faithful friend Gareth Travers, Lady Aline Carrington, and to everyone's surprise, Grenville's new paramour, Marianne Simmons.

"We are all old and wise enough to allow one of the demimonde in our midst without fussing," Lady Breckenridge told me when I discovered she'd invited Marianne. "We are widows and wives or world-wise spinsters and will not faint because a woman has been an actress."

Marianne, at least, behaved herself. She was well turned out in a lovely but modestly cut frock that breathed the same elegance as the gowns Lady Breckenridge wore. Her only jewelry was a thin string of diamonds in her golden hair that winked and shone as she turned her head.

Her manners were impeccable, and even Lady Derwent spoke to her without dismay. Occasionally Marianne flashed me an ironic look, but I could see she was trying hard not to embarrass Grenville.

All this polish did not come entirely from Grenville, I surmised. Marianne, I had suspected before, must belong to the middle or upper-middle class. What circumstances had led her to eking out a living on the stage at Drury Lane, and whether the birth of David had anything to do with it, I had not yet learned.

After supper, we went all together to the sitting room, rather than having the men linger in the dining room over port. I preferred the company of the ladies, in any case, their softer voices and finer smells more appealing to me than sitting with loud-voiced gentlemen who became drunker by the hour.

Lady Breckenridge raised her glass of wine. "To the safe return of Miss Gabriella Lacey."

"An excellent toast," Grenville said, looking at me.

Murmurs of "hear, hear" filled the room as glasses flashed upward, raised in honor of Gabriella.

Lady Breckenridge had invited Auberge and Carlotta with Gabriella, but Auberge had declined. Too soon, he said. Gabriella had agreed to give evidence at Payne's trial, and she was recovering from that ordeal.

I had explained to Gabriella that she did not have to appear as a witness. She could go back to France, with no one the wiser to her ruin. Payne had not raped her, she said, but I knew that the kidnapping would scar her even so. Society being what it was, there would be people who blamed Gabriella for making herself available to be kidnapped at all.

Gabriella, however, had resolutely decided to appear as

a witness. Payne had frightened her very, very much, but he'd also made her deeply angry. She wanted justice, and I am certain she wanted more than a little revenge. The stubborn outrage that had flashed in her brown eyes I'd often seen in my own. She was her father's daughter.

"The trial was splendid," Lady Aline said, beaming. "So satisfying to see a beast get his comeuppance."

"Pomeroy got his conviction," I added. "And his reward. He is most satisfied."

"But he lost his sweetheart," Grenville pointed out.

Black Bess had also agreed to be a witness in the trial for Mary Chester's murder, and had spoken in loud, clear tones everything the monster Payne had done. Gabriella had not had to answer many questions, after all, only to confirm Bess's story. Bottle Bill, sober and meek, had sang Payne's guilt with the fear of a man still believing he'd be blamed for everything.

Sir Gideon Derwent and Sir Montague Harris had worked between themselves to fill the jury with gentlemen sympathetic to the plight of game girls, reformers who tended to blame men like Payne for their downfalls. Payne, standing fearfully in the dock with his face sporting half-healed bruises, was condemned to hang, and taken down.

Black Bess and her laborer lover, Tom, had been tearfully reunited, and Bess had scarcely let go of the man as they met up again after the trial. Pomeroy had been surprisingly cheerful even so. "Got my man," he said. "Congratulate me, Captain."

"And Bess has hers," I remarked, shaking his hand.

Pomeroy shrugged. "Aye, well, she's proved too fickle for me. Besides, I have me eye on another." With that he flashed a grin across the cobbles in front of the Old Bailey. I followed the grin to see it caught by Felicity, who returned it with a sultry smile.

I raised my brows. "Good lord. I thought you did not trust her."

"I don't," he said. "But I know where I stand with her, and just how far to take things. Besides, she's a beautiful thing, ain't she?"

"You are a brave man, Sergeant."

He laughed. "Right you are, Captain. I'm off then. Call on me when you find another dead body." He'd strolled away in Felicity's direction, whistling.

Soon after, Black Nancy kissed me good-bye and departed for Islington and her hostler. "He's a good man," she reiterated. "He does well by me, and he must be missing his Nance."

"Thank you, Nancy," I said. "For all your help."

She grinned and patted me on the shoulder. "Anytime for you, Captain. You know, I could take to this investigating business. Next time you hunt a kidnapper, or a murderer, you just sing out for me, and Nance will come a-running."

I'd laughed and hugged her hard, to her delight. Giving me an impish wink and a pat on my backside, she'd gone away home.

In Lady Breckenridge's drawing room, we turned the talk to the upcoming summer months. The Derwents were going on holiday to Italy, taking Leland and their daughter and Gareth Travers with them, to hopefully warm the treacherous cough from Lady Derwent's throat.

Grenville spoke of his own estate and the hunts he'd join. He had invited me to accompany him, and then, in an act of generosity that touched and humbled me, he told me that the stallion he'd purchased at Tatt's had been intended all along for me. He could stay in Grenville's mews, tended by Grenville's grooms, but he was mine.

"This is a stunning gift," I'd told him. "Especially after I spit in the face of our friendship."

Grenville waved that away. "I learned that you still loved to ride, but lacked a horse. And so . . ." He shrugged, as if the matter were unimportant. I remembered telling Lady Breckenridge that I missed riding in almost those words. The two of them had been embarrassingly kind.

Grenville planned to take Marianne with him to his es- tate this summer, and be damned to those who were shocked by it. He and Marianne had traveled together to Berkshire to visit David before the trial, and he'd returned home much subdued.

"Dear God, Lacey, what she has borne," he'd said to me. "She can have everything I have. All of it."

They had much to smooth out between them, but I sus- pected the process had already begun. Marianne clung pos- sessively to his arm tonight, and the looks he gave her were openly fond.

Lady Aline said she would make a round of country houses before returning to her own in August, and she spontaneously invited all of us to spend time with her there. We accepted with pleasure.

When our party began to break up and drift home, I found myself at one point alone with the Brandons. "Lacey," Brandon said. He shook my hand, then I gave Louisa a light embrace and a brief kiss.

"We retire to Kent for the summer, as usual," Louisa said. "Please say you will join us for a time."

I looked from Louisa to her husband. Louisa would not ask unless she meant it, but it all depended on whether my former mentor wanted me or not. To my surprise, he nod- ded. "Do, Lacey. Perhaps we do need to find out what hap- pened between us."

I saw the plea in Louisa's eyes. For her, I said, "Very well. Set aside a bed for me that is on the hard side; I am used to it."

Louisa's smile flashed, relieved. She had been worried

that I would blame her for Gabriella's disappearance, as she did herself, though I had tried to reassure her as much as I could. She would always regret it, but at least she had the knowledge that Gabriella was safe at home.

As the Brandons departed, the last guests to do so, Lady Breckenridge slipped her hand in the crook of my arm and smiled warmly at me. She'd dressed her hair how I liked it, in long curls, a few caught and held by a diamond pin.

"So many country house visits for you," she said. "Lady Aline, Grenville, the Brandons." She squeezed my arm. "And I promised my mother I would bring you home to Oxfordshire with me at the end of June. Shall you come?"

I touched her chin, bent, and kissed her. "I would be delighted."

BEFORE I ran off to enjoy my summer bliss, of course, I had to settle the question of the divorce of my wife and my guardianship of Gabriella.

Carlotta and Auberge met with me and Denis in the parlor at the boardinghouse with some trepidation. Carlotta had said very little to me since Auberge and I had returned Gabriella, and she barely wanted to look at me at all as we waited for Denis to seat himself and spread the long pieces of parchment he had brought with him on a writing table.

Gabriella reposed on a Sheraton chair with fading paint, her hands calm on her lap. She insisted on being there, although Carlotta had tried to dissuade her. She was seventeen now, Gabriella had said, and this was her fate as well.

Gabriella sent me a serene look, which I returned with a smile. She had endured much, I could see in the shadows beneath her eyes, but she sat upright, determined not to be broken by it. My heart swelled with pride in her.

Denis cleared his throat, sounding as dry as any solicitor. "Captain Lacey has asked me if the process of freeing the both of you can be expedited," he said to Carlotta. "As I outlined previously, dissolving a marriage entirely is a long and expensive process, designed to discourage such a thing."

Carlotta looked downcast, Auberge, stoic.

"However," he continued without pause, "I am a man of means, and a man of special circumstance. I have— business acquaintances—in the Doctors Commons and in Parliament, many of whom owe me rather large favors."

Since one of Denis's practices was to maneuver men into seats in the House of Commons and other high places by means of manipulation and outright purchasing, I knew he was able to control the outcome of certain issues put forth by the government. A man owned by Denis did exactly what Denis wanted.

"The official separation will be easily achieved," he went on, "and in fact, I have a gentleman who should be signing the papers for that even as we speak. The conviction of criminal conversation will be handed down without a lengthy trial, and without you having to appear, Mrs. Lacey. The captain will have to make a nominal testimony, and I have provided for that as well. The private Act of Parliament to dissolve the marriage entirely will take more time, but I believe it can be done by the autumn."

I stared at him, and so did Auberge.

"This must cost you much," Auberge observed.

"Quite." His cold blue gaze flicked to me. "The captain will pay me back for the endeavor."

"I will," I said. "Every ha'penny."

Denis inclined his head, pretending to acknowledge my resolution. "I have a few papers for you to sign, Mrs. Lacey," he said, "and then you may go back to France and lose yourself as Colette Auberge. I will notify you when the divorce is final so that you and the major may return, sign the final papers, and begin your life of wedded bliss."

"Thank you," Auberge said. He took Carlotta's hand in his and squeezed it hard, looking down at her. "We both thank you."

Denis moved another paper, unconcerned by Auberge's sentimentality. "The next issue concerns Miss Lacey—Gabriella Auberge, as you call her. As you know, Captain Lacey is, by law, her guardian. It is his decision where she goes and with whom she lives until she comes of age or marries. And then it is his decision whom to allow her to marry."

Auberge and Carlotta flicked their gazes to me at the same time. Gabriella kept her eyes straight ahead, as still as if she were made of marble.

I remembered her joyous cry of "Papa!" the night I'd rescued her, how she'd pushed away from me and flown into the arms of Auberge. I remembered the knifelike pain in my heart, overlaid with the joy at finding her safe.

Auberge had raised her, had watched her turn from child to youth to woman, had loved her. She loved him as much in return, trusting and admiring him as her father. I was a stranger from her past, one she did not know quite what to do with.

I wet my lips, pulling the words from deep inside me. "Gabriella should return to France with her mother and stepfather. She belongs there."

Gabriella's eyes met mine in stunned surprise.

"Are you certain that is what you want?" Auberge asked, his tone pleading me to say yes.

I studied Gabriella, her honey brown curls trickling from beneath a cap, her brown eyes so like my own. "I love you, Gabriella," I told her. "You are my daughter, and I will always love you. But I cannot take you away from everything you have ever known."

She hesitated one long moment, then she inclined her head. Her expression was neutral, almost as though I'd turned down an invitation for tea, but the ringlets about her face trembled. "Thank you, sir. Might I visit you, though? I would like to get to know you, and your people, to discover where I come from."

My heart caught. "You are certain?"

She nodded. "My father told me what you did to find me. He said that if not for you, all would have been lost."

It was likely true. Auberge alone could not have bullied Pomeroy, Denis, and Grenville to turn out half of London to search for Gabriella. A few patrollers might have looked, found nothing, and sent Auberge home.

"I had resources," I acknowledged.

"For which I am forever grateful," she said, as polite as a duchess, I noted with amusement. "May I begin my visits soon?"

"In August," I said. "I will take you to Lady Aline Carrington's house party in Hampshire. We will have a fine time."

She relaxed her hauteur and gave me an impish grin, as good as Black Nancy's. "Will there be games and country dances? I have read much in the newspapers about games and country dances at English house parties."

"Lady Aline is at the forefront of society," I assured her. "I am certain she will provide exquisite entertainment."

Gabriella clasped her hands. "I will be most happy to go, then."

I felt a sudden stab of trepidation. I wanted to know and cherish my daughter again, but I realized I had no idea how to be a father.

Denis, who had watched the exchange with no flicker of warmth, gathered his papers. "It is settled, then. I will leave documents for Mrs. Lacey to sign and dispatch to me." He rose, tucked the rest of the papers under his arm, took up his walking stick, and bowed coolly. "I bid you good day."

I walked him to the door of the parlor, politely opening

it for him. "I meant what I said. Every ha'penny. You will see it again."

He gave me a wintry smile. "There are a few problems that have come to my attention," he said, "that I wish to consult with you about. You will be just the man to find the answers."

"I do not work for you," I reminded him.

His look turned wise. "Wait and hear the problems first," he said. "And then decide. Good day, Captain."

He was gone, settling his hat onto his head and climbing into the elegant carriage that waited for him in the summer mist.

Auberge asked me to stay and speak with him, but Carlotta wanted to take Gabriella upstairs again, ready to hide her away once more.

"Thank you, Gabriel," Carlotta said stiffly as we parted at the foot of the stairs.

I lifted her hand, though she did not offer it, and pressed a brief kiss to it. She had been my first love; I had kissed the dainty fingers so long ago. "Be well, Carlotta."

She looked startled, then swiftly inclined her head and started up the stairs. Gabriella allowed me to kiss her cheek, although she still behaved as though I were merely a kind stranger. Tears filled my eyes as she gracefully caught up to her mother and slipped her arm about the older woman's waist.

Auberge joined me in watching them. "I cannot repay you for what you have done," he said. "You have my deepest obligation."

I remained gazing up the stairs after Carlotta and Gabriella had gone. "I do not know, Auberge. I cannot help feeling that Gabriella would not have been in danger at all if not for me."

"No, Captain. I, too, feel great guilt, but the one who should bear it is Payne. Were he not such a beast, Gabriella would have gone unaccosted to your rooms and been comforted by you. We might have had a merry argument, but no more."

"My reason tells me this," I said. "Still I go over it and over it, wondering what would have happened if I had said the right things or done things differently."

"Whatever we feel, I am forever in your debt for restoring her to us." He paused. "And for not taking her away again."

I met his gaze. "She loves you. You are her family."

"You have the law," he said.

"The law is not everything."

He pressed his lips together and nodded, as though afraid that if he went on in this vein, he'd lose what he had gained. "You will take care of her when she is here?" he asked.

"Oh, yes," I answered fervently. "You can be assured I will watch her every move."

We stood awkwardly a moment, two men who were, in truth, rivals, and whose bond over a common problem had come to an end.

"Carlotta finally told me," he said after a time, "the reason she left you to stay with me in France. I asked her quite closely about it last night."

I lifted a brow. "And what did she say?"

He slid into French, as though unable to keep up his halting English. "That when you were in France with her, she'd had a letter from her father. He wrote that he would dissolve her marriage to you and drag her home to marry the bounder he'd tried to betroth her to before. Her father was sore in need of money, as I said, and you had little. He convinced her, in her naïveté, that he could do such a thing. Carlotta said that she had no idea until now that divorce and annulment were such difficult things to obtain. You were ready to return to England, and she feared if she came back here, her father would force her into the marriage she'd run to India to escape."

I stared at him in astonishment. "Good lord. The little fool. Why did she never tell me of this letter?"

Auberge shrugged. "She was young, she was afraid, and as we agreed, Carlotta is not one to think things through. She simply acts. She and I had grown to know each other, and I admit, I flirted with her and quite fell in love with her. So, when she came to me in trouble, I had no compunction against taking her away. For that, I am sorry."

"Dear God." I exhaled. "Poor Carlotta. She must have been terrified. And she did not feel she could come to me." The knowledge hurt, even now. "But you made her happy, Auberge. She fled with you into safety, and you loved her."

He nodded quietly. "We have been very happy."

"And she would not have been happy with me," I acknowledged, "not even without her father's threats, which were empty. She would not have had what she has with you."

He sent me a warm smile. "You are a good man, Captain."

"No, I am not." I studied him for a time. "I have always wanted to hate you. But I have to admit that you are a good man in your own right." I shook his hand once more, deciding to begin my life again, free of the past. "Be well."

"*Au revoir*," he said.

I bowed and departed, not returning his wish.

TWO weeks later, a hired coach let me off before a spreading, graceful house, approached by a mile-long drive that wound beneath powerful and ancient oaks. The house, golden brick in the middle of Oxfordshire, welcomed me with promise.

A tall butler met me at the front door, bowed to me,